Praise for

SERVANT: THE AWAKENING

"Unique and fascinating."
—Elizabeth Lowell, *New York Times* bestselling author

"The first book in a new series, *The Awakening* features a unique heroine, a wonderful hero, and a likable sidekick . . . The gritty, atmospheric inner-city setting, graphic violence, and raw language are perfect for a story that unfolds, scene by scene, like a graphic novel and cries out to be graphic-novelized en route to the movies. May this be just the first in a long series."
—*Booklist* (starred review)

"A new name and an enticing new series propel Lori Foster into an exciting new direction . . . *Servant: The Awakening* practically blew me away . . . [It's] brash, darkly edgy, and insightful. And all grown up. Kudos to Ms. Foster for this fascinating, utterly unique fantasy."
—*Romance Reader at Heart*

"Fascinating . . . a new twist on demon slaying." —*Fresh Fiction*

"With *Servant: The Awakening*, L. L. Foster shows she has a true gift for writing dark urban fantasy . . . The Servant series will be addictive."
—*The Romance Readers Connection*

"Brilliant . . . The tone, intensity, and sheer grittiness of this book is awesome. I think Ms. Foster was channeling early Anita Blake, Eve Dallas, and a dash of J. R. Ward . . . A great intro to a series that I will be following religiously!"
—*Night Owl Romance*

"Dark, gritty, raw . . . urban fantasy at its finest . . . As can be expected from the darker alter ego of Lori Foster, L. L. Foster delivers characters that are engaging yet in your face . . . This looks to be the beginning of a really great series. Get your copy today and get in on the ground floor."
—*Love Romances & More*

"Entertaining paranormal romantic suspense that grips readers . . . Romantic fantasy readers and fans of Buffy and the movie *They Live* will want to read the first tale in the human war against demons."
—*Midwest Book Review*

Titles by L. L. Foster

SERVANT: THE AWAKENING
SERVANT: THE ACCEPTANCE
SERVANT: THE KINDRED

Writing as Lori Foster

THE WINSTON BROTHERS
WILD
CAUSING HAVOC
SIMON SAYS
HARD TO HANDLE
MY MAN, MICHAEL

Anthology

WILDLY WINSTON

SERVANT
THE KINDRED

L. L. FOSTER

JOVE BOOKS, NEW YORK

THE BERKLEY PUBLISHING GROUP
Published by the Penguin Group
Penguin Group (USA) Inc.
375 Hudson Street, New York, New York 10014, USA
Penguin Group (Canada), 90 Eglinton Avenue East, Suite 700, Toronto, Ontario M4P 2Y3, Canada
(a division of Pearson Penguin Canada Inc.)
Penguin Books Ltd., 80 Strand, London WC2R 0RL, England
Penguin Group Ireland, 25 St. Stephen's Green, Dublin 2, Ireland (a division of Penguin Books Ltd.)
Penguin Group (Australia), 250 Camberwell Road, Camberwell, Victoria 3124, Australia
(a division of Pearson Australia Group Pty. Ltd.)
Penguin Books India Pvt. Ltd., 11 Community Centre, Panchsheel Park, New Delhi—110 017, India
Penguin Group (NZ), 67 Apollo Drive, Rosedale, North Shore 0632, New Zealand
(a division of Pearson New Zealand Ltd.)
Penguin Books (South Africa) (Pty.) Ltd., 24 Sturdee Avenue, Rosebank, Johannesburg 2196,
South Africa

Penguin Books Ltd., Registered Offices: 80 Strand, London WC2R 0RL, England

This is a work of fiction. Names, characters, places, and incidents either are the product of the author's imagination or are used fictitiously, and any resemblance to actual persons, living or dead, business establishments, events, or locales is entirely coincidental. The publisher does not have any control over and does not assume any responsibility for author or third-party websites or their content.

SERVANT: THE KINDRED

A Jove Book / published by arrangement with the author

PRINTING HISTORY
Jove mass-market edition / September 2009

ISBN: 978-0-515-14690-5

JOVE®
Jove Books are published by The Berkley Publishing Group,
a division of Penguin Group (USA) Inc.,
375 Hudson Street, New York, New York 10014.
JOVE® is a registered trademark of Penguin Group (USA) Inc.
The "J" design is a trademark of Penguin Group (USA) Inc.

PRINTED IN THE UNITED STATES OF AMERICA

10 9 8 7 6 5 4 3 2 1

SERVANT
THE KINDRED

Chapter 1

God please, not now.

For long minutes, what began to feel like an eternity, Gabrielle Cody fought the inevitable. Naked on Luther's king-sized bed, she stretched taut as sweat beaded on her skin and her teeth locked.

The agony grew.

And she fought it.

As her heart pounded too hard in her chest, she repeatedly fisted her hands, clenching and unclenching the smooth, clean sheets beneath her. Exiguous moonlight snaked through a part in his heavy bedroom drapes, sending a silvery dart to cross the floor and crawl, with painstaking slowness, up the wall.

Clean. Organized. Masculine. Everything about Luther's home, a *real* home, felt nice, smelled nice.

So inappropriate to the likes of her.

That Gaby could hear Luther in the bathroom finishing up a hot shower was the only salvation, the only measure to fight the staggering call. It dragged at her, commanding acceptance, gnarling her muscles, relentless in its claim on her.

She squeezed her eyes shut and thought of Luther, remembered his pleasure as she'd capitulated to his demands.

Demands to join him, to try for a normal life—to give them, as a couple, a chance.

He was a fool. *She* was a fool for accepting even the slightest possibility of a normal life, a real relationship.

Before excusing himself for the shower he'd smiled at her, thrilled to have her in his home, anticipation bright in his eyes. Luther thought he'd gotten his way. He thought he had Gaby where he wanted her.

Be careful what you wish for.

Another shaft of pain pierced her. It was always this way—the bid to fulfill her duty was a wrenching agony she couldn't fight. Whenever she'd tried, the pain had grown insurmountable.

As it did now.

Sweat trickled down her temple to soak into Luther's pillow. Already she'd soiled his fine home. If she stayed, she'd turn his entire existence black with depravity.

Her breath caught as the shower turned off. Luther would not expect to find her in his bed. No, he thought she was downstairs, waiting, where she should have been, where he'd left her. He wanted to go slow, to give her time.

But, God knew, time wasn't always something she had.

Tonight, right now, her time had run out before she'd even begun.

Damn her plight. Damn her *duty.*

For so long now, Detective Luther Cross had tried to worm his way into her dysfunctional, psychotic life—and she'd resisted.

With good reason.

No matter his claims of "knowing" her, of "accepting" her and her strange eccentricities. He might think he had an inkling of what she did as a paladin, and why, but he didn't, not really. He couldn't.

Why had she come here?

Tears, salty and hot, trickled along her temples, mingling with the sweat. Her body strained as she tried to find just a few minutes more, just enough time to have Luther. Once. A memory she could keep forever . . .

But the relentless pull and drag on her senses, the encompassing pain that twisted and curdled inside her told her to stop being fanciful.

Should she leave without telling him? Make a clean break of it and let him wonder, let him worry?

Let him give up. On her.

On them.

Or should she try trusting him?

No, no never that. She couldn't.

The pain lashed her, impatient for obedience, and Gaby knew she couldn't resist it any longer. As she sat up, she cried out—and the bathroom door opened.

Luther stepped out, buck naked, tall and strong and oddly beautiful for a man. That stunning golden aura swirled around him, bright with optimism, with the promise of all that was good.

All that was the opposite of her.

Seeing her, he drew up short, stared for a moment. His hot gaze moved over her body, but not with lust as much as concern. "Gaby?"

"I was waiting . . ." She gasped, nearly doubled over with the physical torment of the calling. "For you. I was willing, Luther. I was anxious. But . . ." She staggered to her feet, unseeing, choked with the need for haste. "But now I have to go."

He remained steadfast, still, watching her. "Where?"

How could he remain so composed, so . . . detached, in the face of what she was, what she had to do? "I don't know yet."

She fumbled for her shirt and dragged it on.

Words hurt. Leaving felt like death.

But she was a paladin, and being interested in a man, even a man as irreproachable as Luther, didn't change that.

Luther didn't ask any more questions, he just dried with the speed of a man on a mission—all the while keeping his gaze glued to the naked parts of her.

To her shock, he said, "I'm coming with you."

"Don't be fucking stupid." She stepped into jeans, almost fell, and had to stop, had to gnash her teeth and squeeze her eyes shut in an attempt to contain the overpowering draw, but she knew the only relief would be to give in.

And she would—once she was away from Luther.

It was his nearness now that made the pain bearable at all, that gave her the opportunity to delay, to explain. "I work alone."

"Not tonight, you don't." Already dressed in a black T-shirt, jeans, and sneakers, he reached for her. His hand touched her face, smoothed back her damp hair and some of the awful, distorting agony dissipated.

How could he affect her so strongly? How could a simple touch from him alleviate the agony?

Almost sad, definitely accepting, he reiterated, "Not tonight."

From the day she'd met him, he'd always influenced her this way, bringing clarity in the midst of the turbulent summons, easing her misery, calming her heart.

With the short reprieve, Gaby slapped his hand aside and after stepping into her sandals, grabbed up her knife.

She secured it in a sheath at her back. "I'll say it once, Luther. Stay out of my way."

And then, unable to resist any longer, she gave herself over to her duty.

Once accepted, it lashed through her, jarring her body, rolling her eyes back, straining her spine. On the periphery of her senses, she felt Luther there, not touching her, not deterring her, but keeping pace as she moved forward, out of his bedroom, out of his house—and into the hell that was her life.

She raced so quickly that Luther could barely keep up. The sec-onds it took him to lock his front door almost allowed her to get away. Ignoring the blustery morning air and lack of sunshine, he trotted across his lawn after her. Fallen leaves scuttled over his shoes. The autumn air nipped.

Gaby never noticed. She was impervious to the weather, and to his calls for her to wait.

When Gaby started past his car, he finally caught up and dared touch her just long enough to suggest, "I'll drive."

With her eyes unfocused, eerily vacant, she entered through the car door he'd opened and sat with a sort of charged energy that had her teeth sawing together, her brows pinching, and her chest heaving.

Pained by the sight of her, Luther bolted around to the driver's side and got in as quickly as he could. He started the car, turned on his wipers to counter the heavy fog, and pulled out.

"Other way," she said in a faraway voice, one that was hollow enough to send fingers of unease crawling up his nape.

Striving for calm, Luther turned the car, alternately looking at Gaby and watching the street. Dark clouds that shadowed the colors of changing leaves threatened a downpour. It'd be a cool, miserable day—perfect for his introduction into the arcane phenomena of Gaby's mission.

The astonishment of seeing her naked, in his bed . . . well, she hadn't given him time to assimilate that, to get his visual fill before she'd gone all ominous with recondite purpose.

Her features were now sharper, distorting the way he'd seen before, but amplified beyond anything familiar. This, he realized, was Gaby in the zone. She'd warned him against seeing her like this, tried to prepare him, but the surreal qualities gripping her had no explanation other than supernatural.

Or pietistic.

Vibrating with repressed strength and dynamic force, she paid no attention to the scenery or the direction he took. Perched at the edge of her seat, one of her small hands gripped the dash and the other squeezed the side of her seat, near her hip.

Her pale lips barely moved when she intoned, "Left."

Luther had to cut across traffic to make the turn, but he didn't argue with her. Warring with the need to show his trust, to give *her* reason to trust in return, was the image of her bare body, there for him.

Never had he wanted anything or anyone as much as he wanted, needed, Gabrielle Cody. And that in itself felt influenced by a higher power. From the first day he'd met her, he'd felt a draw to Gaby unlike anything an experienced, educated adult would recognize.

As a man of faith, Luther gave himself over to the desire, to Gaby.

But as a man of law, a man who enjoyed controlling his own fate, he prayed for guidance and understanding. In his guts, he knew he belonged with Gaby. But his mind

balked at the idea of playing a role in her self-devised fight
against evil.

He'd chosen a balancing act—one that left him on the
precarious edge of disaster.

When they reached their destination, how would he stop
Gaby from issuing her own form of punishment? He'd seen
her secure her knife at her back; she never went anywhere
without the deadly blade.

He knew what she could do with that knife, what she'd
likely done in the past.

The rapid turn of his car, the squealing tires and angry
horns from other drivers made no impact on Gaby's ex-
pressionless void. Knowing he had to get a grip, had to
formulate a plan, Luther drew a breath to steady himself
against her unearthly mien.

They'd traveled out of his neighborhood and into another. Occasionally Gaby twitched or jerked, then stilled
herself with obvious pain, accepting it all as any martyr
would.

Already they'd gone quite a distance, surprising Luther
and piquing his curiosity. He glanced at her finely drawn
profile. Her damp hair hung loose, a few tendrils sticking to
her cheek. "Would you have come here on foot?"

She didn't answer, didn't even acknowledge his presence.

Her pallor worried him, but not so much as her fast,
panting breaths and the racing pulse he noticed in her slender throat. Every muscle in her thin body twitched with
fervent edginess. He'd seen that body naked now, knew the
frailty of it, the feminine curves and hollows.

More than anything, more than he feared the consequences of what she intended to do, Luther wanted to haul
her close and protect her, soothe her however he could.

But accepting Gaby meant taking part in her dysfunctions, trusting her aberrant province and inverted moral code, being there for her wherever her mind or body ventured.

A juggling act, for certain, but somehow he'd make it happen.

The early hour of the day and the inclement weather accounted for the hush in the neighborhoods they traveled through. They drove along a street of houses converted to small privately owned businesses. Two black men stood in quiet conversation at a bus stop. A gray-haired white woman pushed a rickety cart out of a mom-and-pop grocery. A dog jumped against a fence, barking as crows dined on indistinguishable roadkill.

The damp day began to sputter from the dark clouds hanging above. The humidity thickened, and the temperature dropped.

Gaby turned to stare out the window as they passed a dress shop, a pony keg, a bar—

"Turn."

Scouring the crowded street, Luther finally noticed the narrow alley barely visible between two parked cars occupying the curb. It ran alongside a ramshackle brick dry cleaner. Over the front door a faded wooden sign offered alterations and fast service. Prices were hand-painted in the dingy picture window.

Having only one option, he turned right into the alley.

Gaby opened her car door with the car still moving. Luther slammed on his brakes but not before she leaped out, landing on her feet like a cat. Her abrupt departure left him no choice but to park with haste and little discretion. He blocked the alley, but that was too damn bad.

Already Gaby had strode straight to the warped, unsecured back door of the establishment. Rain dripped off the leaf-clogged gutters. An overturned garbage can sent soggy refuse fleeing with the wind. Drying weeds punctured the ground of the small yard.

Luther watched Gaby's hands fist, open, fist again. As she stood poised over something to the side of the stoop, she didn't reach for her knife. Expression rigid, she stepped over a rumpled heap, opened the door, and went inside while scanning the area.

Trailing a few feet behind her, Luther rushed forward and almost fell over a . . . body.

A body that Gaby had barely registered.

He took in the dead eyes, the white, shriveled flesh and the signs of dissipation. Rivulets of mud trailed along a sunken cheek to drip into a gaping mouth. Death had contorted the features in gruesome display.

Judging by the skin abscesses and fresher track marks on the exposed upper arms, the dead woman had been a druggie. Probably not the owner, but then who?

"Fuck." Drawing out his gun, Luther dogged Gaby's heels and found her standing in the front of a crowded dry cleaner lobby with a half dozen people looking at her with rank fear.

Not that she cared about her audience. She gave them no more attention than she'd given the dead body. With keen perception, she cut her gaze over everything, the exits, the windows, the people inside.

No better ideas came to mind, so Luther stowed the gun and withdrew his badge. "Detective Luther Cross. I need all of you to stay put." He put one hand on Gaby—not that he had any delusion of restraining her if she decided to bolt—and with the other he withdrew his radio to call for backup.

With that done, he told the woman who appeared to be in charge, "Come out from behind the counter and take a seat. All of you, get comfortable. No one's leaving, and this might take a while."

A dozen questions erupted from the now hostile and confused customers.

Forgoing any further explanations, Luther drew Gaby aside and turned her to face him. Color had leached back into her face, but he wasn't reassured. "Talk to me."

"We missed him." Her eyes narrowed. "You slowed me down."

How the hell could he have slowed her down when he was the one who'd supplied the transportation? "You think you'd have gotten here quicker on foot?"

"Yes."

For now, Luther stowed his disbelief to leave room for more questions. "He who?"

Since knowing Gaby, he'd learned one thing with absolute certainty: trusting her instincts could very well mean the difference between catching a killer and letting a psychopath go free.

She shoved away his hand with disgust. "The guy who sucked that body dry and then dumped it out there. Who else?"

"Sucked dry?" The anxious customers mirrored his incredulity. Their murmurs, this time tinged with panic, filled the air. Luther concentrated on blocking them from his mind. "You want to explain that?"

"Yeah, Luther. Your new guy is a vintage bloodsucker, kicking it new school." Her blue eyes narrowed and she turned with a purpose, heading back to the corpse.

"Gaby, wait."

Of course she ignored him.

"Shit." A patrol car chose that auspicious moment to pull up out front, lights flashing, sirens screaming. Luther jerked the door open. "There's a dead body around back.

I need you to keep everyone inside here until I've had a chance to talk to them. Got it?"

One startled patrolman nodded and headed inside while another started around back, gun drawn.

Luther rushed through the store to find Gaby, but by the time he got back outside, the only body around was the dead one.

Gaby was long gone.

Gaby knew a cold trail when she found one, but there had to be a clue left or she wouldn't have been sent here. Allowing instinct to guide her, she went down the alley, out the back to a street . . . and sickness, like a sticky cloak, infiltrated her every pore.

Another body, drained of blood, used to feed the wickedly corrupted; she knew she'd find it, but where?

Luther wouldn't just wait behind. He'd be searching for her with his misguided notion of protecting her while overseeing the ever-faulty legal process. She had to hurry if she had any hope of keeping him out of the treacherous path of her life.

The power within her had dissipated, but still it churned deep inside. As Gaby scanned the area, the power ripened, began to boil to the surface. Her gaze caught; there, the old building.

She started forward with driving purpose—and a flicker of lightning licked the sky, immobilizing her.

Oh God, no.

Storms always left her inert with scalding, deep-bred irrational fear. A frantic glance at the sky showed ominous clouds—but no more lightning. She strained her ears, but heard no thunder.

A deep breath sent oxygen into her starving lungs. She

dragged herself forward, one foot at a time, sluggish but determined. The decrepit building loomed ahead, taunting her, daring her to brave the impending storm to find the malevolence lurking inside.

She had a duty, not only to herself, but to the person now suffering, the person being bled dry. Straining, her feet heavy and her heart clenched, she took two more steps.

The skies lit up. Nature did a full display, sending a bolt of electricity to splinter the air while a cannonade of thunder shook the ground beneath her feet. Gaby's world squeezed in, turned black and bleak and empty of free volition.

For as long as she could remember it had been this way. Father Mullond, the man who had taken her in and tried to assist her, God rest his soul, had blamed the manner of her mother's death for the irrational fear.

A deadly lightning strike had stolen her mother's heartbeat. As her heart had stopped beating, Gaby came into the world—an orphan.

It was a fucked-up way to be born, and had set the tone for a life that deviated from any kind of normalcy.

Whether it was an honest recollection from birth or a learned fear from the stories told her by foster parents, she didn't know. She fucking well didn't care. Storms paralyzed her. Fear was fear, and for Gaby Cody—paladin, warrior against evil—it was unacceptable.

And still, she couldn't get her fucking limbs to move.

Icy rain soaked through her meager clothes, chilled her down to her bones, and prickled her flesh. She could have stood there and died except that she heard the moan.

Not a loud moan. Not a piteous cry that others would have detected. It was faint with weakness, a meager tone that depicted resignation to death.

"Oh God." Fighting the fear with everything she had, Gaby stumbled forward. Her muscles cramped; her thoughts were wild and scattered. But that sound drew her and she inched closer to it, closer to that deteriorated structure that once might have been a home.

Empty windows framed lush spiderwebs filled with bloated white eggs.

Dead moths littered the pathway, mixed with brittle leaves and some broken beer bottles.

All around the house, a murky aura of misery and malevolence shimmered in and out of the dank air.

The evil lurked inside, doing its foul work.

Another crack of electricity split the skies with a fantastic display of light and power. Gaby collapsed against the side of the house, her eyes going unseeing again. No, not now. God, please not now.

But the rain pounded down in a deafening deluge as the heavens thundered and crashed. Terror pervaded her every limb.

How long she slumped there, shivering and useless, she didn't know. It felt like an eternity. She hated herself and her weakness, hated that someone suffered while she did nothing.

And then warmth enfolded her; lips touched her temple and she knew.

"Luther?" The whisper was strained, barely audible. His nearness cleared her vision and she saw again that tragic aura circling the house . . . and fading.

"It's okay. I've got you." He lifted one of her hands and put it under his shirt, against the heat of his powerful chest and the reassuring thump of his steady heartbeat. His forehead rested against hers. "I don't like it when you leave me, Gaby."

She didn't know if he meant physically leaving him—which she had done—or emotionally leaving him—which she also had done. She swallowed the bitterness of defeat and whispered so faintly that her voice barely carried over the violence of the storm, "Can you hear him?"

Luther went on alert, jerked around, searching the vacant area. When he saw no one, he turned back to Gaby, his big hands clasping her upper arms with urgency. "Who?"

"Inside. He's . . . inside. In terrible pain." This close to Luther, the awful gripping trepidation eased and her voice gained strength. "He's sinking into the abyss, Luther. You have to hurry."

He tilted her back to study her face, and she felt his alarm.

Because he believed her.

His trust helped to strengthen her, too. "Hurry, Luther."

"Where is he, Gaby? Inside where?"

She turned her head enough to look at the blackened, empty front window of that forsaken home. "There." She drew in a shuddering breath. "He doesn't have much longer to live."

Luther's beautiful brown eyes flashed with comprehension. "I'm sorry. I'll be right back." He settled her down on the stoop and reached for the door. The knob turned, and a harsh wind jerked it from Luther's hand, crashing it against a crumbling wall. Plaster and dust rose into the damp, chilled air, caught in the wind, and swirled away.

Gun drawn, Luther ventured into the tenebrous core of evil.

The second he left her, coldness and despondency mauled back into Gaby, sending pain into her restricted lungs, narrowing her sight to pinpricks of indistinct light.

Sometime after tunnel vision had closed in on her, Luther rushed back outside. He gathered her close even as he snapped out orders into his radio. The festering fear made it difficult for Gaby to focus, but she grasped that he wanted his partner, Ann Kennedy, to join him, and an ambulance.

When he said, "And bring some tools—something to cut through chains and locks," Gaby stirred. Chains? Locks?

Voice grim, Luther added to Ann, "Yeah, you heard me right. The poor bastard is shackled down tight to the floor."

By the time the street filled with police cars, lights, and sirens, the storm had turned fierce beyond anything Gaby had ever experienced.

Was this a precursor to her life with Luther?

Did God want her to understand the folly of trying to cultivate a relationship?

Concentrating on that thought, along with Luther's nearness, gave her a means to ward off the phobia. To his credit, Luther managed to do his job and watch over her at the same time. Did he expect her to run off screaming? Or to interfere, as she wanted to do?

He'd seen her in a storm only once before. After this, he'd never forget the effect it had on her.

Shame at the insidious weakness bit into her, but even that couldn't shake the last residue of panic. She was cursed, in more ways than one.

Chapter 2

Frustration decimated Luther's last ounce of patience. The ferocity of the storm didn't help, hampering everything that needed to be done, inhibiting the forensic work. More than two hours passed before he could get Gaby into his car to take her home.

All the while he'd given orders—overseeing the nearly wasted body into an ambulance, assigning a few uniformed cops to keep watch, directing others within the old house—and at the same time, tried to help Gaby. Unsure of how she might react, he hadn't wanted her out of his reach. That meant the only way to get her out of the rain was to take her just inside the house.

She'd sat in a dusty corner, eyes unfocused, pulse racing. Fear held her as securely as the chains held their victim.

Even like this, in a state of sheer panic, she remained untouchable by most. Ann had tried to speak with her, but got no response. Only when he could put aside his duty and touch her did she show any sign of comprehension.

How someone could live with such a debilitating fear, he couldn't imagine. For someone of Gaby's dominating character, it'd be the worst of handicaps. She was a doer, someone who wanted and needed to help others. When fear held her back, it would be unbearable.

Was her phobia of storms due in part to her many years under foster care? Not that Luther could entirely blame people who'd only wanted to help a little girl and instead had gotten a preternatural child with immeasurable abilities few would ever understand or accept.

Seeing the barren perception in her eyes twisted Luther's heart. Only the very certain belief that Gaby would resent herself more if he hadn't done his job had kept him from removing her from the scene earlier. But he had fulfilled his duty as a detective and now he wanted to concentrate on her.

When they were both safely ensconced in his car, he kicked on the heater and rubbed her thigh. "Gaby? We're going home now."

Her throat moved as she swallowed, but she didn't reply.

He drove away from the scene. Rain drenched her clothes and he realized he needed to get her warm and dry. She shivered in misery—and so much more.

"The guy we found . . . he was as close to death as I've ever seen anyone." Why he kept talking, Luther wasn't sure, but he wanted her to know how she'd helped. "Thank you for leading me to him."

A shiver ran through her, but she didn't reply.

"He's lost a lot of blood," Luther said, "so I don't know if he'll make it. But if he does, he has you to thank."

Gaby frowned a little, either in disagreement, or in surprise that she'd heard him, that his voice had registered beyond her palpitating despair.

Understanding Gaby as he did now, he could easily guess how she'd hate her inability to act. He felt a desperate need to reassure her. "I know how hard this is for you. But you got him help, Gaby. You pushed past the fear and made sure we knew about him."

Her lashes fluttered, her mouth tightened the tiniest bit.

"You're the most courageous person I know, and that's saying a lot, given the honorable men I've worked with." He glanced at her, rubbed her leg again while steering one-handed. "I don't know if we got to him in time, though. I've never seen anyone so white or weak. Another hour and he'd have been dead."

He took her left hand, lifted it to his mouth and let his warm breath soothe the iciness away. He saw her eyelashes flicker again, and her tongue came out to moisten her bottom lip.

That encouraged Luther. "He's an addict, Gaby, like the other, with plenty of track marks. But I saw nothing to say he'd been deliberately bled."

Her struggle to focus left her voice raw and deep. "He was."

"Okay." Thrilled to hear her voice, Luther squeezed her fingers. "I believe you."

The car grew almost uncomfortably warm, but he didn't turn down the blower. The fact that she'd spoken proved that some of her abyssal terror had waned. "Once the doctors have looked him over, they'll call me. We can confirm things then."

"They won't know where to look." Her expression pinched in pain, and she closed her eyes a moment to concentrate. "You'll have to insist."

Again he said, "Okay." He couldn't help but smile a little, mostly with relief. Bossiness crept back into her manner, reassuring him that she'd be her old self in no time.

With her free hand, she toyed with the choker he'd bought her, the choker she never removed. "I fucking hate storms."

"I noticed." Her grumbling delighted him; her acceptance of his gift thrilled him more. The choker was the only jewelry she ever wore. "It's better now that we're in the car, out of it?"

She nodded, and turned her face away.

Though she remained too tense, and far too pale, Luther let it go, content to touch her as he drove cautiously along the roads until he finally turned into his driveway. "Want me to pull into the garage?" He usually didn't, but if it'd make things easier for Gaby, he didn't mind.

She stared out the window, filled her lungs with a very deep, fortifying breath, and—without replying—opened her door and got out.

A gigantic lightning bolt ripped apart the sky and crackled along the ground. Deafening thunder shook the air around them.

Gaby froze again.

"Damn it." Luther rushed around to her, gathered her close, and led her inside. She'd again retreated into herself, into some safe haven where he couldn't reach her. Luther wanted to howl at the storm for doing this to her, and he wanted to go back into her past and find everyone responsible for ever hurting her.

"Come here, Gaby. Let me help you."

When he tugged on her arms, she moved as directed, but with a zombielike void of comprehension. On the tile entry, they both dripped puddles. Luther locked the door and turned to her. Her colorless lips trembled.

A tidal wave of emotion rose to choke him.

Luther hugged her close, rubbed her chilled arms, and kissed her throat. She didn't thaw at all. He needed to get her warm, and fast, but he couldn't. Not while she wore cold, rain-soaked clothes.

Kissing her made him feel better, and even now, with her being so emotionally wounded, the taste of her satisfied something deep inside him, something he'd never experienced with any other woman.

Though Luther's ardor grew, Gaby didn't make a single sound, and he hated that. "To hell with it." He knew what he wanted to do, knew the best way to reach her.

Leaving her for only a moment, he went to the adjacent living room and closed the drapes, and then turned on the television. Maybe if she couldn't see and hear the storm, it wouldn't bother her so deeply.

Gaby stood frozen where he'd left her as he went down the hall to the guest bathroom to gather up a few towels. When he returned to her he smoothed her dark hair away from her face. With his heart pounding, he kissed her mouth and, little by little, her icy lips thawed.

"Gaby." His mouth still touching hers, he looked at her, and then covered her left breast with his palm.

Her eyelashes fluttered, so he kissed her again, deeper this time, as he cuddled her breast.

It appalled Luther that he was turned on while she stood paralyzed by terror. Maybe it was seeing her quiescent for a change instead of defiant, maybe it was that for once she didn't scald him with her acerbic disdain.

Whatever logic he applied, he shook with wanting her. Lust roughened his voice as he spoke. "Let's get you out of these wet clothes and warmed up."

For most women, what he was about to do would be unethical in the extreme, even illegal. But for Gaby, it was the only way he knew to help her.

Her shirt stuck to her skin as he wrestled it up and over her head. It hit the tiled foyer with a sodden plop. Luther looked at her, at her small breasts and her nipples drawn tight by cold, and knew he was a goner.

Using one of the towels, he squeezed excess water from her hair and then dried her torso. And because he couldn't help himself, he kissed her again, on her soft, pale lips, her nose, her chin.

"I'll have you warm soon, I promise."

The waistband of her loose, worn jeans curled outward from her thin frame, exposing her narrow hip bones and a tantalizing navel within a concave belly. Around her waist, Luther saw the thin leather belt that held her lethal blade in a sheath concealed at the small of her back. The stark reminder of who Gaby was, and what she did, didn't faze him. He knew her, and he accepted her.

Cautious, because Gaby could be unpredictable at the most unexpected times, Luther unfastened and removed the sheathed knife from her person. Her lips firmed and her brows pinched, proof that even while in a stupor, she didn't like losing her knife.

Keeping his gaze on her, he placed the weapon on the hall table for safekeeping. "It's okay. No one is here but us. The knife's not going anywhere, I promise."

The suffocating fear had such a stranglehold on Gaby that she offered no further challenge or protest. Now, at this particular moment, she looked small and feminine and vulnerable when normally those terms could never be applied to her.

The chilly room gave her a shiver, and Luther's gaze again went to her exposed breasts. For only a few seconds, he covered each breast, cuddled her, gave her his warmth. Then he forced himself to keep his brain on task.

Yes, he planned to pay plenty of attention to those pert breasts, but not yet. First he wanted her more comfortable, and that meant removing the rest of her clothes—and his.

Going to one knee, he slipped off her sandals, thinking to himself that with the cooling weather, she'd need some different, warmer outfits.

When she'd moved in, she insisted on having her own room—not to be apart from him, but for privacy of other matters.

What those matters might be, Luther didn't yet know. Gaby would tell him in her own good time.

To accomplish his plans of getting closer to her, he'd gladly given her the spare room. Refusing his help, she'd carried in a few small boxes and a larger trunk that held God only knew what. She'd stowed it all in the room. Maybe she had some warmer clothes in there.

After she came around, he'd ask her.

Her soaked-through jeans, even a size too large, proved tricky to get down her hips. But once Luther had them to her knees he discovered her lack of panties.

Damn. He'd forgotten her rush in dressing, and her general lack of modesty. Gaby gave no more notice to her body than she did her attire. She lacked any real grasp of her sexual appeal.

He was only a man, and he wanted her, had wanted her for a long time. Seeing her naked again, her fair skin teased with goose bumps, tested his control.

On his knees in front of her, Luther reached around her body to palm one firm cheek. He wanted to kiss her belly— and more—but Gaby made a small sound that jerked him back to reality.

Standing in a rush, he grabbed a towel and dried off the rest of her body, lingering on that sweet ass, and over her belly, between her thighs. By the time he wrapped the towel around her, he had enough heat to warm them both.

Naked except for the towel and choker, Gaby stood there before him and did nothing.

"Hang on, honey. Let me get rid of my clothes, too, and then we'll get . . . comfortable."

Saying it caused his dick to flex, to stiffen, but he couldn't help that either. He'd made up his mind and it was the only way he knew to break the spell.

He stripped his clothes with swift urgency, putting his badge, gun and holster, cell phone, radio, and wallet on the table by her knife. Seeing the items side by side gave the differences in their lives a harsh reality.

He had everyday items used by most of society to stay in touch with others, to label him as a cop, and to defend. For Gaby, there was nothing to identify her, nothing to communicate with; she had a honed blade meant to kill, period.

Luther refused to ponder the contrasts.

Leaving the soppy pile of clothes in his entryway, he took Gaby's arm and drew her to the couch with him. He drew her down onto his lap and covered them both with a soft throw.

Gaby was a tall woman, willowy in build, sleek with muscle. In comparison, he topped her by three inches in height and at least a hundred pounds. As he settled them both, her head fit under his chin, her hand rested over his heart. Holding her felt as right as anything he'd ever done in his life.

Luther stroked up and down her back, sometimes going over her hip, sometimes her waist. He kissed her shoulder, the side of her neck around the choker he'd bought her, the choker she never removed. Soon he forgot his own motives. He was a man on the make, pure and simple.

Little by little, Gaby relaxed. She even tipped her head to give him better access to her collarbone.

With a soft groan, Luther leaned her back and put his mouth over her breast, drawing on her nipple.

Her fingers knotted in his hair, thrilling him with the sign of life, of response—and of willingness.

The pulled drapes left the room dark, shadowed only by the flickering light of the television. Luther could still hear the raging wind and rain battering against the window, and he heard Gaby's breathing as it deepened.

He lifted back up to take her mouth in a voracious kiss that consumed them both.

She gave a heavy shudder, then suddenly clutched at him, encouraging him without words.

"Gaby . . . " He slid his hand along the inside of her thigh.

After a fractured moan, she scowled at him. "You're doing something to me."

"Yeah." He nuzzled her face and smiled. Finally the fear had left her tone. She sounded accusatory, and angry. She sounded like the Gaby he adored. "I'm seducing you."

Color flushed her cheeks and turned her mouth rosy. Blue eyes bright, tone once again commanding, she said, "Are you going to have sex with me?"

"I haven't decided yet."

She opened her mouth to protest that, and Luther pressed one hand between her thighs and found her warmer, softer.

She went mute, and, slowly, her eyes sank shut.

"Just relax now, okay?"

Thunder clattered, and she stiffened. "Luther . . . "

He was so horny he hurt. "I'm right here." He stroked over her, opened her, and pressed one finger deep inside her.

The storm lingered overhead, jarring the house with flash and rumble; the television went off with a snap, leaving them in utter darkness and a silence broken only by the fury of Mother Nature.

Gaby barely noticed. After a small flinch, her hips lifted and she squirmed against his hand. "The things you do to me . . . "

"I know." He kissed his way from her throat to her mouth. "Kiss me."

She did, without reservation. Though he'd kissed her many times now, he'd be her first, so she was far from experienced. But she showed as much gusto for sexual matters as she did for hunting wicked beings.

Her fevered enthusiasm soon had them both panting.

He'd gotten her off like this once before, in an open parking lot where her savage screams had echoed across the concrete. Now he had her alone.

Now he could finish this as he wanted.

While Luther found a rhythm she liked, he kissed her everywhere, bit her gently, nibbled on sensitive peaks and licked sensual hollows.

Gaby clutched his wrist, keeping his hand against her as if refusing to let him stop. But stopping was the last thing on his mind.

"Luther." She bit his shoulder without the gentleness he'd shown her. *"Luther."*

"Right here, honey." He felt her strong muscles tightening and looked at her face. Never one to be timid, her gaze locked on his, magnifying the intimacy, sharing everything she felt. He watched the extraordinary shifting of her features, the sharpening of her expression. Gaby changed in infinitesimal, subtle ways when she embraced the acute pain of her duty—and when she gave herself over to extreme physical pleasure.

From now on, Luther planned to immerse her in pleasure.

Just as he saw her eyes darken and go vague, he felt the bite of her fingernails on his flesh and inhaled the scent of her desire.

She came with the same primitive abandon she'd shown once before.

As her climax faded, she went limp, and then dropped back onto the couch, sprawled inelegantly, her legs over his lap.

In breathless wonder, she said, "Holy shit, Luther." She kept her eyes closed and she didn't smile. "That rocked."

Outside the wind whistled, but inside, warmth generated by their bodies, scented by their lust, filled the room. Need, satisfaction, rose up to glut Luther. Emotion permeated his soul. He stroked Gaby's calf, over the arch of her foot.

He'd never really noticed before, but she had narrow feet with a delicate arch. Graceful feet—feet that could deliver a kick deadly in intent.

"Hey." She remained still, her chest barely rising with her slow, even breaths. Luther kissed her ankle, just to get her attention. "You're not going to sleep on me, are you?" He had a boner that demanded immediate attention. He would never rush her, but he hoped Gaby's natural curiosity would see their relationship finally, fully, consummated.

"I'm not tired."

Of course she wasn't. Gaby never seemed to show the same weaknesses as others. "Then why so quiet?"

Her sigh was part repletion, part frustration. "Just thinking."

That worried him. "About what?"

Capable hands rested loosely over her pale belly. Baby-fine, tangled hair fanned out behind her head. She shifted one shoulder and didn't quite look at him. "About how much I detest cowards."

She meant herself, and Luther knew it. As the need to reassure her crowded in, sexual urgency took a backseat.

For now.

But it wasn't easy with her lying there nude, relaxed, soft and feminine. Using one finger, he drew a circle on her inner thigh. "People can't help the things that scare them, Gaby."

"Nothing scares you."

His short, sharp laugh corrected her error. "Losing you terrifies me." He bent and kissed her belly. "Too much."

"I don't know why." She tangled her fingers in his hair and brought his head up so she could look him in the eyes. "I'm fucking pathetic."

"No."

"You don't need me."

"But I want you." He thought about that, before adding, "And I do need you." He pulled her fingers from his hair and, moving up and over her, pressed her hand above her head. The full-body contact almost stole his thoughts, but this was too important to sidestep. "You, Gabrielle Cody, are intriguing, and frustrating, and sometimes foolhardy. You're an enigma, and an angel on earth."

"An angel?" She made a rude sound—and stared at his mouth. "Sex must fuck with your head if you believe that crap."

He hushed her with a quick, soft kiss. "You care more than anyone I've ever known. Despite what you do or how you do it—"

Her eyes narrowed, but she didn't verify the many ways she served her unique brand of justice.

"—it's always out of caring. I know that."

With her free hand kneading his shoulder, she shifted under him. "There's a world of difference between what you think you know, and the bloody truth." Before he could reply to that, she wrapped her legs around him. "We're naked, Luther."

"Believe me, I'm well aware of that." He caught her other wrist and brought that hand above her head, too. "I want to be inside you, Gaby."

"I'm not stopping you."

Tacit in her statement was the fact that she could stop

him if she wanted to, and they both knew it. Gaby was more capable, more physical, than any person—male or female—that he knew.

Bypassing that truth, he kissed her again, light and easy and full of hunger. "Knowing it'll be your first time, that you'll only be with me, is making me nuts." He drew in a big breath. "But I need to know that you're okay now. It's still storming—"

"Is it?"

Her teasing made him smile. It was so unique for her to show any lightness at all. She never laughed, never joked, and only at the rarest of times had he ever seen her smile.

That she'd tease now gave Luther hope for progress. "It is. And the way that it affects you breaks my damn heart."

"I won't whimper like a baby, if that's what you're worried about." She pressed her hips up and gave a grudging truth. "Having you close blunts a lot of extraneous influences."

Sometimes the things she said boggled his mind. But she'd said it before, crediting him with the power to soften the harshness of her life. "I'd love it if you told me exactly what that means."

Her brows scrunched as she pondered her explanation. "It's a little weird—but then everything about me is, right?" She didn't give him a chance to correct or reassure her. "Somehow, Luther, you filter the call to duty, and in the process, my neuroses. They're still there like a live beat inside my bloodstream, but your nearness keeps them tamped down and . . . manageable."

Hope, and guilt, stirred in Luther's heart. If he could give her any relief, he'd be thrilled. But at the same time he knew that what she did—and why—was important. The most important thing, at least to her.

"The calling, too?" Was he keeping her from tracking down a bloodthirsty psycho?

At the moment, did he care?

She gave a tentative tug on her wrists, and when he didn't release her, she relaxed again, her expression lazy, cocky as only Gaby could be. "I can get free anytime I want, you know."

Rather than acknowledge that claim, he said, "I would let you—if I thought getting free of me was what you really wanted."

She considered that, and let it go. "He's out there, Luther. A monster in our midst. A sickness of humanity. He'll torture, bleed, and kill innocent people, again and again. He won't care how they scream or beg. He enjoys that. Catching him won't be easy."

Luther sighed. In his line of work, he'd dealt with the criminally insane, and the just plain evil, many times. "It never is."

"It's easier if you don't interfere with me doing my duty."

Not her job, but her duty. How burdensome it must be to feel that the safety of others relied on how well you performed your *duty*—a duty that involved heinous, bloody deaths?

For him, it was different. He was a cop who took great pleasure in seeing justice served. But Gaby's form of justice would never fly in a court of law.

She didn't apprehend evildoers; she eradicated them.

Using that awesome blade, and miraculous speed, agility, and cunning, she wasted the bogeymen.

"I don't want to get in your way, Gaby. I only want to help you." *And protect you, as much from yourself as from a society that would condemn you.*

She tilted her head to study him. "Are you going to fuck me?"

Though he was used to her coarse language, Luther's brain almost exploded. It was damned difficult, but he managed to say "No."

Anger flashed in her eyes, and she started to pull away in earnest. "Jerk."

He fought to hold her still. "I want to *make love* to you, Gaby." A soft kiss to her pinched mouth stilled her struggles. "I'm going to show you that there's a difference."

Curiosity lit her eyes. "Yeah?" Her chin jutted. "Tell me, but do it fast. Having you like this makes me achy. Inside, I mean. I feel almost . . . liquid." Some of the antagonism faded as she admitted, "I'm not used to this stuff yet."

No, as a pariah to society, an outcast in her own mind, Gaby wasn't used to any affection at all. In twenty-one years of life, she'd managed to isolate herself so thoroughly that she was by far the most innocent woman he knew.

Until very recently, Gaby had never allowed others to touch her: emotionally, mentally, physically.

Definitely not in sexual exploration.

But now, with him, her life was changing. Luther remembered when he first saw her, how something about her had struck him hard, laid him low, and drawn him to her irrevocably. After that meeting, he would never be the same.

And he planned to see to it that she wasn't either.

Now he only had to ease Gaby into that reality.

With her pinned beneath him asking for sex, he was off to a good start.

It was so novel to see Gaby like this, sexually aroused, disgruntled with physical need. Her normal demeanor was balls-to-the-wall brazen, gutsy beyond common sense, so daring and determined that she risked her life without reserve.

He liked both aspects.

He liked her. Too much.

Luther stared into her eyes as he released her wrists, reached down between their bodies, and positioned himself. Thanks to her recent release, the head of his cock entered slick, moist heat.

His muscles bunched and his heart expanded painfully in his chest.

Her breath caught, then released on a low, shuddering moan.

And a knock sounded on the door.

Chapter 3

No fucking way. Gaby glared at Luther and ordered, *"Ignore it."*

Eyes squeezed shut as if in pain, Luther cursed low and long.

Frantic need encompassed Gaby unlike anything she'd ever felt before. Even her other sexual experiences with Luther didn't compare. Those times when he'd touched her, he was fully clothed, somehow apart from her.

But now . . . now she felt his body in places she'd never before had reason to consider.

He could not leave her like this.

Her voice sounding like a growl, she said, "Don't even think it, Luther. Whoever it is will go away."

The knock sounded harder, and Luther's partner, Ann Kennedy, shouted, "Open up, Luther."

Gaby tipped her head back and yelled toward the door, "Go *away*, Ann. We're busy."

Luther stared at her in appalled silence. What? Did he expect her to just give him up at such a crucial moment?

Ann knocked harder.

"No." Seeing the inevitable in Luther's eyes, Gaby shook her head. *"No."*

"I'm sorry, Gaby." His big hand smoothed along the side of her face, cupped her skull. He put his forehead to hers. "Though I'd conveniently forgotten, I'm still on duty."

God knew she understood duty, but that didn't mean she was appeased. It'd be a long time before she forgave him.

"This fucking sucks, Luther!" She shoved him aside and left the couch.

Luther grabbed her hand, and with his gaze flickering over her body, he swallowed hard. "You can't open the door like that."

A sneer formed. "I'm not opening the door at all, but it looks like you are." Pissed off and frustrated beyond all measure, she marched naked to the stairs. She glanced back once to see Luther standing there, wrapped in the throw, watching her retreat with undivided attention to her backside. "Perv."

"Only you would think so, Gaby."

His gaze followed her up the steps; she felt the burn of his scrutiny, the near tactile pressure of his interest. Sexual need sucked.

She'd just reached the top of the stairway when she heard the front door open.

Ann, in her characteristic way of acceptance, said, "I gather you forgot we have a dead body to contend with."

"Dead? So he didn't make it?"

"Died on the way to the hospital. I got a call, and they said so far, other than an obvious loss of blood, they're not sure what killed him."

Hiding her nudity, Gaby peeked around the wall to yell down, "He was drained. Try checking between his toes, in the crease of his groin . . . hell, maybe behind his ear.

Somewhere on his body, you'll find a pinprick big enough for an IV."

Ann appeared at the bottom of the steps. She looked at Gaby's disheveled hair, and then her bare shoulder. One slim brow lifted.

For the very first time in her life, Gaby felt slight embarrassment over her physical appearance. "What?" she asked Ann. "You have something to say, just say it."

Ann's mouth tilted in a smile. "I'm sorry that I interrupted."

For some reason, that infuriated Gaby even more—especially when she saw Ann's gentle amusement. The woman was a freakin' saint.

Ann was not only beautiful on the outside, with golden blonde hair, soft dark eyes, and a slender, womanly build, but she also possessed a gigantic heart and a temperament that reserved judgment against others—even against a freak like Gaby.

At times like this, Ann's graciousness grated on Gaby's nerves. "Fuck off."

Gaby heard Ann laugh and Luther apologize seconds before she slammed the door to the spare room that she'd commandeered. Putting both hands in her hair, she stalked to a window to look out.

Rain continued to fall, but in a peaceful, cleansing way now, rather than with the turbulent rage that had so badly disarmed her.

She hated weakness of any kind—in herself. In others, she expected it.

She had superior skills, both mental and physical, that made most seem frail in comparison.

But not Luther.

Oh God. Just thinking his name set her body to throbbing with a pulse beat of hot need. Her breasts ached. Down deep inside herself, her belly burned around a churning demand for *something*. It wasn't like the vague necessity for food she sometimes felt, or the need to rest. And it didn't resemble the driving urge to protect others.

This was different, and twice as gripping.

She needed to do something to distract herself because she didn't know how to assuage the need on her own. In this, Luther had her at his mercy.

Untenable.

Somehow, someway, she'd have to overcome this awful requirement of him.

Going to the trunk at the end of the unused bed, she opened the combination lock and removed her current work in progress. Writing graphic novels served as the only outlet for her frustrations. She needed to write and draw now more than ever.

Because the room didn't have a desk, she arranged everything on the floor and then sat cross-legged and went to work. Downstairs she could hear Luther and Ann speaking, and then a few minutes later, she recognized Luther's familiar tread on the stairs. He didn't come to her room, but instead went to the room she would sleep in with him.

The room where she'd presented herself naked on his bed, only to be called away.

Fuck.

Concentrating anew, Gaby threw herself into the ink depictions of a long-toothed bloodsucker feeding off an innocent who screamed in soundless agony as her lifeblood drained away.

Heart racing, Gaby let her muse take over—until she really saw the woman she'd drawn.

This woman was different from the corpse they'd found. Darker, younger.

Shit, shit, *shit*. Would she be next?

Pausing, Gaby studied the drawing that her subconscious had conjured. Gaunt, fragile, eyes hollow with abuse, the dark-skinned woman looked like any of a hundred addicted transients who clogged the alleyways.

Somehow, Gaby had to find her, and save her.

Then, hand shaking, she noticed something that showed from just behind the woman's leg.

A child.

"Gaby?" The doorknob twisted, but the lock kept Luther from entering.

Sick at heart, Gaby stood and stared down at the pages on the floor.

A young girl, not more than ten years of age.

God no. *Please*. Not that, not an innocent kid.

But the image remained, mocking her with the portent of what would come.

She backed up, removing herself from the harsh reality and going closer to Luther's soothing voice.

"Gaby?" His fist struck the door in an annoyed knock. "Open up."

Gaby rolled in her lips, breathing hard. "Yeah, hang on." Not until her hand touched the doorknob was she able to draw her gaze from the papers. After a deep breath, she stepped to the side of the door and opened it a little. "What?"

His jaw loosened.

She hadn't bothered with clothes yet, and he was now fully suited in a way befitting a detective. He looked nice. He smelled nice.

The way he'd touched her . . .

"Damn, Gaby." His chest expanded. In a low, nearly reverent voice, he whispered, "You're still naked."

She stared at his throat and at a small bit of chest hair showing from the open collar of his shirt. His tie hung loosely around his neck, his dark blond hair was mussed. "Yeah, well I didn't feel like getting dressed. Sue me."

"I'd rather eat you up."

Her gaze shot to his gorgeous brown eyes. She could tell that what he said held some significant sexual innuendo, just by the way that he said it. But the meaning escaped her.

"Damn, Gaby, you'll be the death of me." He trailed a finger along the curve of her breast, down to her nipple. He circled it once—and his hand dropped away. His eyes closed, his jaw locked, and then he firmed his resolve. "I have to go."

Of course he did. Now that he had her heart pumping too hard again. *Jerk.* "So then why are you bothering me? Go."

He cupped the back of her head and his voice gentled. After several heavy beats of silence, he asked, "You okay?"

"What do you care? You have a job to do—go do it."

His palpable irritation struck her. "I care, and you know it."

"Then stay and finish what you started." She knew he wouldn't. She knew he couldn't. But, damn it, she didn't really care about his problems at the moment.

Pained, he dropped his hands and stepped back from her. "Ann is waiting in her car."

Some strange emotion that felt too much like jealousy took a bite out of her pride. Gaby shoved him back several feet, using more strength than she meant to. "Then fucking go to Ann! Damn you, Luther. Nobody asked you to hang around anyway!"

"You did."

"Well I take it back."

So quickly that she didn't have time to think about it,

Luther jerked her through the doorway and slammed her to the wall. One of his pants-clad legs came between her naked thighs, his chest pinned her. And then his mouth was on hers, kissing her hard and deep, giving her just a small taste of what she so desperately wanted and needed.

Gaby considered leveling him.

It'd be so easy to make him hurt the way she was hurting. But she held back.

That kiss of his . . . it robbed her of spiteful intent, and instead ignited new fires.

Easing up, his mouth still touching hers, Luther whispered, "Please be here when I get home. I promise that I'll make it up to you."

Before she could answer, he kissed her again, his tongue in her mouth, his hot breath on her cheek. It was wonderful and scorching, and it melted her temper.

"I swear, Gaby, I'll be thinking of you every second that I'm gone, and that's dangerous. So tell me you'll be here."

Lying never fazed her. Gaby did what she had to do when she had to do it. But right now, feeling Luther pressed to her, she didn't have enough wits to consider a more prudent reply. "I don't know if I'll be here or not."

Fury took him two steps from her.

Not that Gaby gave a damn about his anger issues.

"Look, Luther, the truth is I have some stuff that I have to do." She rolled a bare shoulder, cocked her hip, and crossed her arms. "I don't know how long it'll take me. Might be a few minutes, might be all night."

His gaze burned.

Outside, Ann laid on the horn, causing Luther to curse. He ran a frustrated hand through his brown hair.

"What?" He narrowed his eyes in demand. "What do you have to do that's so important?"

Gaby enunciated *"Stuff"* in a way guaranteed to annoy.

But how could she clarify more than that when she didn't yet know herself what had to be done?

His jaw worked, he breathed hard, and then, very slowly, he smiled.

An evil smile.

God help me. But, as usual, God ignored her, leaving her to palpitate over what Luther planned.

Leaning in close to her, he breathed in her ear at the same time that his hand pressed between her legs. "When I say that I want to eat you—that means my mouth on you, Gaby." His hand pressed against her. "Here."

A shock of sensation ran over her.

His tongue touched her ear and stole her breath. "Everything I do to your mouth, the way I lick with my tongue, the way I suck on your tongue . . ."

She swallowed and said, "Yeah?"

"That's what I'll do to you here—" His fingers toyed with her, long enough to send her need skyrocketing, too briefly to give her any satisfaction.

He leaned away, removed his hand, and left her wanting.

Deadpan, he said, "But I can't if you're not here when I get back."

Knowing what he'd done to her—and why he'd done it—sent fury erupting to the surface. Blind with rage, Gaby swung at him, but he ducked and the momentum turned her so that he caught her back to his chest.

"Easy now." His whisper held amusement.

"You miserable fucking jerk!" She considered maiming him. "It wasn't enough to leave me wanting you. No, you had to go and amp it up."

"Take what you feel, multiply it by a hundred, and that's what I'm suffering, too." His lips teased her ear as he spoke softly to her. "Be here when I return, and we'll both get some relief."

"Fuck you."

His sigh was long and filled with frustration. "If you're going out, do you need any money?"

Her spine snapped straight so fast that it hurt. Without thinking it through, Gaby stomped his foot, and when his hold loosened, she brought her elbow back hard into his midsection.

He wheezed—and released her so he could fold in on himself.

Breathing hard and nearly blinded by her pride, Gaby spun around to face him. Through her teeth she ground out, "I will never, *ever* take money from you."

One hand rubbing his ribs, his expression a mix of pain, anger, and resignation, Luther slumped back against the wall. "You could have just said no."

Well, yeah . . . she could have. Gaby eyed him, saw she'd truly hurt him, and wilted.

Now feeling guilty, Gaby reiterated, "I don't need your money."

"You have your own?"

"Yes." Oh God, now he was going to ask her how she got money. Gaby waited, her brain churning for possible explanations other than the writing and drawing of a popular underground graphic novel.

But all Luther said was, "Good. But, Gaby, if you ever do need anything, I hope you'll come to me."

And with that, he turned and went down the stairs and out the front door. Before closing the door behind him, he said, "Remember to lock up when you leave. You can take a spare key from the basket on top of the refrigerator."

Gaby stared down the stairs at the closed door.

Why did he have to be that wonderful? So macho but so caring, so capable and still pure of heart.

She didn't deserve him, but she wanted him. And he wanted her.

Then she thought of that small child she saw in her drawing. The kid was still safe, for now. If the child had been in imminent danger, duty would have sent her for it.

She had to believe that.

Gaby thought of a person vile enough who, for twisted reasons unfathomable to the sane, would want the child. It sickened her, but she feared that the same bloodsucker who had already been at work draining others now wanted the child for nourishment.

Maybe taking a child was easier than capturing an adult. Maybe a kid would be more resilient, quicker to heal if the maniac wanted a reliable blood resource.

Somehow, starting right now, she'd find that kid and protect her.

And then she thought of Luther's request. A shudder passed through her, filling her with equal parts dread and longing. He had a terrible hold on her.

And God help her, she prayed she'd be home when he returned.

The body, long ago quartered into more manageable hunks and stored in a refrigerator, offered nothing more to him.

After the awful intrusion into his domain, a primitive building used only for the delectation of his prodigious appetite, he'd been able to salvage only a portion of the last sacrifice.

The rest of the body had been stored in an industrial refrigeration system in the basement. Soon it would be discovered by the intruders.

For now, Fabian Ludlow would make do with what had

been left to him. He preferred the liquid fulfillment of warm blood, the sweet sensation of it passing over his tongue and sliding down his throat. He savored how it settled in his belly.

He needed it, like some needed the sunshine and sleep.

Long ago, he'd discovered how ingesting blood and, when necessary, human flesh, had added to his health, making him stronger, faster. Keener of mind and more astute to his surroundings.

He hadn't known that he'd be denied his most recent kill.

Thinking of the trespass, his skin itched and his soul screamed in hollow demand. Damn the judgmental law officials for unchaining his captive.

How dare they make moral decisions against vices they couldn't begin to understand?

From a secluded vantage point, Fabian had watched in impotent rage as a skinny woman, indistinguishable from so far away, had collapsed on the porch. The police ignored her as they scoured over the site and gathered ridiculous clues that would lead them nowhere. Eventually the idiots sent his prey on a fool's trip to the hospital.

He might have been able to get another cup or two from the vagrant if they hadn't interfered. And, of course, he would have kept that delectable, tasty body for when the blood flow failed.

Now he'd be forced to kill someone new.

Someone younger, fresher.

More tender.

Saliva pooled in his mouth, on his tongue. What he imagined, what he *craved* with mammoth preoccupation, was something of which he hadn't yet partaken.

But now the time was near.

He ran his thickened tongue over his lips and dreamt

of it, how it'd be, how the blood might taste transcendent and the underdeveloped muscles might be softer, more malleable . . .

All around him, the others laughed and danced. To his right, one young couple mistook the bloodlust for lust of another kind; they fucked wildly, without discretion.

Fools. They reveled in their freedom without discerning that it was all *him*.

He was the one who had transformed them. *He* was the one who had enlightened them on the veritable pleasures of the flesh.

He'd shown them how to take what they needed from those useless souls born only to give.

Worthless individuals unfit for sustaining life cluttered the earth in nauseating proportion. Unlike most, Fabian comprehended that they were there by contrived design, no different from cattle or pigs sent to the slaughter.

They were meant to nourish those with appropriate initiative to partake of the offering.

Those who *he* enlightened with the benefits of ingesting the blood, often straight from the vein, had also been taught the pleasure of taking another's life. He'd taught them to sate themselves with the power of another human, even one too weak to survive.

With each soul he captured, he felt his own strength expand to undeniable proportions. It wasn't an illusion, as one now-dead fool had dared to suggest.

It was actuality. Sweet, undeniable truth. He was near superhuman, with immeasurable cunning and aptitude. He understood that, even if some others yet failed to recognize it.

"Fabian, come join us."

Bored, he looked at Georgie, a young man who favored Goth fashion and an overabundance of tattoos and body piercings. Georgie didn't understand the merits of subtlety, or that sometimes less was more. Fabian had met him, along with most of the others, through the shop.

It amazed even him that people proved so easy to lead when one had leadership qualities, as Fabian did. But then, tattooing was a personal business, and it didn't take long to get to know a person when you put a needle to their skin.

He didn't hold the body art against Georgie. In fact, he often appreciated the beauty of an intricately inked human form. It had almost the same splendor as a body torturously carved of all meat.

But Georgie was stupid. He took drugs that Fabian had not approved, and that was forbidden. Only the narcotics that Fabian himself supplied were permitted. It was yet another method of control, another means of maintaining the upper hand. No one was allowed to ingest any narcotic substance that Fabian did not personally hand out.

Georgie knew that—but he thought he could show up high and Fabian wouldn't notice.

Fool.

At present, Georgie partook of the bounty Fabian had supplied, his eyes glazed and his movements sluggish. He took extraordinary pleasure in being egregious.

For Georgie, it was the shock factor, not a proper understanding of the merits involved in partaking of sweet sustenance, consuming the very essence of life. He didn't fathom the cerebral and sentient fulfillment of what they did.

As Fabian watched Georgie, his temper spiked.

Given a choice, Georgie would probably be stupid enough to eat the brains or even the spinal cord, both of which were prone to carrying disease.

Running his tongue along the blunt edges of his capped teeth, Fabian considered a punishment that might befit Georgie's irreverence.

Yes, he knew what to do, knew exactly how to teach the

others by using Georgie as an example. His heart began to pound in feverish anticipation.

God, he loved the adrenaline rush when he planned an attack.

Parting his lips, Fabian slipped his fingers into his own mouth and loosened the snug-fitting porcelain caps. One by one he removed them, leaving his real teeth exposed. He dropped the caps into the pocket of his coat.

With consummate delight, he skimmed his tongue along the honed edges of his predator's bite. Long ago, his front teeth had been filed and reshaped to accommodate his inexhaustible hunger. There were no smooth borders, only jagged rims and his razor-sharp, elongated eyeteeth, meant to pierce the skin and flesh with ease.

An inferno of heat burned behind Fabian's eyes when Georgie laughed too loud. He made a mockery of them, ridiculing their sublime practice, when in fact he should have shown due deference to the offering.

Fabian's shoulders curled; his long fingers tightened. "Stop it," he whispered, "right now."

But Georgie didn't hear the warning. He swiped a sleeve along his mouth, wasting the bounty—and Fabian lost the fragile hold on his maniacal rage.

On a thunderous roar, he launched himself at Georgie, knocking him backward. With a solid thud, Georgie's head smacked against the chilly cement floor of the abandoned home Fabian had chosen to carry out the delectation of their avocation. Georgie groaned, flailed, and then sank into a stupor.

Someone screamed. Bodies scrambled to get out of their way.

In a blind frenzy of need and fury, Fabian sank his teeth into Georgie's soft white throat. His tongue stroked, located the jugular, and he readjusted his bite.

Yes. Fuck yes. His eyes sank shut as he fed at the ripped throat.

He felt Georgie's futile, insensate struggles. But he was a pathetic boy, not more than twenty, and as weak in body as he was in mind.

At six feet, two inches tall, Fabian was far stronger. He'd fed many times and gathered the strength of multiple sacrificial souls.

Nothing had ever tasted as good as this. He relished the raw, wild feeding from a live body with the heart still pumping hot blood throughout the veins. Because of societal intrusions, he'd long denied himself this splendid pleasure. Instead, he'd been making do by hooking IVs to wilting bodies, ensuring the blood supply lasted.

Now, with this frenzied meal, he moaned with bliss.

All around him, the others were silent, maybe with awe, maybe with fear.

He fucking well didn't care.

Caution made it necessary to plan out the menu, to make each kill last. For far too long now he'd had to resort to a discreet drinking of the stored liquid mixed with anticoagulants and blood thinners, and to meting out the supply in small doses.

He was an alpha male, savage by nature, at the top rung of the proverbial food chain. His basic nature prodded him toward pursuit, domination, and slaughter. At least, on occasion.

When it was well deserved.

The others crowded closer. He felt their palpitating fascination. Slanting his gaze to the side, he saw one woman lick her lips and stroke her own nipples.

His cock hardened.

His pulse thrummed.

Filling his mouth with the metallic blood, he sat up and let Georgie, now a lifeless entity, drop limply to the floor.

He turned to the woman—her name escaped him—and saw her big breasts were heaving, her eyes slumberous with sexual excitement. Many would see her as a perverted soul, defective in her desires.

Fabian relished her reaction.

He grabbed her wrist and hauled her in close, then closed his mouth over hers and let her take Georgie's blood directly from him. It was the rarest of gifts he bestowed on her, and she didn't disappoint him.

She moaned, choked, and then her tongue slicked over his, over his lips and chin. He ripped her shirt away and squeezed her nipples, twisted. Crying out, she bit his chin, launching into her own primal derangement.

Fabian liked it that everyone watched them, that he would be the center of attention as befitted his importance.

With Georgie no longer a viable member, he had an audience of six, which was perhaps one too many.

He shoved his hand beneath the woman's skirt and fingered her roughly through her panties. She panted, fell back with her legs spread.

A dangerous offering to a man in the middle of a bloody fete.

Fabian smiled and bent to her hot, fleshy thigh. He licked, nuzzled, testing the give of her soft body, aware of the warmth from her own flowing blood just beneath her smooth, silky skin.

He looked up at two other young men, both of them wide-eyed with fascination, watchful with expectation. As he recalled, one was an accountant, the other a cashier for the local grocery.

They were both easily led. "Hold her."

At his order, the woman jerked with new awareness of her precarious position. Now panicked, she tried to fight, but oh, it was far too late for that.

His minions were quite willing to do as he bid them, if for no other reason than a macabre curiosity as to his intent.

One of the lads held her arms against her furious struggles; the other caught her free leg and pinned it back painfully so she couldn't kick Fabian.

If she did, he'd kill her for certain. In fact, her outcome was yet undecided. But he inclined toward leniency; after all, they needed a new source of nourishment and Georgie was dead.

With her plump proportions she'd likely suffer them for a week or more, especially if they showed due moderation.

Salty tears, blackened with makeup, tracked her cheeks, mixing with the blood on her mouth and chin. She sobbed and pleaded to no avail.

Beside her, the scent of Georgie's body, his blood and his violent death, spurred on their passion.

"Silence her," Fabian said, and someone cupped a hard hand over her mouth, muffling her entreaties for a mercy that none of them possessed.

Hooking his fingers in her panties, Fabian pulled them to the side, exposing the soft white groin, the thin skin and most fragile flesh. He could see the delicate blue veins, could almost feel the life flowing through her.

His heart threatened to erupt with the grisly provocation of it.

Her snuffling sounds of terror blurred in Fabian's mind, receding until all he could envision was the steady pumping of her blood through her veins. Slowly, relishing the moment, he bent and sank his teeth into her groin.

He could smell her pungent, aroused sex, and *taste* the piquancy of her luxuriant fear. The sensual, potent medley put him into an anesthetized languor.

She screamed in agony, but the sound only incited them all.

She wouldn't die, Fabian decided; he wouldn't allow her that easy release. Her exquisite taste would not be squandered in a loss of control.

Her wound would heal, and she'd be anointed in the ritual of serving others.

Seeing her plight would surely inspire the rest of his minions to greater understanding.

She tasted even better than Georgie had, but Fabian no longer fed from hunger. No, Georgie had taken care of that.

He fed now to show his superiority.

He fed from sheer pleasure.

He fed as a show of dominance.

And then, like any good master, he stepped aside and let the others take a turn.

He didn't mind sharing. And besides, he had to leave for work soon. Today, he would arrive at the shop more fulfilled than he'd been in ages.

Maybe, with the added drug of fresh blood, he'd be able to surmise how he knew the skinny woman he'd seen with the cops. He'd been too far away to see her clearly. All he'd noted with certainty was her weakness, her vulnerability. Yet when he'd looked at her, despite her pathetic flaws, he'd felt a strong familiarity.

Somehow they were acquainted. But how?

He would figure it out, Fabian decided as he stood back and watched the others descend on the woman.

She made a most delectable meal.

But somehow he knew, if he captured that skinny woman and tasted her, she would be the most sublime.

Anticipation gnawed on his serenity; he could hardly wait.

Chapter 4

Gaby dressed without hurry, distracted by the mayhem of her thoughts. She wasn't sure where to look for the girl, but staying in Luther's home wouldn't elucidate things. She needed to be doing . . . something. *Anything*.

Hanging around, waiting for Luther to return, made her feel doubly dependent and pathetic.

She couldn't abide either.

She locked away her manuscript for safekeeping, hoping that by the time she needed to finish it, the child would have an ending that ensured safety and security.

Because she wasn't certain where the bus route might be in Luther's neighborhood, she bundled up in a dark hooded sweatshirt. She might be walking for a while, not that she minded. Strolling around the area would help her familiarize herself with the new surroundings. She needed to find a good place nearby to stow her beat-up car. She needed to learn the various routes and where they led.

After clipping a digital audio player to her waistband

and putting headphones in her ears, Gaby ventured out. Luther had bought her the music player, and she enjoyed it more than she'd thought possible. Even the music he'd initially chosen for her, edgy and loud with a hard thumping beat that she felt inside herself, was perfect for her.

In some ways, he knew her well.

In other ways, he didn't know her at all.

The gray sky and brisk wind added a nasty chill to the air, but Gaby paid no heed as she concentrated on the side streets and main intersections, learning the area and committing it to memory.

After several miles of walking, she found a bus stop and joined others huddling under a lighted metal enclosure that would protect them from the rain.

Recognizing the difference between the squalor of the areas she usually frequented and Luther's middle-class comfort, Gaby stuffed her knotted hands into her sweatshirt pockets.

Truth be told, she felt more comfortable near the dregs of society, in the projects and government housing units. There, surrounded by crime and immorality, around people driven by indifference and desperation, she felt at home.

Mort, her old landlord and now a friend, had kept his building clean and semi-secure, especially since the comic book store he owned was attached to the living quarters. But at night, she could hear the drunken arguments, the domestic abuse, the drive-by shootings and gang disruptions.

And it . . . comforted her.

There had been a bus stop not two blocks from Mort's front door, but not even a bench remained at the designated location. Miscreants of the serious and not-so-serious kind had repeatedly demolished it, as much out of boredom as a display of street cred. No one had bothered to replace the seat or the shelter.

Though she hated to be fanciful, Gaby missed the old place. At least while staying there, she'd understood her life and her purpose.

Then she'd met Luther, and he'd turned her whole existence upside down. Running from him had seemed the safest bet. For a time, she'd stayed with hookers and put up with Jimbo, their pimp.

She'd changed her look, changed her location, changed almost everything about herself except her duty—and still Luther had found her.

Bliss claimed they were destined to be together.

So dumb. How could that possibly be?

Gaby hunched her shoulders, driven inward by her thoughts.

She did believe in Bliss's intuition, but Bliss was little more than a child, as much an outcast as Gaby herself. Until Gaby stepped in, she'd been a hooker.

Now she was a friend.

Damn, how many freakin' friends did she need, anyway? She was starting to collect them the same way a mangy dog collected fleas. She'd gotten by for a long time all on her own. Other than Father Mullond, the priest who'd helped her understand her calling, she'd had no one.

And she'd been fine and dandy all alone. It was better. For her, for everyone else.

But things had changed irrevocably.

An older woman gave Gaby a sympathetic smile, and she realized how darkly she scowled.

Shit. She turned away from the granny and turned up her music until it made her eardrums vibrate.

Disgruntled by the rapid changes taking place in her life, Gaby kept her distance from the warmly clothed men and stylishly dressed women at the stop. Leaning on a brick structure, she surveyed the traffic, both human and automotive.

People laughed or talked, some with umbrellas open, some with collars up. A few had devices in their ears and appeared to be in deep conversation with . . . no one.

Even those waiting for the bus were in a hurry to get somewhere, likely nowhere important. That mind-set, the on-the-go lifestyle, made no sense to Gaby.

These people acted safe, as if anyone ever truly could be. They had no awareness of the ugly societal deformities that loomed around them. Homicidal psychopaths lurked everywhere, disguised as neighbors, family, friends, or lovers. Fiends of every disorder existed hand in hand with innocents.

Yet none of these people had a clue.

And Gaby could never forget. Not for a second. God, she was out of place here, and sooner or later Luther would realize it.

The bus finally came and Gaby waited until everyone else had boarded before taking a seat toward the back. No one sat by her, but several people stared.

Was she that transparent? Did even strangers recognize her deviant presence among them?

Their auras filled the bus with a churning hue of expectation, urgency, boredom, and complacency. Not one of them understood the day-to-day peril they faced.

Choosing to ignore them, she turned to stare out the foggy window. Like veins on emaciated flesh, raindrops traveled haphazardly over the dirty glass, occasionally crisscrossing and blending, only to branch out again.

Gaby contented herself by watching as tidy buildings gave way to shops with crumbling bricks and peeling paint. One by one, the social scale of the bus's occupants changed. The "nice" people got off, and a new element boarded.

The hypnotic hiss of bus tires on wet pavement, the gray day and drizzling rain, softened the reality of bars and tattoo parlors that replaced groceries and salons.

Falling into a lull, Gaby lost herself in her raucous music—until her unfocused gaze snagged on one particular tattoo parlor. Beautiful swirling colors and font shapes drew her attention to an ornate sign indicating the artwork available inside.

But around that sign, encompassing the façade of the tidy, well-kept building, a thick, dark impression of reality swirled. This aura wasn't so much a glow as a smoky film in dirty colors of sulfur and mustard, rich with pain and anger.

Gaby pressed a hand to the window and stared. Black boreholes pierced the shades, and through those holes, small white explosions, spurred by artificial stimulation, told Gaby that the tattoo parlor partook of some serious drug use. Shades of grave imbalance indicated a lack of sanity. A crazed sociopath lurked inside.

Gaby's senses kicked.

This wasn't a true alarm, but more like sensory awareness of things being out of place. It thrilled her to have found a firm purpose.

Adrenaline rushed through her lax limbs as Gaby stood to make her way to the front of the bus. The second the driver stopped, she got off, removed her earphones, and surveyed her surroundings.

Even the air smelled different here, not as green, crisp, or clean as it did near Luther's home. Here, she smelled the smoke of factories, the odor of rotting garbage, and the sticky stench of unwashed bodies.

This was her world.

She knew what to do here.

Renewed by familiarity, Gaby started back up the street toward the tattoo parlor, but before she'd gone more than a few steps, the vicious snarling of dogs drew her gaze.

Across the street, three young men with two pit bulls

on leashes approached the gated area of an old elementary school. The school's windows were all shattered or boarded up, but in the yard a ramshackle playground inhabited by an old moldy sofa and a few treadless tires remained.

The men were muscular guys, tall and cocky, and their dogs begged to be unleashed.

A young, dark-skinned woman quickly gathered up three children and left the area. A husky woman yelled something at the men and shook a fist, but quieted when the dogs lunged, trying to get free of their restraints. The men laughed, and the angered woman snatched up a child off the old couch and fled.

More children remained, climbing in and over the old tires, bouncing on the broken springs of the couch, risking hazard on the rusty, ruined playground equipment. Most of them were unattended by adults.

So, Gaby thought. She had children aplenty, and obvious drug dealers claiming real estate. This was a perfect opportunity for her to shake off her introspection.

Alive with anticipation, Gaby started across the street. The tattoo parlor could wait.

She needed this. Oh yes, she did.

Before she could reach the men, someone caught her arm, startling Gaby so that she swung around in a defensive stance.

The petite girl, who looked to be twelve or thirteen, wore a comprehensive expression of worry far beyond her immature years.

"Lady," she said in a frantic whisper, "what are you going to do?"

Strangers seldom got explanations from her, but the girl's lyrical accent, long dark hair, and dark eyes softened Gaby. "What I do best—get rid of trouble."

Putting a delicate hand to her forehead, the girl mumbled in frustration before saying to Gaby, "You should not do that."

Intrigued by her daring, Gaby crossed her arms and gave the child her full attention. "Why not? You going to tell me those punks aren't trouble?"

The girl's eyes darted to the men; fear clouded her expression. "You should not mess with the likes of them. They are very dangerous."

Gaby leaned down close. "Here's a secret for you, kiddo. So am I."

A small, thin hand clamped on to Gaby's arm. "You do not understand. They do not like interference. They will . . . retaliate."

Gaby scoffed. "They'll try."

The girl rolled her eyes and her whisper went harsh. "Do not be foolish. Please. They will . . . burn you."

That took her aback, not in fear but in curiosity as to what this child had been through. "Burn me, huh?"

Nodding, the girl again glanced at the men. They were currently harassing a boy close to the girl's age. The boy strained away, anxious to escape, but they kept him in place with a painful grip on his shoulder and a lot of mean-mugging intimidation.

That in itself, the physical detainment of a young boy who wanted to be free, was reason enough for Gaby to intervene, to execute her own form of devastation. But she wanted details on what the girl meant, and at present, the boy didn't look to be in immediate danger. Scared, yes, but they wanted something from him, so they wouldn't hurt him. Yet.

If things changed, well then, Gaby would be on the men in a heartbeat.

"How about you explain to me—real fast—exactly what you're so afraid of."

"And then you will go?"

"Then I'll understand." No way was Gaby leaving.

The girl nodded. "There are few places for children to play, and they often gather here. Then the men showed up and began selling their drugs. Things were not the same. There were gunshots and loud arguments about who could sell here and who could not. A man was beaten, and another was cut with broken bottles. When they started to bother the children, my aunt asked them to sell their drugs at another block, to leave the children here alone."

"Other than the obvious danger, how were they bothering the kids?" Gaby already had an idea, but she wouldn't mind having it spelled out.

The girl looked down at her clasped hands. "They get the children to be lookouts when they sell their drugs. My aunt did not like that."

Had they tried to force the girl? Oh yeah, she'd bet on it. And now Gaby would make them pay. "Your aunt sounds like a gutsy lady."

Remembered heartache added pain to her tone. "After my aunt complained, they attacked her. Her house was burned to the ground." Her stark gaze came back to Gaby's. "She and my uncle both died."

Pain as sharp as her blade sliced deep into Gaby's conscience. Why hadn't she been called on to help the aunt? God knew she couldn't be everywhere at once, but for this child to have suffered such a loss . . .

"Damn it." Gaby looked up at the sky. "You know, You could have let me know."

The girl backed up a step, and Gaby realized she'd scared her. Around here, few probably talked directly to Him.

Around the tightness in her throat, Gaby asked, "When was this?"

"A few months ago."

Had the girl been living with her aunt when the fire happened? If so, where did she live now?

Gaby didn't like the probability of her on the street. "The police did nothing?"

"There is nothing that they can do. They try, but they never catch the men doing things they should not. There is no way to prove that they set the fire."

"But you know they did?"

She nodded, and a weighty maturity showed in her stiff-shouldered posture. This girl had seen life's uglier side, and nothing would ever negate the bitter reality.

She looked at the men with angry hatred. "I know."

"That's good enough for me." Gaby straightened with commitment. "What's your name?"

The girl shrank back. "I am no one important." New concern crumpled her pretty face. "I . . . I only wanted to warn you."

"And I appreciate it, I really do." Because Gaby well understood the need for secrecy, she didn't push the girl. "Do me a favor, will you? Head on home and leave the creeps to me. I promise you, I can handle them. After today they won't bother you again."

The child took in Gaby with experienced scrutiny, noting her lack of bulk and no doubt finding her inadequate for the job.

She shook her head with sad acceptance. "You refuse to listen."

Gaby touched the girl's cheek, surprising herself with the affectionate gesture, given that affection of any kind seldom had a place in her life of deleterious persuasions.

It was Luther's influence, and she wasn't at all sure she liked it. "When I'm through here, maybe you'll trust me just a little."

"I wish you to be careful, please." She looked beyond

Gaby to the men. "They have terrible friends. You cannot imagine how scary."

Gaby winked. "They don't have anyone who is scarier than me, I promise you."

The girl's voice went faint. "But . . . there are some who . . . " She trailed off.

"What?"

After an audible swallow, she looked down at her feet. "Nothing. I have said too much already."

"No problem." She hoped the girl would share her fears later, after Gaby reassured her of her abilities. "I'll probably have to split after I dispatch these goons. But I would like to talk to you some more. Do you come here pretty often?"

"Yes. My sister likes to play here."

"Good." Gaby couldn't preset a date to meet again, just in case the girl shared that info with the cops who were sure to get wind of this. But Gaby wanted to see her again, to know that she was safe and in good care.

Children in general had such pure hearts that Gaby always felt an exceptional urge toward protecting them. Gaby sensed that this girl had already suffered far too much.

"I will see you again, then?"

With a nod, Gaby said, "Count on it. Now scram before you *really* get scared—by me." She turned and strode directly for the men.

The boy looked up and saw her first.

Gaby stared at the youth. "Go home, kid."

Alarm widened the boy's eyes, and he strained away, but didn't get far with the tight hold one man had on him. The bullies didn't like her intrusion, which suited Gaby just fine. Even as the dogs spit and growled and strained against the leashes, she kept walking.

When the men focused their entire attention on Gaby,

the boy jerked free and ran hell-bent into the playground area. He disappeared amid the other kids who were all now gawking.

Gaby locked eyes with one foul individual. He looked clean-cut enough, with close-cropped hair, a pricey diamond in his ear, and immaculate clothes. But a murky, sick aura hung like a wet blanket around him and his cohorts. They were malevolent, unconscionable men, but apparently not sick enough to warrant a call to duty.

Again she glanced up at the sky. "I think I should start picking."

One of the men laughed. "Baby girl, who you talkin' to?"

God's lack of response didn't matter. Looking at the three of them sickened Gaby, and at the same time, it sent her antagonism surging to the surface.

She gave her icy rage free rein. "Hey, bitches."

That got their attention.

"It takes a real pathetic bully to push around little kids. And you three look about as pathetic as anything I've ever seen."

One man, taking the role as leader, smiled at her. "You play a dangerous game, sweetness. My dogs are hungry for fresh meat."

Gaby didn't even bother looking at the vicious animals. "I'm not playing, asshole. And a word of warning—if you let the dogs loose, they won't make it, and that'd be a shame, because I have nothing against animals."

Antagonism brought one of the guys forward. "Bitch, are you stupid or insane? Cuz if we turn even one dog loose, you're fuckin' hamburger."

Gaby stayed a mere inch beyond the reach of the dogs' snapping jaws. "So on top of being a wimp, you're a coward who needs animals to protect you. What a laugh." But Gaby didn't laugh; she didn't even smile.

Most times, she wasn't sure she knew how.

Dark eyes flared, and a strong jaw locked. "J.J.," the man said in an ominous but commanding whisper, "maybe you ought to show her how we deal with stupid bitches who don't know the right way to use their pretty mouths."

Showing large white teeth, J.J. stepped around the dogs with a swaying walk and a shitload of attitude.

Exhilaration sizzled along Gaby's nerve endings. She let him get close enough to take a swing, which she ducked without effort.

Having a strong propensity toward violence, Gaby relished the attack.

She *loved* to fight, especially at times like this, when she knew she fought against rampaging cruelty and injustice.

Hoping the girl had left the scene, Gaby came back up with a punch to the guy's balls. Then she planted another, just for good measure. Given the unnatural force of her fisted strikes, he'd be lucky if he ever pissed again, much less fathered children.

And that, too, she figured to be a public service.

He doubled in on himself and would have fallen forward in a pain-induced stupor if Gaby hadn't planted a solid kick to his face, sending him backward.

She saw a tooth go flying, sprayed by blood and spittle. His jaw hung loose, clearly dislocated. One eye bulged grotesquely from the socket.

Well. She'd done adequate damage with that one. Old J.J. went down and he wasn't going to get back up anytime soon.

Smelling the blood and seeing the violence, the dogs jerked at their restraints with berserk fever. They concerned Gaby because if they got loose, they could be a threat to the children who remained nearby, held in place by gruesome curiosity.

It broke Gaby's heart to hurt an animal, any animal, but these beasts had been raised for barbarous aggression. They were a threat to the children, to anyone who got within their reach, and she couldn't have that.

Looking up at the remaining two men with incandescent fury burning in her eyes, she grated, "You'll fucking well pay for what you're about to make me do."

Jaw slack and face livid, the head honcho stood there staring at J.J.'s bloodied, unconscious form.

He regained his focus with a burst of indignation and theatrical antics. His face contorted as he stormed forward.

"Fucking whore!" he shouted. "Now you done it. You fucking well deserve what you get." And with a toss of the leashes, he let loose the dogs.

Gaby had her knife out before the first dog reached her. The animal didn't get a chance to get his teeth into her flesh before she cut his throat in a wide arc that opened to reveal muscle and sinew. The wound smiled wide, gushing blood and limiting the dog to mere gurgles before he stumbled, crumpled, and fell to his side.

Leaping in the air, fangs bared, the second dog tried for her throat. A kick to the muscular head staggered him, giving Gaby enough time to sink her knife into the thick chest. She planted the blade hard enough to lift the dog off the ground, and as he descended again, she twisted the knife, ripping through the canine heart.

With no more than a faint yelp, the poor creature fell back, twitched, and went still.

Gaby's chest ached and her heart squeezed tight with the awfulness of what she'd just done, what she'd been forced to do.

Sadness suffocated her, making it near impossible to swallow around the clogging anguish and remorse.

Even now, in death and sticky with blood, the dogs were

beautiful animals—and they'd never had a chance, thanks to the inhumanity of men.

Tears burned her eyes.

"Whore! Fucking cunt!" Strutting toward her, the leader drew out a gun and took aim. "You'll pay for that, bitch. I'll bury you!"

Gaby spun to the side—and the bullet grazed the middle of her right forearm. Heat exploded and a strange numbness tried to settle in.

It didn't matter. She wouldn't let it matter.

The burning pain only served to incite her inherent response.

Knife still clasped in her hand, she threw it with venomous accuracy and it sank hilt-deep into the shooter's shoulder. Pain forced him to drop the gun from his slack hand and it scuttled over the paved lot, out of his reach.

"Tylek," he hissed through his teeth to his cohort, "kill that crazy bitch for me. Make her pay. Make her fucking suffer."

Tylek looked a little wary of that order, but he dutifully mustered his courage.

Duty, Gaby thought. It ruled so many. It made some do the most foolhardy things—like challenging her.

"That's right, Tylek. Come make me pay." Using the fingertips of both hands, she beckoned Tylek closer. He was the biggest of the three, but he posed no legitimate challenge.

Not for her.

Balancing on the balls of her feet, Gaby took a loose-limbed stance. When Tylek leaped at her, she went to her back with him, rolling and using her feet to launch him away. He landed on his back, giving her an opportunity to move over him in a dominant position.

With a knee planted squarely in his groin, she took aim

and punched him in the throat. He gagged hard, wheezed for air he couldn't get.

Somewhere in the distance, police sirens split across the gray, depressing day with shrill intrusion. No way in hell did Gaby intend to be anywhere nearby when the cops showed up and started asking questions. Luther would have a fit, but she could deal with him.

Being arrested she couldn't abide. Not ever.

She rose from Tylek and kicked him in the temple to ensure he wouldn't get back up. Dispassionate, Gaby watched him go blank; his eyes rolled back in his head and he lolled to the side.

Knowing the shooter, despite his incapacitating wound, would scramble for his weapon, Gaby made a point of beating him to it. She kicked the gun out of his reach, but ever aware of the children, she didn't move it so far that any of the kids might get hold of it.

"You're making a big mistake, bitch. I swear to you, I'm going—"

Without real effort, Gaby stomped his chest, cutting off his threats and knocking him back on his ass. "I'm getting tired of you calling me a bitch." Another kick to the chin leveled him flat.

Relaxed, comfortable, Gaby knelt over him. "So big shot, what's your name?"

"Fuck off."

Gaby stared down at him, and with the knife hilt in her hand, she worked her fingers tight around it and bore down steadily until she felt the tip of the blade meeting bone.

He howled in agony, trying to fend her off without success.

Dispassionate, she studied him, saw his state of shock brought on by loss of blood and amplifying pain. Softly, she said, "I won't ask again."

Breathing in compact, gasping breaths, he nodded with grudging reluctance. "Bogg."

"You shitting me? What kind of stupid name is that?" Knowing the extent of his injuries, Gaby didn't really expect an answer. She studied the ink on his neck. "And your gang?"

"Crazy Crypts."

"You guys aren't real big on creative names, are you? I think you should be called Whiney Wimps."

He coughed out a moaning complaint, and managed to say, *"Bitch."*

"A bitch who kicked your sorry ass, huh?" After opening his jacket, Gaby retrieved an assortment of drugs and paraphernalia. Some of it she recognized; some she'd never seen before. "I'm not real up on this shit. What is it?"

Through a haze of pain, Bogg blinked at her. "It's the popular stuff, woman. Crack, weed, meth."

Gaby held up a pill between finger and thumb. "What about these?" A mixture of pills and tablets in pretty colors and shapes filled several plastic sandwich bags.

Not that long ago she'd been deliberately drugged by a psychopath, and Luther had been put at risk. Looking at the pills now, at any drugs really, set Gaby's teeth on edge.

"Just ecstasy, speed, Viagra. I don't know. I carry a lot of shit." And almost bragging, he added, "Anything you need."

"Like you actually think I'd ever need anything from you?" She snorted, but studied the pills again. "What's Viagra do?"

He choked on an anguished laugh. "You don't know Viagra? Shit, lady, where you been living?"

"In hiding, mostly." Not that it was any of his business. "So what is it?"

He closed his eyes in an effort to control the physical

torment of his injury. "You loopy cunt, the cops are coming. We're all gonna be in trouble if we don't get the fuck
out of here."

"Wrong." Gaby checked the rest of his pockets and
relieved him of a large roll of bills, a switchblade, and a
lighter. "You're a drug dealer, Bogg. I don't like it that you
exist, but I especially dislike it that you drew animals into
your fucked-up dealings, and that you were here by the
kids. What were you doing with that boy anyway?"

"Recruiting. Now get off me."

When he started to rise, Gaby leaned on the knife again.
Blood gurgled out around his wound, soaking his shirt
and causing him to saw his perfect teeth together around
a guttural, animal groan of pain. The fist on his good arm
thumped the ground.

To her, his agony mattered not a whit. The animals had
mattered. The kids mattered. That little girl's aunt and
uncle mattered.

This jerk did not.

"You're not going anywhere, Bogg, so forget it. You get
to greet the cops, but without me."

"What the fuck do you care about any of this?"

"I don't like you, Bogg. In fact, I loathe you."

"You don't even know me."

"Sure I do." Gaby rested her wrists on her knees, at her
leisure. "You're a miserable bully, a drug dealer, a mur-
derer, and on top of that, you abuse animals. But it's your
lucky day." She caught his chin and turned his head so he
had to look at her. "Much as I'd like to, I won't kill you."

No, if she cut his throat like she wanted, Luther really
would have a fit. And somehow, she just knew he'd find
out. Luther might not possess her extraordinary abilities,
but he had something almost as effective: a cop's intuition
and a golden aura of purity.

Bogg eyed her. "Glad to hear you don't have killing on your mind." He jerked his chin free of her hold and his look turned calculating. "Here's the thing, baby girl—"

"I like that even less than *bitch*, so save it."

"But I have a little over ten grand on me. How about we—"

Gaby interrupted the bribe. "Even though I'm going to let you live, I can't take a chance that you'll get away from the cops, that you'll taint another animal or threaten another kid or"—she looked at him—"burn anyone else."

He was quick to scoff at her accusation. "You can't hang that rap on me."

"Course not." Gaby looked over his wounds, his lanky, strong body, and made a decision. "On second thought . . . I guess it's not really your lucky day after all."

She slid the knife free of his body, impervious to his raw, shuddering moan.

The dismal sky cast no shadows. Rustling wind agitated the abhorrent scents of fear, and stirred dead leaves that clung tenaciously to brittle, barren trees. An expectant hush poised in the rank air.

Being sure that she positioned herself in a way that shielded his body from the view of the young onlookers, Gaby pushed Bogg to his side and, without remorse, slashed the blade across the back of his right knee.

The knife sliced through skin, sinew, and tendons like warm butter, leaving behind a gaping, exposed wound. Bogg's hysterical screams cleaved the silence, sending blackbirds into frantic flight and causing the crowd to back up a step.

Gaby eyed her handiwork and nodded to herself. Bogg wouldn't be going anywhere.

Dropping his cash, Gaby let the bills flutter around his writhing body. She tossed the packets of pills between his legs, into a puddle of pooling blood. She glanced to the gun to make sure it was visible enough that the cops wouldn't miss it.

One down, two to go.

No way would she let any of them walk, hobble, or even crawl away. They didn't get the end she wanted to mete out, but they would get Luther's form of justice. And if somehow the cops failed, well then, she'd be back.

But until then . . .

Bloody knife in her hand, Gaby stepped toward Tylek. In tangible horror, he tried to scramble away, but he didn't get far. Flipping the knife around in her hand, Gaby again shielded her actions from the onlookers. With a nimble wrist, she slicked the blade across the back of both of his thighs, all but severing the muscles, definitely rendering the leg useless.

He went down like a rag doll in a soggy swamp of his own gushing blood.

J.J., that poor schmuck, still hadn't stirred. Maybe she'd given him a concussion. Maybe he'd never revive.

Didn't matter to Gaby.

Lifting his right foot, she cut his Achilles tendon, and even that didn't bring him around.

Glancing up, she saw that the young Hispanic girl had remained nearby, watching in horror. All around her, festering carnage proved just how effective Gaby could be.

Trust her? Ha. The girl would hate her now. But at least she'd be a little safer, a little less threatened by the monsters that scoured the earth.

The scream of the sirens reverberated around the area; the cops were on the same street now, closing in.

Time to go.

And as Gaby turned, the girl stepped forward and raised a hand.

A simple wave—but for Gaby it felt like a harbinger of acceptance, maybe even . . . understanding.

Her arm burned and a thin trickle of blood exuded from the sleeve of her sweatshirt, down her wrist, and over the back of her hand. Her blood commingled with the blood of her victims still staining her knife.

She'd have a lot to deal with—later.

For now, she had to distance herself from the bloodbath. And fast.

Gaby weighed her options, and decided on heading up the street. Sprinting, she made the intersection in no time at all. But even as she fled, she again looked at that tattoo parlor. SIN ADDICTIONS.

She knew she'd be back.

In fact, a tattoo might be just what she needed to obscure the gunshot wound on her arm.

Mulling that over, she cut across the street, down an alley and through an old abandoned building, and emerged into another alley. Rats scrambled at her disruption. A crow took angry flight.

By the time the police parked at the playground, Gaby was far enough away that she could hear nothing beyond the low drone of distant sirens.

Being resourceful, she had no problem swiping a different sweatshirt, this one advertising some sports team. Using her old sweatshirt, she bandaged her arm the best she could with limited means.

Finally, more than an hour later, she made her way to Mort's.

Chapter 5

Fabian watched as every minion took nourishment off the woman. He wouldn't allow them to finish her, but by allowing them all to take part, he ensured their commitment to the act, and their devotion to silence.

That she was attractive made it more acceptable to them. As a being superior in intelligence, he'd made many observations about mankind. There were vast correlations in how people reacted to cannibalism . . . and to sex.

A beautiful woman was preferable to a hag, a young woman more desirable to the palate than a matronly elder.

As with sex, the thought of dining off a relative, or even a close friend, repulsed at the same level as incest.

And children . . . oh yes, those most sacrosanct of God's gifts, exempt from all perversions by most. Society thought children were to be protected, cherished. They didn't see the potential, the delectability of young, tender flesh.

It was the most reviled of taboos—and perhaps that's why it tantalized Fabian so.

He would bend them to his will. He would convince them, force them if necessary, but they would do as he requested.

For Fabian, that was perhaps the biggest thrill of all.

"That's enough." The stupid whore lay sprawled, all but unconscious, stained by blood and saliva. Bruises marred her pale body, evidence that many of his followers still lacked control.

They would learn with time and practice.

Reluctantly, the last man pulled away. He licked his lips and breathed deeply, still in the throes of profound enlightenment.

Yes, they pleased him. They took proper enjoyment as they should, and reacted promptly to his orders.

"Because our last meeting residence was compromised, we need to make this new building home. I know it is not ideal." The abandoned property, once owned by an elderly woman who had no close relatives, was cold and musty and cluttered with ridiculous furnishings and knickknacks.

The lack of decorating finesse assaulted his senses, but the water and electric remained on, and the solid basement walls would ensure secure attachment of necessary manacles and chains.

Located on isolated land, long forgotten by the nearest neighbors, it provided all they needed. No one would come here; they would be free to do as they pleased, for as long as Fabian deemed proper.

"I'm needed at the shop soon, but before that, I want to see her cleaned and her wounds tended. After that, secure her so that she cannot escape." With a benevolent smile, he told them, "We will use her for as long as she lasts."

They accepted his edict without comment, as they should. Like mutts, they hungered for a single kind word from him.

He'd found it beneficial to align himself with society's outcasts; the mentally challenged and the psychotically cruel. Every being, he'd found, had a use—be it for taking orders, accepting blame, or supplying nourishment.

"No one is to feed from her without my permission. Is that understood?" After each man and woman nodded in compliance, Fabian glanced at Georgie's gory body. "I'll get an industrial freezer out here soon, but in the meantime, carve him up and place all salvageable parts in coolers. When I return, I'll dispose of the waste."

Fabian trusted no one else for that particular task. It was a tricky thing, dumping bodily remains in a way that would lead others away from them instead of to them. Not that he worried overly about capture. The only link to him would be Georgie's tattoos, and those would be in a freezer with his meat attached, where police would never see them.

"All of you," Fabian added as he looked around the dank room of the building, "after she's properly secured, do what you can about cleaning the place. I want this blood mopped up, and the cobwebs removed. Someone buy some air freshener. It reeks of the old lady who died here."

Knowing he required his own share of cleaning, given that blood stained his face and shirt, Fabian rushed through the rest of his instructions.

He nodded to one sturdy fellow possessed of a low IQ and a fevered bent toward sadism. "You, begin fastening the restraints into the wall. Adjust them for her height so that her feet reach the floor. I want her able to stand." Delight glimmered. "To *watch*."

Knowing his order would be fulfilled, Fabian bestowed his attention on a small woman afflicted with a twisted need to please men. "You can secure what we need from the hospital?"

"Yes." Her head bobbed in animated enthusiasm. "I work tomorrow, and I'll gather the items then."

As a nurse's aide, she had access to the anticoagulants necessary to keep the blood flowing freely. However, the sedatives Fabian used to keep their cattle calm were obtained from a local thug, a miscreant of the worst order.

Fabian neither liked nor feared the crude brute, which made him tedious to endure. But Bogg delivered without fail and he didn't ask questions, and those redeeming qualities kept him a valuable asset.

He supplied the most modern and effective selection of tranquilizers. Victims could stay endlessly in a realm of surrealism, without ever realizing the fate they faced—until the key moment.

Seeing their fear was part of the rush for Fabian, so when they decided to feed directly from her again, he would let the numbing effects of the drugs wear off.

It elated him to get the proper reaction from his prey.

"Complete your tasks," he told his audience, "and you'll soon be rewarded with a special treat."

A low buzz started over what the treat might be, but Fabian chose not to say any more. If he told them now, they would rebel. He needed to present the gift to them first, to work them into a frenzy of wanting it, so that their flagging and seldom-used morals and scruples would be put to rest.

After he procured their special meal, he would entice them into committing the gravest perversion.

Thinking of that moment, he could barely contain himself. Best that he remove himself now before he gave anything away.

With all in order, he headed upstairs to where water and a change of his clothing could be found. He needed only the most rudimentary of cleansings, just enough that no one would notice him. When he reached the tattoo parlor he owned, he could be more thorough.

Despite his proclivity for cannibalism and drinking of blood, he was a fastidious man who always presented himself in a complimentary light. He was handsome, well built, and a good businessman who had turned Sin Addictions into a thriving business—with a believable façade for his predilection.

Peering through the pristine front window of the comic book store, Gaby spied Mort with customers. He didn't notice her, so she bypassed him and, using her key, went into the connected two-family and up the stairs to the living quarters separate from his.

She wanted to visit Bliss.

Proving she could be a wraith when it suited her, Gaby located Bliss in the kitchen without being heard.

Bliss stood at the stove, stirring what smelled like stew and appearing just like a little Martha Stewart. Since transitioning away from her debased existence of prostitution and into Mort's upper apartment—the apartment that used to be Gaby's—Bliss had transformed.

Brassy highlights no longer tinged her soft brown hair, and harsh makeup didn't age her pretty blue eyes. Instead of wearing clothing that exposed too much skin, she dressed in casual jeans and a long-sleeved shirt.

Now eighteen, Bliss looked like any other teenager instead of a homeless, mostly unloved girl who'd once sold herself to anyone willing to drop a few bills for the pleasure.

The thought of Bliss's past life stabbed into Gaby's heart with the force of a poisoned spear.

She must've made a sound, because Bliss turned and saw her standing there.

"Gaby! I didn't hear you come in."

Something in Bliss's expression put Gaby on alert. "Just got here." She strode to the table and pulled out a chair. "Whatever that is, it smells good."

"You hungry?" Before Gaby could answer, nervous energy carried Bliss across the kitchen to get a bowl and spoon. "It should be ready enough for you."

Eyes narrowed, Gaby studied Bliss's frenetic aura. Something was wrong, but she'd give Bliss a little time before she grilled her. "Thanks."

Bliss dished up enough stew to feed two grown men.

Gaby looked toward the empty coffeepot and sighed. She could really use a kick of caffeine. "What's up, Bliss?"

Her narrow shoulders stiffened. Keeping her back to Gaby, she ladled in yet another serving of the aromatic stew. "Nothing . . . probably." She jerked around with a forced smile. "Are you just visiting or is . . . anything wrong?"

"So I'm to go first?"

Bliss rolled in her lips, and nodded. "Yes, please."

"All right." Gaby lifted her arm. "You got a first-aid kit around here anywhere?"

"What?" Bliss almost dropped the bowl. "Oh my God, Gaby. What happened?" She rushed forward, plopped the bowl on the table, and stared wide-eyed at the seeping wound. She swallowed twice. "You're bleeding."

"It's a little flesh wound, that's all." But she wanted to have it properly cleaned and bandaged before she returned to the tattoo parlor and, ultimately, to Luther.

"You're not hurt anywhere else?" Her hands twisted together. "You're sure?"

"I'm fine." Bliss had a burgeoning special ability that she'd yet to master. Had she seen something happening to Gaby?

"I think Morty keeps a kit downstairs. I'll be right back."

"Wait." Detaining her with a hold on her arm, Gaby met her gaze and infused her tone with command. "This is just between us, Bliss. Got it?"

"I won't say anything." She patted Gaby's hand on her arm and tried another tentative smile. "I'll be right back."

Gaby pulled the stew around in front of her and started to eat. Before Luther, she'd never paid much attention to food. She could go days without eating, and often only fed herself out of boredom, or when she saw others eat and remembered that she should, too.

Mort, much like an anxious lapdog, had taken great pleasure in badgering her into sharing meals with him. For the longest time she had resisted his efforts at friendship. The idea of anyone caring about her, knowing her beyond a brief exchange, had been . . . unsettling.

And sure enough, the moment she decided to accept the idea of friends, she'd become inundated with them. Mort, Bliss, Luther . . . and Ann. They were all unique, different not only from Gaby, but from each other.

And Ann was the oddest friend of all.

Morty and Bliss she could understand. Like her, they had survived the dredges of society, accepting abuse as commonplace, taking it as their due. That sort of background bred familiarity, an affinity that outsiders couldn't fathom.

And Luther, well, he claimed some bizarre sexual chemistry—and more. He wanted her, and maybe after that happened he would lose interest. She wasn't versed enough in men, or relationships, to be sure.

But Ann proved an enigma. She was a beautiful, confident, educated woman with a career in law enforcement. She had breeding and class, and one of the biggest hearts ever.

Gaby would never comprehend why any of them wanted

to be a part of her life, but the idea grew on her each and every day.

She had just wolfed down her last bite when Bliss returned with an armful of ointments and bandages and such.

Setting it all on the table, she pulled around a chair for herself and reached for Gaby's arm. "Let me see."

"I can do it. But if you want to help, make some coffee, will you?"

Bliss hovered, her big eyes wounded and worried.

"Bliss, seriously, it's not that bad." Something other than her meager injury had spooked the girl. Gaby would find out what it was before she left.

"You really do want coffee?"

"Desperately. It's colder than a dead witch's left tit in a brass bra out there."

Choking on a snicker, Bliss moved away to start coffee preparations. As Gaby unwrapped her makeshift bandage, she asked, "The food was good. When did you learn to cook?"

"Ann's teaching me."

Hearing the smile in Bliss's tone, Gaby rolled her eyes. Didn't Ann have enough to do by being Luther's partner and Mort's lover? "She's a fucking saint, isn't she?"

"Yeah, just about."

The wound didn't look too bad, Gaby decided. In a few days, she'd be almost healed.

"Ohmigod." Bliss stood over her again. "Gaby, what happened?"

"An accident, that's all." Gaby rose from her seat and went to the kitchen sink to wet some paper towels. She scrubbed at the skin blackened by the heat of the bullet and removed the dried blood encrusted around it until she could see the inch-wide furrow gouged out of her flesh.

Already it looked better, but then, she'd always been a really fast healer.

"What kind of accident?"

Glancing at Bliss, seeing her white face, Gaby said, "Nothing."

"It looks like something." Bliss swallowed hard. "You know you can trust me, Gaby, right? I can keep secrets. I promise."

Because Bliss looked so damned hopeful, Gaby gave in. "It's just a gunshot that missed, that's all."

Bliss faltered back a step. She looked sick and scared. "It did *not* miss!"

"Mostly missed. Trust me, he was hoping for a kill shot."

Breathing hard and fast, Bliss put a hand to her heart. "He?"

"Just some idiot gang thug."

Bliss studied her face. "Did you kill him?"

"No, so don't go fainting on me." No way in hell would Gaby tell Bliss what she *had* done to the cutthroat dealers. "Why so damned curious? If you have something to tell me, Bliss, just spit it out."

Bliss hesitated, and that annoyed Gaby even more. Then, with a determined expression, Bliss said, "First things first. Please, sit down and let me help."

She urged Gaby back to her seat.

Gaby gave an aggrieved huff, but what the hell, why not? If it made Bliss happy, she could put up with her fussing. "Isn't that coffee done yet?"

"Not yet. Soon." Being more careful than necessary, Bliss took out a tube of ointment and coated the wound, put a clean gauze pad over it, and taped it in place.

As she smoothed the edge of the tape down, Bliss whispered, "I keep seeing you with a kid, Gaby." Other than a quick glance at her face, she didn't meet Gaby's gaze. "Not a child of your own—"

"Course not." Nothing could be more absurd. She was only just learning to deal with adults.

"But . . . a little girl who's in a lot of danger."

"Good." Gaby sat back and crossed her arms.

"Good?"

"I saw it, too, Bliss." Unwilling to expound on that for fear that others might discover her pastime as a graphic novelist, Gaby said, "Not the way you did. Not like a vision or anything. But I just sensed that she's there and in some kind of trouble. Really bad trouble."

Tears filled Bliss's eyes and she nodded. "Really bad."

"If you saw it, too, then maybe you have some details that'll help me to find her before it's too late."

"I wish to God I did, Gaby. But all I keep seeing is you with this scared little girl who . . . "

"Tell me."

She squeezed her eyes shut. "I don't know if I can. It's . . . it's just so horrible."

A gnawing shaft of fear crawled up Gaby's spine and coiled around her neck. Fear was such a foreign emotion that she shot out of her seat and went for coffee, just to have something to do.

After a scalding drink of the too-strong brew, Gaby faced Bliss again. "I've heard it all," she claimed with a fallacious bravado that couldn't beat back the surge of anxiety. "So just spill it, and then I can take care of everything."

Keeping her head down and her hands folded together, Bliss stood, too. Trembling with fear, she struggled with herself.

And finally, in a whisper so faint Gaby had to strain to hear her, Bliss confessed, "He . . . he wants to consume her."

A tidal wave of rage swelled over Gaby, warring with incredulity. Everything in her vision turned as red as fresh blood. A crushing weight bore down on her chest, on her heart. "What did you say?"

Bliss gave a sob. "Oh God, Gaby, someone wants to bleed her, and then . . . then *eat* her. Like . . . like food." She looked at Gaby with tears spilling from her eyes, and stated, "The blood wasn't enough. Now they're cannibals."

And Gaby, a powerful paladin, a mortal with untold powers and astonishing abilities, did something absurd.

She lost her meal.

Ann put the car in park at the curb out in front of Luther's house. He didn't look at her. He didn't need to. He knew what she thought. They'd been partners—and friends—too long for it to be any other way.

"What will you do if she takes off again?"

Staring out the wet windshield to the dark street, Luther shook his head. "I don't know."

"She's involved, Luther. Again."

"I know that. But she's not the one draining those poor bastards."

"I realize that. Gaby is many things, but she doesn't hurt innocent people."

Luther's muscles tensed. "She puts herself at risk all the damned time, trying to protect people."

"Yes, she does. But that doesn't change anything. Her involvement puts you at risk, too, you know. She crosses the line—"

"Our line, not hers."

Ann touched his arm. "Luther, our line is the one that matters. Whatever Gaby is, whatever her reasons for playing vigilante, she's on the wrong side of the law." Ann sat back. "And that's a complication for me."

Turning only his head, Luther met her gaze. "What do you want from me, Ann?"

"The truth."

"Fine. I think Gaby is . . . otherworldly. I think she sees and feels and understands things that we don't." Putting his head back and closing his eyes, Luther gave Ann what she wanted. "I don't understand it. But I trust Gaby, as much, maybe more, than I've learned to trust you."

"Gee, thanks."

His eyes opened again. "I've seen her . . . pick up on stuff. It affects her physically. And somehow, I swear to you, she just knows when shit happens."

It was Ann's turn to look away. "Maybe she knows because she takes part in some way. No, I'm not saying Gaby is bad. I wouldn't. There's something about her . . . "

"The same something that draws you to Mort?"

"Maybe."

"But only after his involvement with Gaby. I saw him before that, Ann, and I swear, you'd have felt nothing but pity for him." He let out a long breath. "You've seen the change in Bliss, right?"

Ann smiled. "She's a darling girl. It breaks my heart to think of anyone abusing her. Somewhere she has a family who threw her away. Their loss."

"Bliss is bright and cheerful and she's getting her life together—because of Gaby."

"How did they meet?"

Luther smiled, though the first acknowledgment of the tale had filled him with rage, both at Gaby's audacity and the danger she'd put herself in. "Gaby saw a guy abusing Bliss, and she stopped him."

"Dare I ask how?"

He shrugged. "Nothing worse than what you're

already imagining. She sank her knife into his shoulder and then threatened to castrate him if he ever again hurt a woman."

"Wow." Ann took a moment to assimilate that, then she, too, shrugged. "Effective."

"Gaby does what we'd like to do. And somehow she always gets away with it. But that particular time, she'd only happened onto the conflict. She hadn't . . . " He refused to say she hadn't been summoned. "She didn't have any intuition or anything. She was strolling with Mort and saw what was happening."

"Mort was in on this?"

"If you haven't already figured it out, Mort always covers for Gaby. They have a special bond of sorts." Luther studied Ann. "And Mort is a better man for it."

"Maybe." Ann flattened her mouth in consideration. "She does seem to inspire him to improve himself. Not that I approve of her methods—"

"Insulting him with ease."

"Yes. But Mort cares deeply for her." She tipped her head. "As do you."

No longer in denial, Luther just nodded. "As do I."

"So that brings us back around to where we started. How do you think you're going to work a relationship with Gaby when you're still a cop, and she gets on the wrong side of the law with alarming regularity?"

Unwilling to share all of Gaby's secrets, Luther didn't mention his affect on her perception of evil. Gaby detested any form of softness or weakness, and she wouldn't want others to know how his nearness blunted her ability to focus on malignant immorality.

But if he could keep her near enough to him, if he could get her to trust him, then maybe they could work together. Gaby would point him in the right direction, and he would handle things for her—within the boundaries of the legal system.

He said only, "I have a few ideas."

"That you won't share?"

"Not yet." Time to quit stalling. Getting his sack of purchases from the floor of the car, Luther opened the door and got out. He didn't want to acknowledge the dark windows and apparent emptiness of his house. "Just know that I'm on it, okay? I won't let you get caught in the backlash, I promise."

Bending to see Luther through the open door, Ann huffed out a breath. "I'm here if you need me, Luther. I have a feeling that this is going to be an uphill battle all the way."

Luther knew she was right, just as he had known all day that Gaby wouldn't be there when he returned.

And still he'd held out hope.

After checking the entire house and the backyard, he went in, slammed the door, and threw the bag on the kitchen counter. Purchases spilled out, including two videos and a boxed cell phone with extra charging cords.

It was only eight o'clock. Not late, but later than he'd intended for his return. Had Gaby been here, and then left? Or had she been out and about, doing God only knew what, all day long?

He'd called her at least a dozen times, but she hadn't answered at the house, and she didn't have a cell phone.

That's why he'd stopped on his way home and bought her one. She'd be pissed, but for him, it was like a leash, a way to stay in touch with her for his own peace of mind. If she liked it half as much as she liked the digital music player, she'd carry it with her always.

The two popular horror movies had been an impulse buy. He figured they would entertain her.

For certain, he wasn't enough to do the job.

His head hurt and his guts cramped. He needed to get a handle on himself before she got in.

She would return tonight.

She had to.

He *needed* her to come back to him.

Hands fisted, Luther went upstairs for a shower. When he saw the closed door to the room Gaby had commandeered, he hesitated.

But if he so much as stuck a toe in there, she'd know it. Then what little headway he'd made would be shattered, and he'd have to start all over with her.

Storming past the room, he went into his bedroom, threw off his clothes with an uncharacteristic lack of concern, and turned on the shower in the bathroom. The evening was cool enough that steam immediately fogged the air.

Luther stepped under the spray, hoping it would help to dissipate his disgust.

Praying it would help to ease the awful gnawing worry.

A fucking bloodsucker.

That's what Gaby had claimed, and of course she was right—as always. Some sick fucks were playing vampire, preying on the innocent and . . .

He squeezed his eyes shut. God, to even think it made him feel foul. He'd seen a lot in his lifetime, but now, knowing Gaby's involvement, it all felt worse, more dangerous. Scarier.

How could he keep her safe, from herself and her warped sense of duty, if she wouldn't even give in enough to be at his house when he got home?

Head back, Luther let the hot water pound on his skin, easing his cramped muscles but not doing shit for his oppressive mood.

Come home, Gaby.

But she didn't miraculously appear.

And Luther accepted that it was going to be a very long night.

Staying in the shadows, Gaby kept hidden until it was time for Sin Addictions to close. At nine o'clock, the daylight had long faded, aided by the ominous storm clouds that skirted an eerie half-moon. The wretched chill in the air would bring gooseflesh to most, but not to Gaby.

Her honed senses had fashioned a hermetic shield against mundane matters.

This place was her only lead, the only clue she could follow. One way or another, she would protect the child that Bliss saw in her vision and that Gaby had produced in her novel.

In a small, secret, pathetically wimpy and female part of her, she wished she had Luther with her. But that was an impossibility. His presence fucked with her instincts in a big way, and as much as she wanted him, she couldn't risk that.

She had to move forward with care. Demanding particulars on cannibalism would only alert the fruitcakes to her involvement. If that happened, they might scuttle off to places unknown, possibly out of her reach, to carry out their sick plans unhindered.

She'd die before she let that happen.

Her eyes burned as she stared at the shadows through the closed shades over the big front window. When the light in that room went out, Gaby slipped around to the back entrance. A young man came out, laughing at a comment said by someone unseen. He had tattoos everywhere, including his shaved head.

He wasn't the one Gaby wanted.

She made no move to detain him as he got on a motor-cycle and drove away.

Hell of a night to be on a bike, Gaby thought, watching without concern as taillights faded into the foggy darkness and the rumble of the engine grew dim.

Oblivious to the peril lurking, a young woman stepped out next. As she kept her back to the alley to lock the door, Gaby approached her. Standing only a few inches behind the woman, Gaby asked, "Anybody else inside?"

The woman jumped and let out a small screech. Pivoting to face Gaby, a hand at her throat and her other arm laden with a large satchel, she took in Gaby's looming proximity with barefaced terror. "Who are you? What do you want?"

A shroud of bitter disappointment settled over Gaby.

Accepting defeat—for now—she moved back a step. This woman had no audacity. At a very young age, Gaby had learned not to judge people by appearances.

The rankest immorality could exist beneath the most angelic veneer, just as hideous, distorted features could conceal a heart of gold.

Gaby rather admired this girl's appearance. She decorated herself in a way designed to draw attention: ornate tattoos colored her throat, one shoulder, and her collarbone, while her pierced ears, eyebrows, and one nostril sported silver jewelry. Despite outward appearances, she carried a grayish blue aura of timidity, defensiveness, and fragility.

"Who else works here?"

The girl's dark eyes blinked fast in a display of nervous fatalism. She expected abuse, but wasn't used to it.

Hugging her purse to herself, she tried to press backward into the locked door. She was so worried about surviving the moment, Gaby knew she wouldn't lie.

"There are five of us who take shifts. I do bookkeeping

only, but we have two tattoo artists and two body-piercing specialists."

None of those hit a chord with Gaby. Even standing on a step below the girl, she looked her in the eyes. "Who else?"

"There . . . there's the owner, Fabian. It's his shop."

Fabian. Gaby tasted the name in her mind, let it bring forth a vision, and knew he was the one she wanted.

"When will Fabian work again?"

Fear had the girl glancing left and right before offering a response. "He, uh . . . he'll probably be in tomorrow. Usually midafternoon."

Gaby smiled. "You can tell him to expect me."

Breath expended, it took the girl a moment to realize the import of those words—that she'd have to live to relay the message. "Oh. Yes, yes, I will. I swear."

Taking a step back before her quarry fainted, Gaby asked, "One more thing."

Voice tremulous, she asked, "Yes?"

Gaby pulled up a sleeve and dragged aside the bandage covering her wound. "How soon can I get a tattoo around this?"

Chapter 6

After stowing her car a few blocks away in an area unnoticed by most, Gaby started walking and found herself in front of Luther's house. No way could she have parked her disreputable looking Ford Falcon amidst the middle-class family sedans visible in driveways and along the curb.

Primer in key places, dents and scratches aplenty, led most to believe that the car was a junker. That ruse had allowed her occasional transportation to blend into the neighborhoods where she'd always lived.

It wouldn't blend in here.

Hiding it nearby would have to suffice; if she needed the car, she could get to it fast.

Now she had nothing more to do than to turn in for the night. But where?

Undecided on her welcome, she gazed at Luther's cozy, clean home, making note of the normalcy, the lived-in, welcoming feel of it. Yearning pulled at her, urging her forward. Sick at heart, she dug in and held back.

Uncertainty was a new affliction for her, and she didn't like it worth a damn.

Trying for reason, she reminded herself that Luther had told her to return, had all but pleaded with her. But now . . . did he still feel the same?

Had he heard about the drug dealers? If not, she'd have to tell him, and that would surely negate any hospitality he had extended.

Darkness shrouded the house.

Had Luther gone on to bed? Was he, even now, sound asleep?

And did she, a paladin who fought evil without fear, have what it took to go in, climb those stairs, and disturb him from his rest?

Gaby clenched her jaw, despising indecision as much as she did vulnerability.

Maybe she should just curl up on the porch. God knew she'd slept in worse places. Then she and Luther could sort things out in the—

Her thoughts shattered as the front door opened and Luther filled the space. He stared right at her as if he'd known, as if . . . he'd been watching and waiting for her.

Gaby's sharply inhaled breath burned her lungs.

The sudden furious pounding of her heart made her sway.

Even from the street, with only the faintest yellow glow of a streetlamp that barely reached him, she could see that Luther wore nothing more than unsnapped jeans. He didn't shiver in the cold breeze that ruffled his already untidy hair.

It didn't take a paladin's acute vision or limitless intuition to read his dark mood. Relief, rage, and something so much softer, all churned the bright aura limning his powerful, seductive, and comforting presence.

For an indeterminate amount of time they remained that way, separated by space but connected just the same, each unwilling to make the first move. The longer Gaby delayed, the more she hurt. Not the pain of a devout calling, but pain from sharp need, a need she'd seldom experienced before Luther had forced his way into her melancholic life.

A need she had long ago denied existed.

"Fuck it." Gaby took one step, then another. Her heartbeat and the racing of her pulse sent a cacophonous echoing through her brain. Each step grew harder, faster—and she saw an infinitesimal relaxing of Luther's broad shoulders.

The closer she got to him, the more she convinced herself that she had more reason to be disgruntled than he did.

Hadn't he left her high and dry earlier that day, after getting her all hot and bothered? Sure he had to work. She understood that.

But knowing he might have to leave, he'd still gotten her primed to experience new depths of sensuality—and then he'd walked away from her.

Because of her anger, he'd left her with a promise, a carnal tease about intimate matters to be completed.

And, by God, she would demand he fulfill that promise tonight.

Carried forward by resentment, Gaby bypassed the walkway and stomped over the dew-wet lawn. A stiff, cool breeze moved through the heavy branches of the trees in his front yard, shaking loose raindrops to dampen her hair and skin.

Gaby didn't feel the chill.

Focused only on Luther, her gaze locked on his, she marched up the porch steps and to the open doorway where he waited with crossed arms and copious macho attitude.

Close enough that their breaths mingled, she stopped.

He stood there in austere inflexibility, his brown-eyed gaze locking onto hers with such strong, conflicted feeling that her knees went rubbery.

Today, she had been forced to kill two beautiful animals.

Today, she had seen misery in a young girl's face and learned the intended fate of an innocent child.

All in all, it'd been a super-sucky day.

Gaby didn't want Luther to start chastising her. She didn't want to argue with him. The past few hours had been so fraught with fears and disappointments that she wanted only the unique, opulent contentment he could give.

He didn't reach for her, but so fucking what?

She was used to taking matters into her own hands. And this time, she would do so . . . literally.

Luther felt every punching beat of his heart as forcefully as he felt Gaby's resolve.

But resolve to do what?

His lungs labored for air, but a pressure on his chest kept the deep breath at bay.

"I came home," she told him with her chin in the air and a sour tone of accusation.

His chest grew so tight that speaking proved impossible, so he only nodded.

Then Gaby grabbed his crotch.

That got his air moving in a strangling inhalation. His arms fell to his sides, his stomach knotted.

She put her mouth to his throat. "No games, Luther. No lectures or long inquisition. I need you. I need everything you promised." She bit him, but then soothed the sting of her sharp teeth with the damp stroke of her tongue. "In all my twenty-one years, you're the only person who's ever made me forget the ugliness."

Leaning back, she demanded from him with glittering blue eyes, her features already shifting in that anomalous and hotly appealing way of hers.

"Help me forget, Luther. Right now."

A thousand thoughts rushed through his mind; with Gaby's propensity for finding the goriest of evil, anything might have occurred. He needed to know details; he needed to talk with her.

But that thought was obliterated by the anxious way her slender fingers cuddled his length through the denim of his jeans. When her breath hitched he was so lost that he didn't know if he'd ever find his way back.

Scooping one arm beneath her small derriere, Luther lifted her up and against him. Their mouths met, hungry, demanding, frenzied with pent-up need.

He moved them both into the house and kicked the door shut, then shoved Gaby against it to kiss her harder, deeper. Her long legs wrapped around his waist and she sank her fingertips into his shoulders.

Keeping his mouth on hers, he used one hand to shove her shirt up, to get to her small, firm breasts. She freed her mouth with a harsh groan.

Arching into him, she said, "Let's get naked."

Oh God, the things she did to him.

Luther fought for control. He wanted to make love to her gently, to show her how much she mattered to him, to show her all the pleasure to be had between them.

But she bit his chin, his jaw. "Naked, Luther. *Now*. Don't make me fight with you."

A reluctant smile worked through the lust. Yeah, Gaby would probably wrestle him to the ground if she didn't get her way. "No problem."

He loosened her left leg from around his hip and helped her to stand. Before she'd even gotten both feet on the ground, he pulled her shirt up to expose her naked breasts while she unfastened that damned sheath and let her knife drop to the floor with a clatter.

Using his foot, Luther kicked it to the side. Keeping his gaze glued to her now-taut nipples, he went to work on the snap at her waistband.

But Gaby was just as busy undressing him, and before he could do more than shove her jeans down her hips, she had his cock in her hands. Staring down at him, she licked her lips and groaned.

He lost whatever semblance of a rational, reasonable man he'd ever possessed. It had been too long, and there'd been far too much between them for him to hold back any longer.

Again locking her against the door, Luther put a foot to the bunched material of her jeans and stepped down, shoving them to her ankles. He used his knee to open her thighs as far apart as possible. It wasn't much, given that she was practically hobbled, but he'd make do.

Gaby grabbed his ass and pulled him closer, saying in a low, thrumming growl, over and over again, *"Yes."*

Raging need had such a stranglehold on Luther, he couldn't see straight. Blind lust drove him as he cupped one hand under her bottom to lift her enough to align their bodies. With his other hand he guided himself to her, and found her hot, slippery wet, so damn ready.

"I'm sorry, babe." Grasping her hips with both hands, he drove forward with a hard thrust that buried him completely and lifted her toes from the floor.

Going stiff, Gaby sucked in a sharp, startled breath that froze Luther—until she let the breath out in shuddering, purring pleasure. Against the restriction of her jeans, she brought her knees up to clasp around his hips and wrapped her arms around his neck.

Sinuous and sexy, she squirmed, trying to get more of him.

Her heavy-lidded gaze met his. Her eyes were smoky, intense, the shape more defined with her arousal.

Slowly, she stared down at his mouth and demanded, *"Again."*

Luther gave up. He took her mouth even as he pulled out, only to hammer back into her again. Like a cat, she curled closer, hugging herself all around him.

Knowing he battered her but accepting that she loved it, that she was every bit as turned-on as he was, he found a hard, thrusting rhythm that soon had them both on the brink.

How could he have thought, even for a second, that Gaby would be any other way?

She went through life full-force, without constraint or modesty. She didn't know half measures, had no grasp of social propriety.

For most of her life she'd been without friends, without understanding, without a single caring touch.

Luther vowed to show her the individual satisfaction of tenderness, and lovemaking.

Later.

For now, Gaby demanded a hard fuck, and that worked just fine for him.

"Hold on to me," he told her through clenched teeth. He wanted to touch her breasts, and more. He wanted to learn every inch of her.

"Yeah, okay," she agreed around panting breaths. She pressed her head back against the door and pushed her hips forward, matching his rhythm the best she could in their awkward positioning.

When Luther felt the near-painful grip that secured her hold on him, he took one hand from her backside and, using only his fingertips, teased over her stiffened nipples.

Her lips parted on a fractured moan.

Luther saw her through a haze of carnality and . . . much, much more. "You are so incredibly sexy, Gabrielle Cody."

Maybe because, even now, she couldn't accept a compliment, Gaby kissed him hard again, making it impossible for him to talk to her.

Luther didn't mind.

He had the snug clasp of her body on his cock, her mouth sucking at his tongue, and her hands holding him like she'd never let him go. No other man had touched her like this.

No other man ever would.

And that thought pushed him so close to the edge that he was grateful when he felt Gaby's climax erupting.

Tangling her fingers in his hair, arching her back, she moaned low and long. He bent his head and caught a nipple in his teeth—and she came.

Her reaction was so strong, she damn near toppled them both. Luther flattened one hand on the door behind her head and braced his legs apart to support them both. While his own release boiled up he watched her face, saw all the small nuances as her features shifted, sharpened, and finally softened again.

There was no other woman like Gaby.

And there'd be no other woman for him.

Secure in Luther's embrace, Gaby rested her head on his sweaty shoulder and tried to assimilate everything that had just occurred. He was still a part of her, still inside her, but not so much now.

She felt the trembling in Luther's arms, his legs, but she didn't care.

He wouldn't falter. Not Luther.

Not ever.

A tsunami of overwhelming euphoria had swept away all remnants of her arrant anxiety. The monstrous depravity of the world remained, but now, somehow, it didn't cut so deeply into her peace of mind.

Opening her eyes just enough to see Luther's jaw, Gaby whispered in extreme understatement, "Not bad, cop."

He turned his head a little and pressed the most tender of kisses to her temple.

Just that, nothing more, but it nearly flattened Gaby.

Because she rested on him like a needy woman. Because she liked it so much.

Because she . . . loved it.

Her heart ached with tremendous trepidation. She wanted Luther to always kiss her like that, with so much unspoken meaning. Never before had she loved anything or anyone.

But that kiss . . .

It amped the euphoria right back up there. Not physically, but emotionally. Phenomenal bliss filled her near to bursting.

So unlike her and her normal state of mind.

It occurred to Gaby that she no longer knew herself. She wasn't a woman who partook of physical pleasure with abandon.

She wasn't a woman who allowed others to soothe her.

She didn't even let others touch her.

With her insight into the evil that existed all around her, and her never-ending duty to extirpate it, she wasn't a happy woman. Ever.

How could she be? Her understanding of societal monstrosities refuted any thoughts toward true happiness.

And yet, right now, peacefulness permeated her being.

Oh God, it was a scary thing to feel this level of happiness.

Fear got its ugly fangs in her. If she changed for Luther, who would she be? *What* would she be?

"Shh," he said ever so softly. "Don't go there, baby. Not yet. I need a few minutes to recoup before we get started on all that."

All *what*? Eyes widening, heart pumping fast and hard, Gaby wondered if he'd somehow read her mind. Did he know her internal struggle, the demons that plagued her, that left her weak and ineffectual?

Tense with apprehension, she asked, "What are you talking about?"

He released an exaggerated, grievous sigh. "So there's to be no respite, huh? You won't even let me wallow in the languor a few minutes more?"

Having had no idea what the hell he meant, his nonsense grated on Gaby. The rush of irritation helped her to regain herself.

She went full force with familiar bitchiness. "Stop the bullshit, Luther." She pushed at his shoulders. "And let me go."

If anything, he snuggled her closer, cuddling her butt and breathing in as if smelling her, her skin and her hair. "Why would I want to do that?"

Lots of reasons presented themselves to Gaby's beleaguered mind, but she said only, "I'm . . . wet." She could feel a certain stickiness on her thighs that wasn't altogether unpleasant as much as very unfamiliar.

"Yeah." As if that pleased Luther, his voice deepened. He pressed his mouth to her shoulder in a slow, open-mouthed kiss. "Wet with you," he whispered, "and wet with me."

Why stickiness turned him on, Gaby didn't know. "You're being weird, Luther."

He sighed again. "I can't believe I forgot to cover up."

"Cover up?"

"I didn't use a condom, Gaby." He leaned away from her and gave her a look rife with affection and sincere apology. "I took risks with you, and I'm sorry."

She started to ask, "What risk?" when Luther's gaze went to her arm. She followed his line of vision and saw that blood had seeped through the bandage and sleeve of her stolen sweatshirt.

Shit.

Tensing, he stepped back and obliterated their intimate connection. It was the oddest thing, as if losing him left a void in her heart as well as her body. Gaby wanted him back. All of him.

But she'd be fucked before she admitted that to him.

To her surprise, he didn't say a word about her arm. Instead, he wrestled her shirt off over her head and looked at her upper body. She hadn't realized that her tussle with the drug dealers had left behind a few bruises.

Luther, damn him, managed to locate each and every one.

Naked except for her jeans and panties around her ankles, Gaby crossed her arms beneath her breasts and leaned back on the door. No way would she let him discomfort her with his scrutiny.

Jaw tight, Luther hitched up his jeans and raised the zipper. He didn't bother with the snap before going to one knee and clasping her calf. "Lift your foot out."

Gaby huffed in confusion. "I can undress myself, you know."

He looked up at her. "We just had sex, Gaby. Afford me a few gentlemanly courtesies, please."

How dumb. "Fine. Whatever. For you." Now she felt horribly inelegant. Not that there'd ever been a single elegant thing about her anyway. "But I don't need that nonsense."

"I do." Luther went about relieving her of the rest of her clothes.

He even took his time folding her jeans and sweatshirt and hanging them over his arm. "Let's go upstairs."

Maybe for more sex? Gaby had no argument against that. "Okay. But first things first." She locked the front door, even secured the deadbolt, and then retrieved her knife in the sheath. "You need better locks on your house."

He didn't argue. "I'll get a security system."

His quick compliance wrought a questioning glance, but he wore no real expression at all. "When?"

"I'll make some calls tomorrow." He gestured up the stairs. "Now let's go."

Confused by his complaisance, she started up the stairs. "I need a quick shower first."

Closer than she'd realized, his breath touched her nape when he said, "I was thinking more about a bath."

"A bath?" She stopped, and Luther bumped into her.

His hands went to her waist. "I don't yet know how badly your arm is hurt, but given how you shrug off near death, I'm assuming the necessity for a bandage means it's significant."

"Not really." To chase off the lethargy, Gaby took the rest of the stairs two at a time. At the top step, she glanced over her shoulder and said, "Got grazed by a bullet, that's all."

She went on down the hall and into the bathroom before she realized Luther hadn't followed. Wondering what kept him, she started back out just as he came stomping in, and they nearly collided.

Gripping her shoulders in an iron hold, Luther took deep breaths that flared his nostrils and brought a flush to his face.

Rolling her eyes, Gaby pulled free of him and began unwrapping the bandage. "Get a grip, Luther, it's not all that. And I'm a quick healer, if you remember. In a few days it'll be fine."

He didn't look appeased, but Gaby paid no mind to his fast-shifting mood. "In fact, I plan to get a tattoo around it to hide any scar that might be left behind. I was told that normally a person has to wait at least a year for that, but I'll convince the tattoo artist otherwise, no problem there."

He smashed a finger to her mouth.

Not a good thing to do to a person like her. Gaby no sooner had that thought than she was struck with the realization that there were no other people like her.

She swatted Luther's hand away with an overdose of irritation. "Don't push it, cop."

Still visibly struggling, he gave a stiff nod. "But do *not* start calling me that again. Use my name, damn it." He turned and started the bathwater.

Gaby crossed her arms and stared at the gorgeous muscles in his back. "I prefer a shower."

In a carefully moderated tone, he asked, "Have you ever had a nice long bath?"

"Well . . . " She looked at the steam rising from the water as it filled the tub. The thought of soaking in that heat, relaxing, made her muscles go weak. "Not really, no."

"Why?"

Most times, cautious of being caught off guard, she rushed through even her showers. "Showers are quicker."

"You're telling me you don't have enough free time to indulge in a bath?"

"It's not about having free time. It's about being preoccupied." When he still didn't understand, she made a face. "I can fight naked if I have to, but it wouldn't be my first preference."

He paused, turned to stare at her, and then: "What?"

"Lounging around in a tub is a good way to be taken unawares."

He seemed to droop before shoring up his determination again. "You're safe enough here."

"Yeah, right." Her tone reeked of disdain. "No one is truly safe anywhere."

"Right." He ran a hand through his hair. "I guess that explains the steel door and all the locks where you used to live, huh?"

Where she used to live—because he thought she had completely moved in here. Gaby relented . . . a little. "I suppose that once the water is off, we'll be able to hear if anyone breaks in." She lifted her chin. "I have superior hearing, you know."

"You have superior everything."

He said that with visual attention to her too thin, too lanky body.

She shook her head. "You're deranged."

"Only with you." Luther opened his jeans and stepped out of them. He folded them and placed them on top of her clothes. "I'll join you in the tub, if that's okay."

They'd both be naked in there? Together? Gaby made up her mind. "A bath it is."

Chapter 7

Luther swallowed all his demands for details until after he'd gotten Gaby settled in the steaming water in front of him. He positioned her with her back to his chest, her injured arm resting on the side of the tub, out of the water.

Though she hadn't elaborated, just knowing that a bullet had caused the blood-crusted, burned furrow filled him with rage. That bullet had no doubt been meant to hit something more vital. Only Gaby's quick reflexes had saved her from more serious injury—or even death.

And Gaby treated it as a trivial nuisance.

Any other woman, and most of the men he knew, would be popping pain pills and pampering that gruesome injury.

But not Gaby. Hell, she barely acknowledged it.

Lifting her wrist so he could examine the wound more closely brought a wave of guilt over Luther. His throat tightened. "Did I hurt you?"

"No." She snorted as if he lacked the ability to do so, then thought to ask, "When?"

All around the area where the bullet had abraded her, the swollen flesh felt hot to the touch. "When we were"—he started to say *making love*, but to keep from alarming her anew, he changed it to—"having sex."

"God, no." She tilted the back of her head to his chest and looked at him upside down. "That was great."

Even in the face of his staggering worry, Luther gave a small smile. Knowing he had satisfied Gaby went a long way toward keeping him on course with his plans.

He kissed her wrist. "That was what we call a quickie." He fetched a washcloth and the soap. "Sit up a minute."

"Why?"

Gaby never gave over easily. Life with her—which he was aiming for—would be one struggle after another. "I want to take care of you."

Half turning to face him, she gave him a speculative glance. "Like . . . sexually again, you mean?"

She looked so hopeful that he almost relented. "No, I meant that I want to wash you. Then I want to bandage your arm again."

Her scowl showed what she thought of that plan. "I'm able to wash myself."

"Trust me, Gaby." He smoothed aside her wet hair and, using the sudsy washcloth, started on her nape. It took a few minutes, and he was working the cloth halfway down her spine before she relaxed and let her head drop forward.

"That is . . . nice."

He wanted to care for her always. And somehow, he would. After using the cloth to massage her back and shoulders, he put it aside and used both hands to rinse her. "Get on your knees and turn to face me."

His heart hammered as she complied without a word. The steam in the room left her lashes spiky, her cheeks flushed and rosy. He knew well that Gaby considered herself a less than pretty woman. Sometimes she barely acknowledged her own humanity. Her life as a tool to combat gross iniquity had left her with a far from complimentary view of herself.

To him, she was by far the most striking, admirable, and appealing female he'd ever met.

Staring at her breasts, he soaped up the cloth again and started on her slender throat. Just beneath her pale skin, her pulse beat frantically. When he shifted, bathwater lapped at her narrow waist.

Gaby was all straight bones, sleek muscles, and female pride.

Slowly, Luther massaged over her shoulders, her collarbone, down over her nipples. She tipped her head back a little and held her breath.

Dropping the cloth, Luther covered her soapy breasts with his hands.

"Luther?"

"Hmm?" The soap made her nipples slippery, adding a new sensation to his touch.

"You're not going to get me all excited and then stop again, are you?"

"No." He teased her nipples with his thumbs, gliding around them, under them, not quite touching her as he knew she wanted. "How did you get shot, Gaby?"

She stiffened, but he'd anticipated that reaction from her, and lightly caught her nipples, tugging, rolling.

Her tension coiled tighter. "Drug dealers," she managed to say.

Luther held the burgeoning anger at bay, anger at Gaby for putting herself in peril—again—and a hotter rage at whoever had dared to try to hurt her. "What about drug dealers?"

"They were hanging out . . . at a playground." She covered his hands with her own, but she was too new to this to know what to do, and her hands fell away again.

"You ran them off?"

"No. I disabled them. As a warning." She breathed faster. "The cops found them where I left them, there near the playground."

Luther released her and while he gently cupped water over her chest to rinse the soap away, he asked as judiciously as he could manage, "Disabled them how?"

To his surprise, she started to shake.

"Gaby?" Alarm mushroomed. Never had he seen Gaby tremble. "What is it?"

In a sudden rush, she crawled up over his lap, putting her legs around him, with those puckered nipples at eye level. "I had to do something terrible, Luther. I can't talk about it now. Please."

Please? From Gaby! Fearing for the worst, Luther caught her hair and pulled her head back so he could see her face. "What happened? What did you do?"

Her quivering lips compressed, and grave sadness filled her beautiful eyes. She looked away. "I had to kill two dogs."

Jesus. He felt like the wind had been knocked out of him. Tragic, yes, but nowhere near the possibilities summoned by his imagination.

She hugged herself around him. "Help me forget, Luther. Just for a little while."

Two dogs. His eyes closed in profound relief. But, of course, it made sense. Gaby would always consider children, animals, victims of any kind, to be innocent. If she'd had to exterminate the dogs to protect others, it would be an atrocious burden for her, an albatross of guilt that she'd never lose.

And she had actually asked for him to help her.

Strides, Luther told himself. Great strides.

"It's all right, Gaby. Let me help you." He adjusted her just enough that he could lick her left nipple, circle it with his tongue, and then suckle her softly.

Her thighs tightened and she squirmed. He wedged a hand between their bodies and, given her wide-open position around him, easily pressed his fingers to her. Touching her would never be a hardship. He loved touching her.

He loved . . . No, he couldn't let himself get sidetracked that way. Concentrating on their physical relationship would be enough.

For now.

Within minutes, Gaby was breathing hard and fast, and she moved against him, showing him what she liked, what she needed. Learning her preferences, her body, proved a distinct pleasure.

When she came, Luther held her close, glad that he could share this with her even as his heart broke for the high level of accountability she placed on herself.

Afterward, she lay sprawled over him in the tub, her legs still around him but her spine relaxed, her head fitting perfectly beneath his chin. Her warm breath teased his shoulder, and her injured arm remained out of the water only because he ensured it.

Hating to disturb her, Luther trailed his fingertips along her back, raising gooseflesh, bringing forth a sigh or two.

Several minutes passed, and he thought she might have fallen asleep.

"Sorry, but I need to hear the rest of it, Gaby." He moderated his tone, treating the obdurate phenomenon of her routine existence as mundane, hoping she would follow suit. "You know that."

"Yeah, I know." She shifted a little, maybe tightened her hold on him. "I don't care that I hurt the men. They were drug dealers preying on kids. One of the guys had so much money on him and so many drugs that I know he had a lot of exchanges planned for the day."

"But they had dogs, too?"

"Pit bulls."

Luther couldn't suppress a shudder of dread. He had to close his eyes to regain his composure. He never blamed an animal for attacking, especially when trained to do so. But he'd had experience with vicious dogs before, and pit bulls were known for their strength and tenacity once they went after a victim.

"We've had officers badly injured by that breed."

Ducking her head, Gaby tightened again. When she spoke, her voice crawled with a level of pain unfathomable to most. "No animal is to be blamed for what monsters force it to do."

Luther heard repressed tears in her tone, and while it devastated him, the sign of human emotion also offered encouragement. Like the mistreated animals, Gaby had been given few choices in life except to desecrate perceived evil.

He would give her choices, and pray that she adapted.

"No, it's not," Luther agreed, determined to reassure her on her decision to put the dogs down. "Unfortunately, an abused dog can be a threat to others, especially to the elderly, and to the small children nearby."

She nodded. "There were two of them, Luther." Her free hand fisted against his side. "Beautiful, strong animals, with so much spirit." Her breath shuddered. "I tried to make it quick and painless for them. I couldn't . . . didn't want them to suffer at all."

He couldn't bear it. He needed eye contact, to let her see his conviction that she'd done the right thing. "Gaby, look at me."

She clung tighter, a silent refusal that Luther accepted with subdued frustration.

God, if only he could take some of the responsibility from her. Her narrow but proud shoulders bore the weight for protecting all in her realm. In doing so, she'd had a lifetime of absorbing many inflicted hurts and defensible deaths.

Gaby truly believed in what she did, but that couldn't make it any easier.

"Tell me about the men."

After a moment, she collected herself. "All three of the bastards would have still been there when the cops arrived."

"You're sure of that?"

"Yes." Sleepily, as if maiming men mattered little in comparison to killing helpless animals, she detailed the way in which she'd ensured their capture.

She must have mistaken Luther's palpable frustration for a struggle to accept her, because she straightened her arms to sit up over him.

Luther had a struggle, all right. Gaby straddled his lap, her body bare, wet, and still flushed from sexual activity. And grief lent a softer edge to her usual strident demeanor, making her seem even more womanly, more vulnerable and approachable.

It wasn't easy to keep altruistic motives at the forefront of his thoughts.

Until Gaby straightened with sharp-edged antagonism. "You want me to leave now, cop?"

His gaze shot from her breasts to see the unmitigated resignation on her face. Damn her, would she never accept him and what he felt for her?

His own countenance severe, Luther shook his head. "No, never."

Surprise shifted her expression. "The police will be looking for me, you know."

"Was there anyone to identify you?"

At his continued equable discourse, she eased. "Some kids."

He cupped a breast and looked at her mouth. "You protected them. Not just for the moment, but in the long-term."

"It won't be enough. It never is." Her inhalation pushed her breast more firmly into his palm—a circumstance they both noted. "I personally talked to two of the kids, one girl who told me about the drug peddlers burning down her aunt's home. And there was a boy they had trapped near a fence. I ran him off before I took care of them."

Took care of them. Because he needed to hear it all, Luther released her. "The kids will talk. And," he said, trying for a smile that wasn't entirely feigned, "they'll tell how vicious the dealers are, and how one of them shot at you."

"Bogg," Gaby confirmed, giving Luther a name to research. "He was sort of the head honcho, but I wasn't impressed much."

"You never are." He examined her arm again, thinking of how close that bullet had come to really hurting her. Oh, he'd check into Bogg's file. And he'd make damn sure the bastard spent his life behind bars.

She put a hand to Luther's face in the most affectionate gesture he'd ever gotten from her. "I'm impressed with you."

His smile now was genuine. More often than not, Gaby insulted him with regularity, and at other times, she fought him over everything from murder to bathing. "Yeah? Since when?"

"You bowled me over the day I met you." She tipped her head to study him. "I saw your golden aura and I knew you were everything I wasn't."

He didn't want her impressed by perceived differences. "We're more alike than you think, honey. We both care about protecting those who can't protect themselves, right?"

"Our methods differ by a long shot."

Unable to refute that, Luther said only, "Our intent is the same." But he saw the exhaustion in her face and knew she needed to rest, whether she'd ever admit it or not. "Have you eaten?"

"I stopped by to see Bliss." Her eyes darkened with the memory. "Did you know that Ann is teaching her how to cook?"

"Ann is teaching her a lot of things, all of them good."

"She made stew." Gaby looked annoyed by that accomplishment. "It wasn't half bad."

Luther secured his hold on Gaby and sat up. He didn't understand why it bothered her, but maybe her close bond with Bliss made her overly protective. "Between the two of you befriending Bliss, she'll soon have all the self-confidence she needs to make her own way in the world." He tipped up her chin. "You do realize that you have as much if not more influence on Bliss than anyone, right?"

That thought didn't please Gaby. "God, I fucking hope not."

"Why not?"

Her mouth twisted in a quirk of ill humor. "What I do and how I do it . . . I'm damned good at my duty, but I wouldn't wish it on anyone else and I sure as hell wouldn't want Bliss to see me as an example."

"With you, Gaby, it's easy to overlook the grisly effect of what you do for the reasons you do it, and the end results." With wet tendrils clinging to her cheeks and a pugnacious frown, Gaby appeared as deceptively frail as any other woman. "You know what I think Bliss sees when she looks at you?"

Gaby rolled her eyes. "Is this going to be some sappy shit?"

Luther spoke over her cynicism. "She sees a woman who isn't afraid to stand up for her beliefs. A woman who makes her own way by her own rules, and who doesn't let the opinions of others veer her off course. She sees a woman who helps others. A woman who is strong and capable, with a bone-deep core of honor."

Leaning back, Gaby stared at him. "Damn Luther, your perception is sadly skewed."

"After the abuse Bliss suffered from people who should have cared for her, she needs your type of influence a lot more than she needs to learn domesticity. And no, I'm not talking about meting out justice. I'm talking about the core of you, your pride and independence, caring and intelligence. By example, you can show Bliss how to overcome obstacles, to make her own way." He brought her close again. "And before you object to that, I know you've shielded her from the more graphic examples of your ability."

"As much as I could, anyway." She eyed him. "Besides, who would believe it? You're the only one who seems to think you know me well enough to understand what I can do."

"And I would never share your secrets." Forestalling more arguments from her, Luther brought them both to their feet and reached for the towel. "Now, if you're not hungry, how about we turn in? I'm not superhuman like you, and I do need sleep."

New doubt brought a scowl to her face. "I don't know how this all works."

That he understood exactly to what she referred showed a new depth to their relationship. "We'll sleep in my bed," Luther explained with no room for argument. "Together. Naked."

She didn't object, but she did require elucidation. "Sleep as in . . . sleep?"

Striving for physical detachment from the act, Luther began drying her. "Soon, yes." First, he had a promise to keep.

"No more questions?"

"We do need to talk more, but it can wait until the morning." He didn't want to say too much yet, so he summarized with, "I don't have to go in early, but I'm going to have to work late."

Gaby's thoughts remained elsewhere. Puzzled, untrusting in her own impression, she sought eye contact. "This is nuts. You really don't mind what I did to the drug dealers? I mean, I cut them up pretty bad. I might even have maimed them for life."

Time for stark honesty. Luther put his hands on her shoulders and met her gaze. "I would have preferred that you call me, to see if I could offer an alternative solution to . . . maiming them. Sometimes, you know, the legal system does work."

She snorted.

Yeah, he already knew her thoughts on going by the book. "But, Gaby, as I've told you many times now, I trust your instincts."

"So you're not pissed?"

That she'd chosen once again to handle life on her own terms saddened him, but he couldn't be angry with her for doing what she could to protect others. He shook his head. "I'm not mad."

Her brows scrunched down in disbelief. "No fucking way."

"Way." Luther pressed a kiss to her frown. "Trusting you won't stop me from worrying, or from trying to convince you to do things along a more legal path—and we'll save that lengthy discussion for the morning. But, no, Gaby, I'm not going to lose sleep over cretins who would prey on the vulnerability of children."

Her chin came up and her small fists clenched. "I could have killed them without remorse."

"But you didn't, and I appreciate that." Showing restraint was new for Gaby, but Luther believed it was more her own sense of right and wrong that kept her from butchering the men. They were bad, but she could handle their immediate threat, and so she did.

He'd come to realize that Gaby annihilated only those she believed posed a bigger menace to mankind, the truly heinous, soulless fiends who, even while imprisoned, would find a way to indulge their immoral debauchery.

"You, Gabrielle Cody, have your own sense of fair play. Besides, having them in custody might help lead us to other drug distributors, buyers, and even pimps. It all trickles down a dozen different ways into society. Like dominoes, if one goes down, the others topple, too."

He stepped out of the tub and helped her out, then finished drying her legs.

"I don't understand you," Gaby said to the top of his head as he kneeled before her.

"For now, that's okay." He stood and patted her pert backside. "I know you haven't completely unpacked yet, so I have a spare toothbrush if you need to use it." He ran his fingers through her hair. "My comb is on the sink."

Taking the hint, she turned to the sink and rummaged through his belongings until she found what she wanted. Seeing Gaby naked at his sink, doing a routine chore like cleaning her teeth, gave him a sense of inevitability.

Sooner or later, Gaby would accept him as part of her life.

When she did a ruthless job attacking the tangles in her

short hair, Luther winced and took the comb from her. She had baby-fine hair, inky black and liquid soft as it slipped through his fingers.

Her physical appearance was a stark contrast to her hard-edged personality and purpose.

When her hair lay smooth, Luther kissed her on the top of the head. "Why don't you wait for me in the bedroom? I'll only be a minute."

With a shrug of her shoulder, she agreed and went off to the bed. After Luther drained the tub and picked up their dirty clothes, he gathered the medicinal items he'd need for her arm.

There were many things he wanted to do with her, to her, but her injury precluded those activities. Still, he had told her what would happen if she came home to him, and he couldn't wait to show her exactly what he'd meant.

Propped against the headboard on top of the covers, one leg straight out, the other bent at the knee, Gaby awaited him. She had one of the DVDs he'd rented and was reading the back.

"Look interesting?"

She turned the movie over and looked at the front. "What is it?"

"A movie. We watch it on the television. I had hoped to watch it with you tonight, but . . . " His turn to shrug. "You had other things to occupy your time."

She tossed it onto the nightstand. "Don't expect me to feel guilty. Not for that. We can watch it tomorrow night, if you want."

Tomorrow night he'd be at a local rave known for catering to deviants of all sorts, but most especially to wannabe vampires.

"Maybe." If things worked out, he could get home early enough to crash on the couch with her. He seated himself beside her, causing the mattress to dip. "Let me have your arm."

"This is getting out of hand." But she offered up her arm and then watched closely as he applied a healing ointment, a clean strip of gauze, and fresh surgical tape. Though the wound was still raw, Gaby never made a sound.

"You'll get used to me caring for you." He hoped. "It's what a man and woman do for each other when they're . . . " A proper word to explain their relationship eluded him, so he settled for, "involved."

Forced to scoot over as he slid into the bed, Gaby again went quiet as she assimilated the new suggestions.

"If you're saying I should pamper you, too, you're bound for disappointment."

That made Luther grin. Gaby didn't have it in her nature to hover over anyone. But she did, in her own unique way, show extra care when needed.

"It's different for men." He tossed the covers to the end of the bed. "Right now, pampering me means letting me pamper you. And no, I won't explain that tonight because there's something else I want to do."

Her eyes went smoky with interest. "What?"

Catching her hips, he pulled her flat to the mattress. "You'll see." And with that he started kissing her—her throat, her shoulder.

She tipped her head to give him better access. "I don't know why that feels so good."

Luther smiled against her skin. "Women have lots of sensitive places on their bodies." He licked the inside of her elbow, then moved over to her ribs.

Her hand knotted in his hair and she brought his face up. "Listen up, cop. I don't want to hear about you with other women."

"I wasn't going to go there, I swear." He had to fight

his amusement. A jealous Gaby could be deadly, so he shouldn't provoke her. "Just saying that's why you like it."

She let him go, but continued to scowl. "It sort of makes me shiver."

"Mmm-hmm." Holding her waist, he kissed his way down to her navel, then a hip bone.

Gaby let out a soft sound of pleasure. She tipped her head back and closed her eyes.

"You remember my promise, honey?" He urged her thighs farther apart and moved between them. "I told you how I'd kiss you."

"Where you'd kiss me." Her hands knotted in the sheet. "I'm ready."

Like a sacrifice, she braced herself. Damn, but everything about her pleased him, most especially her sexual willingness.

Luther took a minute to toy with her, to tease with his fingers until she squirmed, until she tightened all over.

When he knew she was tense enough to break, he used his thumbs to open her, licked over her distended clitoris, and then drew her into his mouth.

Her long, broken groan rewarded him for his patience.

"Oh God, Luther . . . "

To keep her still, he flattened one hand on her stomach. With the other, he pressed two fingers deep into her, withdrew, pressed in again.

She cried out, already on the edge of a climax. But he wanted to be with her, so with one last leisurely lick, he rose up over her.

Her parted lips and heavy eyes proved her need. As fast as he could, Luther rolled on a condom, lifted her hips, and drove into her hard and fast.

With that first deep stroke she started coming, her legs tight around his waist, her fingers digging into his shoulders.

She was wild, hot, and so damn perfect for him.

Arms straight, Luther stayed over her, watching her face, loving the way pleasure contorted her features. It pushed him past his own restraint and he felt his own burning release.

Afterward, he collapsed atop her. She hugged him, her legs still around him, her soft mouth touching his neck. When he started to move, she squeezed him, so he settled back to her and just held her.

"I'm not squashing you?"

"Don't be stupid."

Damn it, even an insult from Gaby, at such a special time, could make him smile. He rolled to his side but brought her with him.

"I need to get rid of the condom."

She smoothed a hand over his sweaty chest. "It's crazy how much I enjoy your body."

"Ditto." He kissed her, and then eased from the bed. When he returned only moments later, Gaby was just as he'd left her. She looked to be asleep. All in all, this was turning out to be easier than he'd first expected.

He settled back into bed with her, pulled her in close, and closed his eyes.

Then out of the blue, she turned her face up to his. "I meant to ask—what's Viagra?"

Chapter 8

Humming to himself, content to transport his cargo, Fabian drove along the serene streets until he found a neighborhood offering what he required. Beneath scant moonlight and the occasional streetlamp, garbage cans and lawn bags waited at the end of each driveway.

The houses were spaced far apart, and the denizens had turned in already, leaving the area dark and quiet. Not even a dog barked.

Perfect.

Ensuring that no one loitered near a window, he dimmed his car lights and coasted up to the curb of a tidy upper-middle-class home. Snickering to himself, thinking of how easy it was to dispose of the unused body parts, he released the latch to his trunk and put his car in park, but left it running.

Donning surgical gloves, he dragged a weighty bag from his trunk and dropped it next to those already near the street, waiting for garbage pickup early the next morning. It blended right in.

Snickering to himself, he gave a furtive check up and down the street, got back in his car, and maneuvered without headlights to the next block. As soon as he turned the corner, he turned his lights on, and, whistling, drove toward another house.

In a fit of whimsy, he'd decided to scatter the body parts. Imagining the police trying to piece them together like a grisly jigsaw puzzle filled him with macabre amusement.

Every time he drank, each time he feasted off another, his intellectual superiority expanded and his physical attributes grew more youthful, more dynamic. He possessed a sagacity and elite taste that exceeded those of everyday man.

The police couldn't stop him; they couldn't even name him as the culprit.

Through careful design, he'd re-created himself as an omnipotent leader. No one would uncover his select lifestyle unless he deemed it so.

Soon, his agile calculation would manifest the ultimate sacrifice due him, a succulent meal that he'd bestow on the others. As a unit, they would commit the ultimate depravity.

All he needed now was to find the perfect target.

But first, he needed to finish ridding himself of the waste.

Dry-eyed, skin rippling with chills, Gaby stood naked, staring out the window. Fear was so new to her that she couldn't fathom how to cope.

She didn't want to awaken Luther . . . but then again, she did. Fuck. In a very short time she'd become a needy, whiny fool.

"Gaby?"

Closing her eyes, she swallowed and attempted to regulate her voice, to hide the repulsive despair. Too much depended on her being a paladin.

Without looking at Luther, she said, "There's more that I should tell you."

A heavy pause preceded Luther's calm concern. "Why don't you come back to bed and we'll talk?"

No, if she got back in bed with him, she'd want things she shouldn't. Like respite from duty. Like . . . normalcy. "No, Luther. I can't." An odd constriction in her throat made it difficult to squeeze the words out. But the import of her words demanded voice. "It . . . it's eating me up inside until I feel like I'm going to . . . I don't know. Explode. Destroy something."

She heard the creaking of the bed, then felt Luther's arms come around her. And oh God, it felt good.

Too good.

"You can tell me anything," he whispered, "and somehow, we'll figure it out."

That he believed such nonsense only added to her agitation. Some things, like her purpose on earth, would never be so easily divined.

Breathing hurt, but then, she'd hurt for so much of her life, what did that matter? Pain kept her sharp, in senses and in body. She needed the pain now.

Pain she could handle.

It was the invasive weakness that would be her undoing—and still she turned into Luther's comforting embrace, holding him so tight that her arms ached.

She shouldn't share her appointed onus with anyone, much less someone as pure as Luther. It wasn't fair to burden him.

But he'd changed her, and she no longer had the internal fortitude to bear it all alone.

Unable to face him as she detailed the awful, ugliest of possible crimes, Gaby told him about Bliss's vision—and her own.

"Your bloodsucker is still on the loose, Luther."

As if to soothe her from her worries, his hands rubbed up and down her back. "I know that. We'll get him, Gaby. I swear. It might take some time—"

"Yeah, well, unfortunately time is something you don't have. Hate to break it to you, cop, but your guy isn't just a bogus bloodsucker." She had to take several quick, shallow breaths before giving him the truth. "The sick fuck also likes the taste of human flesh."

Luther stiffened. The ugly word barely squeezed past his abhorrence. "Cannibalism?"

Gaby nodded. "Not just a cannibal, fucked up as that is." Sick to her soul, she whispered, "He wants something special now. He wants . . . fresher meat."

With each word, Luther grew more rigid, until now, it was his hold that crushed.

Gaby didn't mind, though. Somehow, for whatever inane reason, being held by him made the possibility for resolution more plausible.

Careful not to hurt her arm, Luther levered her away from him. At her disclosure of what she believed, what she had considered keeping from him, what she had thought to fight alone . . . Oh God.

Fury and fear rolled together to obliterate his control.

He struggled to keep his temper concealed from her. He knew Gaby, and if she suspected he wanted to lock her away for her own safekeeping, she'd leave him and never come back and everything they'd shared wouldn't sway her one bit.

His fingers bit into her shoulders, but he couldn't help it, and she didn't seem to notice. "I understand about Bliss. This isn't the first time she's claimed to have a strange foreboding about things, most often with morbid circumstances."

"And she's been right every time."

Did that mean Gaby considered Bliss right in proclaiming them an item? According to Bliss, they were meant to be—and Gaby knew it.

He let that go to tackle a bigger, more monumental question. "What I don't understand is *your* vision." He managed one leveling breath, and then another. "Care to explain?"

She shivered, and then in a burst of energy she shoved him away. "I fucking hate this."

"This?"

"Feeling this way." She pressed a fist to her belly. "I'm *cold*, Luther. I've never been cold a day in my life. Other than thunderstorms, I don't even notice the stupid weather."

He had no idea how to console her. Never had he known her to be susceptible to the cold, so she *was* changing. He'd already sensed it, and understood how hard it was for her.

And still he relished it.

But changing wouldn't be an easy thing for Gaby to advocate.

Her gaze sought his before she stepped away, putting a deliberate physical and emotional distance between them.

"Always, every second of every day, there's been this awful yawning pit inside of me. It's been a part of me for as long as I can remember. It's bleak and hungry and sick, but it's buried deep where I can't change it, and so I ignore it. It's there, but I've made it unimportant."

"You've learned to function with it."

"I had no choice, damn it." She pressed the heels of her

hands to her eye sockets. "Jesus, Luther, I want that awful, indifferent pit back."

Hurting for her, Luther stepped closer. "Because it's familiar? Or because it was replaced with something that's worse?"

"Because now I can't compartmentalize things." She dropped her hands, but only to slug him in the shoulder, to close in on him with aggression and urgency. "You fucked it all up. You've got me confused and . . . and fucking *cold*." Her trembling bottom lip was stilled only by the harsh compression of her mouth. "And needy."

She swallowed, but he heard the tears in her voice.

"And . . . scared."

That admission cost her, sending savage emotion to wrack her body. She swallowed again, convulsively, but the tears still glistened in her sad, wounded eyes.

He'd never seen Gaby cry and, God Almighty, it ripped him apart.

If he touched her now, she'd resent the compassion, and it might send her over the edge. No matter how badly he needed to hold her, he couldn't do that to her.

Going to his closet, Luther found a flannel shirt and draped it around her. Holding the collar together under her chin, he put his forehead to hers and wished for a way to ease her turmoil.

As a detective, the only way he knew to proceed was to get all the details he could. "Tell me about your vision, Gaby. Let's start with that."

Angrily, she shrugged into the shirt, and then swiped a hand over her eyes. "Why not? It's all so screwed up anyway."

She marched out of the room and down the hall to the spare bedroom she'd appropriated. Going to her knees, she bent at the waist and dug under the bed.

Good God. Even now, with foul talk of a cannibal, she threw him off guard with her manners.

The shirt barely covered her hips. And with her in that position, he saw . . . well, everything.

Lounging in the doorframe to keep from touching her, he said, "You know, Gaby, most women feel vulnerable when they're naked."

She dragged out a box without looking at him. "Why?"

The question threw him. "I suppose because many men are spurred by lust at the sight of a woman's body. Some men, idiots I guess, can lose control."

"So?"

Right. Why would Gaby be concerned with a man's loss of control? She'd flatten anyone who tried to take advantage of her. "Very few women are as capable of fending off rape as you are."

"Interesting. But I'm not naked, so does any of this really matter?"

He felt sweat on his forehead. "Jesus, Gaby, you're mostly naked and you just flashed me an invitation that was damned hard to resist."

Flipping the lid off the box, she slanted him a distracted frown. "Are all men so unflagging then when it comes to sex? I mean, seriously, Luther, I figured you'd want some downtime by now."

She damn well didn't need to know how other men dealt with sexual overindulgence, because she wouldn't be with anyone other than him—but telling her that now wouldn't be a smart move. Especially not when she was so open to him for a change.

Stepping forward, Luther went to his knees and joined her on the floor. "With you, Gaby, I don't think I'll ever get enough."

Unconvinced, she turned away and lifted out . . . a

manuscript. She set it on the floor between them and just waited.

Luther knew in his guts what she'd just revealed. For some time now he'd suspected that Gaby created the popular, underground graphic-novel series *Servant*. The vividly depicted stories of a female paladin on earth had an enormous cult following.

And through secretive sales and hidden identities, only Morty had it available.

In fact, *Servant* kept Morty's comic book store in business. As Gaby's closest cohort, whether she'd ever admit that or not, Morty got the privilege of presenting her work to the world—or at least as much of the world as his small shop could reach.

"It's you, isn't it?"

Her hands flexed over her knees. "And you. And everyone I've met. Everyone I've . . . eliminated." She glanced up at him. "Usually I use the writing and artwork as a way to exorcise the ugliness of what I've done, what has to be done."

"It's cathartic to get it out on paper?"

She nodded. "But on occasion, when I'm working, things show up that I didn't yet know. Clues to the future, direction on what to look for."

"Me?"

She smirked. "No way, cop. You came with no warning. If I'd had even a clue how much you'd invade my life, I'd have steered clear for sure."

"As I recall, you tried to do just that."

Her mouth twisted. "Yeah. A lot of good it did me, huh? You're not very good at accepting rejection."

"About as good as you are at accepting affection." Luther scooted around to sit next to her, letting their shoulders bump, their hips touch. "So what in the manuscript makes you think a child will be a victim?"

"The little girl is an *intended* victim. But no way in hell will I let it happen." She turned the pages around, flipped aside a few, and showed Luther an eerie ink representation with stark details and fearsome impressions. "There. Do you see her?"

Peering from behind a dark-skinned woman in the throes of consummate terror, Luther saw the child's face. The woman had already been attacked, but the child appeared unharmed.

"It's too late for the woman?"

Agitation took Gaby to her feet. "I don't know." She sliced a hand through the air. "Probably."

Luther studied the incredible artwork with new attention to detail. Gaby possessed not only phenomenal physical ability, but astounding artistic talent. "Does Mort know that you're the—"

"No." Her shoulders bunched as she paced, not in dejection, but in profound thought. "Only you. And it better stay that way."

"Because . . . ?" He wanted to hear her say that he mattered more than anyone else.

Instead, she shook her head. "Around you, especially whenever you touch me, I'm not as effective. Since I guess you're not kicking me out . . . " She paused, waiting for affirmation.

"Definitely not."

"Then I guess we should try working together. When my elevated perception fails me—thanks to *you*—you can maybe step up and fill in some of the gaps."

"You're serious?" For what seemed a lifetime, he'd been waiting for her to trust him enough to fully involve him in her life.

She gave a grudging nod. "Sure, why not? After all,

you're not entirely obtuse. You have pretty good instincts and adequate enough skills."

From Gaby, compliments sounded closer to insults, but Luther knew that it wasn't easy for her to admit them to him.

"Such high praise will make my head swell." He looked back at the depictions. "From everything you've drawn here, the woman looks African-American, transient at best, an addict at worst."

"I know. I think . . . I *feel* that she's probably both."

Fascinated, he continued to peruse the pages. "Under those circumstances, and with nothing else to go on, finding her won't be easy."

Her gaze cut to his. "It never is. But she has to be somewhere close enough that I can get to her. I never get called for acts out of my reach. If we check all the slum areas . . . " She started to say something more when suddenly her back snapped straight, so hard and fast that she bowed up onto her tiptoes with a painful gasp.

Luther was on his feet in an instant. "Gaby!"

"He's here." Her voice crooned with frigid intensity. "He's close." She dropped back to her feet with steely purpose and joyful anticipation. Chin tucking in, eyes brightening with morbid objective, she started out of the room.

Luther reached for her—and she jerked out of his reach.

"No! Don't touch me." Eyes unseeing and muscles clenched, she made ready to battle with him if he tried. "Don't fuck with me, Luther. I mean it. I need to get him, and I can't if you start hovering over me, dicking with my perception."

"All right." He held up his hands, showing that he respected her decision. "But I'm coming with you, no arguments."

She said nothing. In less than a minute she had on jeans but no shoes. She'd buttoned the flannel shirt only enough to cover her breasts.

Luther had no choice but to follow her out into the cold, early morning obscurity wearing no more than unbuttoned jeans and carrying his gun in one hand, his cell phone in the other.

"No car," she told him as she reached the sidewalk and launched into a flat-out run away from his home.

"Damn it." Luther ran as hard as he could, but the icy walkway numbed his feet and each pounding footfall sent pain radiating up his shins. He hadn't run barefoot on concrete since he was a young boy. He blocked the discomfort to push himself, and still he couldn't keep up with Gaby.

He'd almost lost sight of her when, for no apparent reason, she came to a dead stop.

At the end of a driveway, near bagged refuse ready for pickup, she turned a full circle, scanning the area, hunting for something.

Or someone.

He'd gotten to within forty feet of her when her face tightened and she took two hard steps toward a cross street—only to draw up short as an idling car a block down the road, hidden by the darkness, suddenly gunned the engine and sped away.

Gaby didn't chase after it, thank God. But her eyes narrowed with a transcendent apperception that Luther couldn't comprehend.

Even as the car passed beneath a streetlamp, thick fog made it impossible to see the license plate, or even identify the make and model, especially since the car kept the headlights off.

Why wasn't Gaby upset at losing her quarry?

"We're not going after him?" Feeling like the wimp

she often accused him of being, Luther bent, hands on his knees, and tried to regain his breath.

"No." Gaby wasn't breathing hard, but he could barely draw enough air into his laboring lungs. "There's no need, not right now."

She continued to stare in the direction the car had fled until the sound of the engine faded into nothingness.

Almost to herself, she mused aloud, "I couldn't see him, but he couldn't see us either. I'd say that's a fair trade-off."

"Who?"

"Not sure yet, but I'll figure it out." Gaby put her nose in the air, inhaled deeply, and closed her eyes with a fervid satisfaction that altered her expression. "Oh yeah. I have him now."

"What is it, Gaby?" Luther straightened as he watched her. What did she know that he didn't?

"I smell it."

Dread knotted inside him. She smelled . . . human remains? He looked at the garbage bags. "Oh fuck."

He started to reach for one, and Gaby grabbed his wrist in an unbreakable hold.

"No." Her gaze was truculent, almost . . . inhuman.

It reassured him. This was Gaby at her best, and knowing she had a handle on things meant fewer people would die.

"Call it in," she ordered. "Have them get forensics here or whatever you cop-type people do."

"Okay." He covered the hand she'd placed on his wrist and pried it loose. Flexing his fingers to restore the blood flow, he asked, "On what grounds? Unlike you, Gaby, I can't claim a sixth sense. I have to give them something more solid to go on."

She turned and crouched down near the stuffed bags. A damp wind blew the flannel open over her midriff, but this Gaby, Gaby in the zone, didn't feel the cold. Her hair whipped past her eyes, and still she didn't move, didn't speak.

Finally, her thigh muscles flexing, she stood. "Tell them you saw him dumping body remains. Bones, brains. Tell them we have the grisliest murder evidence they're ever going to see." Her gaze swung around to his. "Tell them we need this prioritized.

"All right." He lifted his phone.

"Wait." She worked her jaw, solving some inner turmoil. "Tell them to keep us out of it. He doesn't know us, and we don't want him to. As long as we're unknown, we can continue to investigate. Make them understand."

Their gazes held. Luther didn't relish the possibility of being caught in such a farfetched lie. "You're sure about this?"

"Fuckin' A, I'm sure." She all but vibrated with purpose, with devotion to her certainty. She pointed at the garbage. "There is a mishmash of inedible human pieces in those bags, Luther. Body parts already stripped of chunks of flesh because our fiend likes to store his food." She put her head back, closed her eyes. "When we find him, we'll find a full freezer, too."

"Christ." Luther rubbed his eyes. He wanted to take Gaby away from this, but he couldn't. He was a cop down to the marrow of his bones. And she was a paladin.

With her guidance, they'd get the cretin that much sooner, and save lives in the process.

She looked around, eyes narrowed, hands on her lean hips. "If you can get some units to check the rest of the neighborhood's trash, I'm betting you'll find more bags, too." She glanced at Luther. "Our guy is smart enough to scatter around the remains."

Luther's guts knotted in rebellion to the vividness she described. "You can smell that?"

In the slightest movement imaginable, she slowly shook her head. "Oh no, I smell something far more important than blood and guts and intestines."

He straightened. "What?"

Her eyes brightened in the darkness, and she said with enthusiasm, "I smell ink."

Head down, music blaring in her ears, Gaby strolled along the curb toward Mort's place. It was late afternoon, and she and Luther had already had a long day.

"I don't smell it," Luther had said about the ink, as if they operated on the same plane. As if anything about her was perceptible to him.

When would he get it? When it was too damned late?

Not much separated her from the ghouls she killed. When Luther realized that, would he revile her?

She just didn't know, and it made her tetchy.

At least he had believed her, had thrown himself into her instructions without reserve. In record time, Luther had gotten half the damn police force out on the scene. Neighbors awakened to the racket and lights. News crews showed up on the scene.

From inside a dark cruiser, wearing a hat and sunglasses, Luther directed the search. Gaby tucked into the backseat and thought about what needed to be done, and how she'd do it.

Toward dawn they discovered the third and last bag, thanks to stray dogs that sniffed out the feast. At the sight of a mutt gnawing on a human foot, a young female officer puked up her morning coffee and Danish.

Luther didn't relieve her of duty. He kept them all searching until the last of the garbage had been screened.

They now knew that their cannibal refused feet and hands, intestines, brains, and the spinal cord.

Internal organs were missing, so he either ate those or hadn't yet had an opportunity to dispose of them.

After they concluded the search, Luther had trailed Gaby to several tattoo shops. He didn't send other officers to do the same, because he had no legitimate reason to present for the search. He couldn't very well announce that Gaby smelled the ink, especially when the overwhelming scents of dead flesh mixed with refuse presented a cacophonous assault on the senses, enough to drown out every other odor—at least for the average person.

But she wasn't fucking average.

No, she wasn't even in the realm of normal, and because of that, Luther hadn't discounted her theory of a tattoo artist being involved. But neither did he want Gaby harassing tattoo parlors on her own.

The side investigation, Luther claimed, required finesse and subtlety.

They both knew she possessed neither virtue, and so he went with her. She didn't mind his company, but she thought he could have done something more important, especially since the legwork hadn't panned out. Yet.

Gaby was so drawn into her own thoughts that she didn't see the duo of ragtag youths until they stepped out in front of her, blocking her path.

Slowly she looked up and took their measure. Oh yeah. This confrontation showed promise.

Few people in the quiet, disadvantaged area of tenement housing and crime cared when others got victimized. It was an everyday way of life. At the sign of impending trouble, a vagrant scurried away. Two hookers made a point of turning their backs. Across the street, sitting on a stoop, an obese woman in her nightgown smoked a cigarette and rocked a baby.

No cops. No one to care.

There were only two guys, probably between the ages of eighteen and twenty-one. Given their sneers and aggressive postures, they wanted trouble.

A gift from heaven.

Because Gaby had trouble to spare.

Chapter 9

A stiff wind carried the odor of fetid refuse. It wafted around Gaby, but it didn't come from the men. No, an overturned trash can was to blame. The bodies attempting to intimidate her were outwardly clean.

Their insides, their rotten morals and foul intentions, had no discernible odor. But Gaby knew. She saw beyond their young, handsome faces and healthy physiques to the burgeoning savages within.

Gaby anticipated the conflict to come. She could use a brawl right now. Physical combat had proven to be the preeminent release for her churning discontent.

That is, she'd found battle to be the greatest release before Luther showed her the draining effects of sex.

Nothing, absolutely nothing, compared to the lethargy and peace of mind imbued from carnal intimacy with Luther.

The realization of yet another drastic change Luther had perpetrated caused Gaby's shitty mood to ramp up a paramount degree.

Slowly, savoring the possibilities, she removed the ear-buds and turned off her music. She tucked them into her pocket alongside the new cell phone Luther had presented to her, the phone he insisted she carry on her person at all times.

It was a fucking leash and they both knew it, but what the hell? She could give a little on that score. If the cell phone ensured he could reach her whenever he wanted, the opposite was also true. She could contact Luther at any time.

And she would, just to emphasize that their relationship worked both ways. If he worried for her, well hell, she worried about him a thousand times more.

Luther was a prodigious specimen among ordinary people, but his skills didn't come close to hers, and that made him far more susceptible to injury.

Utilizing her keen insight, Gaby surveyed the two males who'd separated to block her way. Their low-hanging jeans displayed a laughable amount of underwear, and their shirts were meant to show off tight upper bodies.

Cruelty and belligerence were now comfortable window dressings for them, but to Gaby, their insecurities remained so transparent that she almost pitied them.

Almost.

"Everyone has a choice," she told them. "You see life, see the injustice, and you can either mimic it or you can do better." Giving them a fair shot, she said, "Now, decide."

After sharing a look, one of them said, "What the fuck is she talking about?"

They laughed as one, finding strength in unity. "Bitch, are you loco?"

The darker and more handsome of the two slid a suggestive gaze over her. "She's butchin' it up, for sure, ain't you, girl?" His sleazy grin matched his sleazy perusal. "Wearin' them ragtag clothes and hiding all the good stuff. But underneath there, mama's got all the right parts, don't ya?"

Mustering serene but disdainful mockery, Gaby said, "Just spit it out already. What is it that you fuck-heads want?"

The other boy was taller and looked like a basketball player with his long, lean, muscular physique. Laughing at her, he said, "The skinny cat has claws." He crowded into her space with cocky obnoxiousness. "I like it. What d'ya say, girl?" He cupped a hand over his package. "You know you want some of this."

She snorted. "Yeah—just like I want my eyeballs clawed out with an ice pick."

He got closer still, and now she could smell him, the scent of testosterone, pot, and nervousness.

Oh yeah, he was nervous. And high. His pupils were so dilated, his eyes looked black. Even in the cool air, sweat popped on his forehead and upper lip.

Idiot.

At her insult, his chin jutted and his chest puffed up. "Check that fuckin' mouth, woman, or I'll take you right here, right now."

Next to him, Gaby felt short but not in the least threatened. She leaned in, saying with ominous threat, "Are you really so anxious to lose your cherry that you want to take me on?"

"Lose my cherry? Bitch, you're trippin'!" His voice shook with fury and insult. "I get laid anytime I want."

"Using force, I'm guessing." Gaby stifled a yawn. "No woman would lie down with the likes of you otherwise."

His clouded eyes narrowed. "Using force," he agreed on a snarl. "When the mood strikes me."

Gaby considered giving him some slack for being a moron, for being a product of his bleak environment, but she said aloud, "Nah." His bragging agreement that he wasn't above forcing a woman, whether true or not, hit a nerve.

And with that, she punched him in the face, hard and fast. A direct hit from her equaled the same force as getting plowed by a baseball bat. His nose shattered, his head snapped around, and bright red blood sprayed out in a wide arc.

Her victim staggered into a crumbling brick wall and barely managed to stay upright. He clutched a broken pipe for balance while cursing her in lurid terms.

Wide-eyed with disbelief, the darker boy stared toward her.

Gaby flexed her knuckles. Oh yeah. That felt awesome. But she wanted more. A lot more.

"Well, c'mon, girls." She taunted them both with a *come and get it* gesture. "I have other things to do today."

"Un-fucking-believable," the second boy muttered through bared teeth as he raised his fists.

He lunged forward and Gaby kicked out the knee on his lead leg. He buckled in surprise, yelled out, and fell to the ground.

Amused, Gaby raised a brow. "Well? Is that it?"

The bloody-faced fellow, whose nose now looked like a football it was so swollen and discolored, pulled a switchblade. It snapped open with a quiet snick.

So dumb. He held it wrong, Gaby noted, and a pellucid aura of fear undulated around him.

Why did the biggest cowards always think they had more to prove?

She tsked—and withdrew her own knife. "Mine's bigger, sweet cheeks. And I'm willing to bet it's been used a whole lot more than yours ever has."

His eyes rounded as comprehension sank in. "Who the fuck are you?"

"Your worst nightmare. Your conscience. Or maybe just the one who's going to put you on a different path. Up to you."

Instead of taking the offer, the idiot jabbed out, trying to gig her. Gaby dodged his lame attempt with ease and retaliated with a series of fast, flawless slices along his arm, his chest, and low on his abdomen. The cuts were superficial, but still they had to burn.

"Now," she said, as he stared in horror at the blood seeping through his clothes. "I don't like abuse of any kind, but I especially fucking hate men who abuse women. So the next cut will be your dick. Tell me, boy, you ready to lose that useless appendage?"

Dumbfounded, he dropped the knife and put a hand to his stomach to staunch the trickle of blood.

Wounded Knee lunged forward with a frustrated cry.

Talk about stupid . . .

Gaby tripped him, took him down to his back hard enough to knock the wind from his lungs, and then dug her knee into the base of his throat. He tried to gasp for air, but could get none past the calculated restriction she inflicted.

Blood oozing from between his fingers, the last man standing pleaded with her. "Hey! He can't breathe!"

"That's the point, moron." Caught on a whirlwind of discordant emotions, Gaby dug her knee in harder.

She needed to hurt him, she really did.

But . . . she didn't want to.

Panicked, the youth came forward. "Lady, please. You're gonna kill him!"

"Yeah, so?" She nodded to his knife, still open, lying on the sidewalk. "I suppose you just wanted to trim my hair with that switchblade, right?"

He ran a bloody hand over his face, adding a sinister

taint to his punkish appearance. "We were just messin' with you. Honest. We ain't never killed no one before."

"You guys bragged about forcing women. You expect me to just forget that?"

"It was bullshit, I swear. We . . . we took some shit that fucked us up, that's all. We weren't thinking straight."

At his pleading, Gaby eased a little. "I'll say you weren't."

Panic added an urgent edge to his pleading tone. "It was a fucking stupid mistake, okay? We didn't mean no real harm."

"Could've fooled me." Unwilling to give an inch, Gaby said, "What if you'd harassed someone other than me? What if you'd pulled this shit on a"—she almost said "normal person"—"a woman less skilled?"

"I'm sorry. We're both sorry." His voice went high and shrill. *"Please, he's my brother. Let him go."*

Gaby had a soft spot for siblings—since she had none. But the mention of drugs intrigued her. "What are you high on? What'd you take?"

"I don't know. Some strong shit. Stuff we bought earlier."

Huh. "Stronger than usual?"

"Yeah." He shifted his stance. "Usually that shit is cut, ya know? This might be, too, but not as much."

Gaby returned the pressure of her knee into his brother's chest. "Where'd you get it?"

Fear flashed over his ashen face, and he shook his head. "I can't tell you that."

That exacerbated Gaby's already pissy mood.

"Don't make me ask twice, you dolt." She did all she could to suppress her fury, marshalling her remaining control to keep the rage at bay.

"But . . ."

"I want to kill him," Gaby explained, and it was only a partial lie. She didn't want the boy's death on her conscience, but the need for violence churned within her. "Be smart and don't push me."

The guy blanched. "We . . . we used to buy from some dude named Bogg. But someone 'bout killed Bogg and left him for the Five-O. They hauled his sorry ass off to some high-security hospital hellhole. His brother stepped up to handle the biz."

Clarity burst inside Gaby. This was why she'd ended up here, tackling these boys today. She glanced heavenward, shook her head at the subtlety of the message, and the fog of murderous rage cleared as a gust of determination washed in.

Oh yeah. Now she felt more like herself, like the Gaby she knew and understood.

The Gaby with a specific purpose.

Clenching her jaw, she tucked her chin in with gleeful anticipation. "Give me the dealer's name."

"I don't know. I swear it. He was handing out stuff free, looking for any word on who got his brother. We took the shit and split. That's all I know."

"All right. Then tell me what the asshole looks like, and where I can find him. I'll take it from there."

His gaze going to his brother's purpling face, the guy swallowed and rushed into speech. "He's tall, a real skinny fucker. But mean, ya know? He shaves his head and has this bitchin' tat on the back of his skull. Like a demon or some shit. He was hanging out on Race Street."

"Near where the kids play?"

"Yeah. Where the cops nabbed his brother. You might be able to find him there again tonight."

"Oh, I'll find him. Count on it."

Drowning in his own strangling fear, he begged, "Please

don't tell him you heard it from me. He'd kill me for sure if he knew I sent you."

"And you think I won't?" Gaby stood, allowing her prey to suck in a strangled gulp of air. He rolled to his side and promptly puked around his gasping breaths.

She paid no mind to his struggles. The numb-nuts would live, and maybe now he'd think twice about who he tried to bulldoze.

Stalking over to the other boy, she locked eyes with him. "Listen up, shithead. You'll never know when I'm around, but believe me when I tell you that I see a lot. Everything that's important."

Something in her gaze convinced him, because he nodded fast and hard. Gaby knew that sometimes an otherworldly light shone through her eyes. Luther had told her she morphed some, just as her evil prey did.

She fucking hated that, but what the hell. For now, it worked to her advantage.

"If I catch you bullying anyone else, if I see you hopped up, if I see you so much as eyeball a dealer, I'll not only kill you, I'll fucking well take you apart piece by piece. You got that?"

"Yeah, yeah, I got it." He walked a wide berth around Gaby and, anxious to be on his way, helped his brother to his feet.

"You'd better." Looking at them both, seeing how terror had replaced their cocky attitudes, Gaby felt devilish and pretended to lunge for them.

They scrambled away, hobbled by painful injuries.

It almost made her snicker, but laughter was so contradictory to her existence that she didn't quite know how to get it out.

If she stuck with Luther long enough, would she turn into one of those twittering fools who found humor everywhere, regardless of the suffering that existed in everyday life?

Did she maybe . . . want that? Did she want to conform and become like every other mundane person in life, oblivious to the reality of iniquity?

If it meant keeping Luther, then she would try.

Now that he had shown her something so special, the thought of losing him left her hollowed out with an invasive sense of despair.

Despite the conflict she'd just concluded, she still twitched with an abundance of energy. And no wonder, considering that she needed to destroy a cannibal, shut down a drug dealer, and save a child.

And she needed a way to do it all without alienating Luther.

She touched the choker around her neck. It was a gift from him—the first gift she'd ever received in her entire life.

Replacing the earbuds in her ears, she turned on the music Luther had chosen for her.

So many remarkable ways that he'd influenced her. He'd shown her a side of life that she'd never before experienced. In a way, that cognizance of everyday normalcy helped her because now she could understand why people chose to remain oblivious to the truth of their own frailty.

With every step, Gaby felt her newest gift from Luther, a narrow cell phone, which was wedged into the back pocket of her jeans.

He'd taken over, changing her irrevocably, and the awful truth was that she craved the changes, scary as they might be.

But could she change enough to make it all matter?

A pale sun attempted to peek through gray clouds as Gaby finished her stroll to Mort's. The old neighborhood lent her a moment of serenity. The debris-covered walkway felt familiar beneath her feet. The smoggy air smelled the same, and the depressed people hadn't changed much.

More than anywhere else, this was her home.

Here, in the apartment above Mort's, she'd found her first friendship—and recognized her own humanity in the bargain. Before Mort, she hadn't felt human.

She hadn't even felt real.

She located him on his front stoop, sitting there with legs stretched out, propped back on his elbows, doing nothing.

Many times she'd sat in that exact same spot, waiting for duty to call, suffering her own existence.

At the sight of Mort, something warm and mellow spread throughout her.

She liked him. Hell, she probably loved him, though she couldn't be sure. Caring was a very new concept for her and she wasn't sure what it felt like. The only strong emotion well known to her was the driving, all-consuming need to destroy evil.

And lately, her profound desire to be with Luther.

Frustrated by that, Gaby kicked a rock, and Mort looked up.

When he saw her approaching, his face lit up with pleasure. Good old Mort. His devotion to her left her humbled and befuddled.

She was the creepiest person he had ever met, and yet he revered her.

Good old Mort—the impetus that had set her on an unknown track.

She owed him much, more than she could ever repay.

Now on his feet, he hailed her with a wide smile and blooming energy. "Gaby! I didn't know you were coming to visit."

It didn't make any sense, considering what an utter putz

Mort used to be. But he looked good. For a man who had previously presented himself with stoop-shouldered insecurity, a paunch, and loads of desperation, he now exuded good health, confidence, and maybe even sex appeal.

Why else would women give him second glances? Men eyed him with respect. Hookers did their best to entice him.

But Mort had eyes only for Ann.

Ann, the miracle worker. Ann, the savior of all pathetic souls. Ann, of beauty and grace, a woman who accepted the faults and lacking nature of others, including Bliss and Mort and . . . Gaby herself.

The woman should be canonized. Her presence made Gaby's faults and shortcomings more conspicuous than ever, and for that, Gaby resented her.

Thanks to Ann's influence, Mort's body was more fit now, leaner and harder than ever before, and his self-assured demeanor gave him a striking edge.

She waved him back to his seat. "You didn't have to get up."

"Of course I did." Laughing, he reached for her and dared to draw her into a tight, friendly hug.

Solid, that was the word to describe Mort: solid in form and in friendship.

"It's always great to see you, Gaby, you know that." He let her push out of his arms, and added, "Especially today."

Why? Gaby wondered. What made today special?

"Let's go in for coffee. Or would you rather have a cola?"

"Cola," Gaby said, no longer feeling the need to rebuke Mort's every gracious effort.

They passed through the front door and Gaby paused inside, looking at the stairs that led to the upper rooms where she used to stay. Much had happened here, and she felt a poignant loss for what she used to be. Her life back then had been stark and bleak and simple.

Now the complications filled her with fear at what she was becoming.

"Gaby?" Mort touched her shoulder, startling her and drawing her from her thoughts. "You okay?"

She jerked away from long-dead memories and nodded toward the upstairs apartment. "Bliss cooking anything? I could eat."

He frowned in concern. "You all right?"

"Just hungry, that's all. Luther and I missed both breakfast and lunch."

Assuming they'd been pleasurably occupied, Mort smiled. Gaby didn't bother to tell him that in their urgency to hunt down clues on a cannibal, they hadn't thought about food.

"She's out interviewing for jobs, but I can put together a sandwich for you." Mort turned to lead the way toward his kitchen.

Thanks to Ann-the-fucking-paragon, Mort's place was now tidy and organized. Everywhere Gaby looked, she saw Ann's influence. The old kitchen table remained, but now it looked pristine, matching the rest of the kitchen. Placemats decorated the tabletop, with matching curtains at the window.

It made Gaby want to puke.

She jerked out a chair and dropped into it. "So Bliss wants a job, huh?"

Mort nodded. "Sure, why not? Ann set up interviews for her with several nice places. We're hoping she lands a job today."

Getting colas from the refrigerator, Mort said, "It'll really help Bliss's self-confidence to earn her own way, instead of relying on friends to help her. Not that I mind having her upstairs."

"But you need the money," Gaby said as he handed her a frosty can.

Confusion stalled him. "You don't know?"

"Know what?"

"Luther pays her rent, so I'm not out anything."

Gaby paused with the foaming can almost to her lips. No, she hadn't known that. But this added example of Luther's compassion warmed her. True, in the depressed area with an apartment so small, the rent wasn't much at all. That's how Gaby had afforded it. Still, it was a real kind thing for Luther to do.

To hide her surprise, Gaby took a long drink, burped, and set the can on the table. "I suppose Luther can afford it."

"He says he can. I tried to tell him not to worry about it. Truth is, I like having the company here, whether Bliss could pay or not. She's a nice girl. But Luther insisted." He gave her a look. "He knows you care about Bliss, and he doesn't want you to worry."

Gaby grunted. "So it's my fault he's spending his life savings?"

Sticking his head in the fridge again, Mort ignored that to ask, "Ham and cheese okay?"

"Anything'll do." Along with now being sensitive to cold, exhaustion, and despair, Gaby grew ravenous several times a day. Feeding herself was a pain in the ass, but it beat the growling in her stomach.

Mort set out pickles and chips, too. "Don't worry about the rent, okay? I doubt Luther will let himself go broke."

Gaby set out the cell phone. "He might if he keeps buying me stupid gifts."

Mort glanced at the phone. "Nice. Now I can call you to chat."

Just peachy. That probability hadn't occurred to Gaby. "I'm not real used to it yet," she hedged. "Don't count on me answering all the time, okay?"

Mort laughed. "Here, I'll get your number and program in mine for you. If anything comes up, you know, like with Bliss or whatever, I can let you know." He cast her a quick smile while fidgeting with the phone.

Mort made it look so easy as he pushed buttons, clicked here and there, and then put her phone back on the table.

"I'm getting your number, too. I can share it with Bliss." He opened a drawer and got a slip of paper, wrote the number on it, and put it on the front of his fridge with a magnet shaped like an apple. "Bliss will love being able to reach you."

Double fuck. The last thing Gaby wanted to do was indulge small talk on a phone. "Make it clear that the phone is only for emergencies."

"Got it." Grinning, Mort went back to the food preparation. It occurred to Gaby that he was now a multitasking man, when he used to be pathetically ineffective at all he did. He was different, better, but still the Mort she knew and felt comfortable with.

If Mort could change so easily, then maybe she could, too.

But then again, Mort wasn't a freak of nature.

"So," Gaby said, harking back to his earlier comment, "what's special about today?"

He glanced at her between layering meat and cheese on white bread. "I was talking about the investigation and everything."

"Some creepy shit, that's for sure." To a guy like Mort, the grisly murders had to be scary.

He glanced up. "I know it's routine for Ann and Luther, but aren't you worried about tonight?"

Trying to hide her ignorance, Gaby narrowed her eyes. She didn't know about anything happening tonight.

Hedging, she asked, "Is there some reason I should be?"

He withdrew a butcher knife to slice the sandwich in half. "I forget that you don't freak out about stuff the way the rest of us do. But let me tell you, I'm plenty spazzed about it. I looked it up on the Internet, and those underground raves are nothing but sex, addiction, and perversion. A lot of people go into those things and never come back out."

Raves?

Mort handed her the sandwich, and before he could step away, Gaby caught him by the upper arm.

Slowly, she reeled him down so that he bent at the waist, his nose almost touching hers. "Okay, Mort, one time, and one time only."

His brows went up. "What are you talking about?"

"That's how many times I'm going to ask. Just once. Got it?"

"Um . . . yeah."

It burned her ass to admit Luther had left her in the dark. But if she wanted details, and she did, she had no choice. "I don't know shit about a rave, or about what Luther and Ann have planned for tonight. But you're damn well going to explain it all, every detail, and you're not going to make me ask twice. Understood?"

Mort puckered. "Uh . . . Luther didn't say anything to you?"

Her hard stare proved answer enough.

"Right." Sighing, he pulled out a chair, sat down, and propped his head in his hands. "Ann told me, so I just assumed . . . "

The mention of Ann kindled Gaby's smoky temper.

"What? That Luther and I share the same kind of relationship? Get real, Mort."

Mort flopped back in his chair and gave in with enthusiasm. He seemed more than gleeful to share what he knew. "Ann said they've been keeping tabs on a few gang members with these weird tattoos. She said they have this vampire obsession that she'd always considered harmless, but now . . ."

"What kind of tattoos?"

"Ann said that one of them has this huge, vicious bite mark tattooed on his shoulder, like maybe someone tried to take a chunk out of him. She said it looks totally real and is pretty sick. Another one is a set of perfect fang marks on a woman's neck, with blood dripping all the way down over her chest."

"What does that have to do with this underground party you mentioned?"

"It's called a rave. According to Ann, all raves have two main ingredients—loud music and plenty of drugs. They keep breaking up the raves when they know about them because there've been so many rapes, and a lot of deaths."

"Yeah, sounds like a party to me." Gaby rolled her eyes. "So people go there and get murdered?"

"Not exactly. Someone takes a pill that someone else hands to them, and then later dies. Ann said it's hard to trace back to the raves, but they know a lot of ecstasy gets passed around. Usually though, it's that something was cut into the ecstasy and that's what kills."

Having only a rudimentary understanding of drugs, Gaby frowned. "Someone tampers with them?"

"The dealer, I guess." Mort shrugged. "I'm not an expert, but I read that said ecstasy could be mixed with anything from caffeine to cocaine. Some sickos are passing off an ingredient in cough syrup as ecstasy. Sounds harmless, right? But mix that in with all the wild dancing and sweating, the alcohol and other drugs, and . . . " He shrugged. "Kids die with heatstroke or something."

Gaby crumbled a potato chip. "Fucking idiots, if you ask me."

"I'll say. But young people sometimes do really dumb things that they shouldn't. It's all part of growing up, I guess."

For her, growing up had meant suffering the agonizing pain, struggling with supernatural powers unknown to the rest of society, and coming to grips with a devout calling against evil too wicked to continue to exist.

She hadn't had time for drugs, much less stupid parties.

Gaby studied Mort. "Did you do that kind of shit when you were younger?"

"God, no." Mort stared down at his hands. "I was never popular enough to be invited to parties. But even if I had been, no way would I have randomly taken drugs. I was always a coward, always afraid of getting caught or hurt." His smile went crooked. "That's partly why it's so fun being around you. You're the most fearless person I've ever met."

"Oh, I dunno about that," Gaby told him. "I've seen you be pretty damned fearless yourself." Not that long ago, Mort had been brave enough to let her escape capture by the police, and for a time, she'd been left thinking he had died for his efforts.

Nothing had ever hurt so badly or cut so deeply as that.

Finding him alive had been the happiest moment she'd ever known.

"Maybe you inspire me," he told her with a laugh. "But more likely it's that I always figure you'll find a way to keep me safe."

"Don't get mushy on me, Mort, or I won't be able to

eat." She picked up her sandwich. "So what's the connection between this rave and the tattooed idiots?"

"Word on the street is that they're the ones setting it up." He shrugged. "It's been organized underground, off the radar, so police aren't supposed to know about it. Ann had a snitch tell her about it in exchange for dropping a solicitation charge."

Ann again. "Good old Ann keeps herself busy, doesn't she?"

Mort missed the sarcasm. "She's a really good cop. She said a lot of college kids, especially girls, were invited. I guess she and Luther hope to find a lead there. At the very least, they'll be able to check on the group with the vampire fixation, right?"

"If Ann's such a stellar cop, then why are you worried?"

"From what I could figure out, the music at raves is so loud you can't talk. Laser and strobe lights, and even fake smoke, make it really hard to see. Everyone is drugging everyone else, so people are really messed up and not thinking straight. And . . . " He blanched, looking away.

"Don't hold back now, Mort."

Color tinged his face. "Well, Ann said this particular group is known for throwing . . . orgies."

"What's an orgy?"

His eyes bulged and his color deepened to crimson. Lowering his voice, he said, "You know. Where everyone is . . . having sex with everyone else."

"You're shitting me."

He shook his head. "Ann could get taken from Luther and by the time he found her again, God only knows what might've happened."

"I could take a good guess." Suffering her own turbulent thoughts, Gaby peeled the crust from a piece of bread. "I'd say you have reason to worry."

Gaby could have stayed home with Luther today, but he'd had his hands full. Though he said that he'd planned to take some time off with her, he was instead organizing the newest task force against a monster so reprehensible that he made women faint and men nauseous.

Gaby knew that eventually she'd have to annihilate the fiend.

But Luther and Ann hoped to locate him at this stupid rave first. Fools.

The atmosphere Mort described would make it difficult for Luther to establish himself as an officer of the law. For that reason alone, he should have asked her along.

Ann had confided in Mort, but Luther had left her out in the cold.

Her stomach grumbled, as much from hunger as discontent, so she started to eat. Mort watched her with due caution and finally, after several minutes of silence, he cleared his throat.

Gaby glanced up at him. "Now what are you squirming about?"

He shifted again in his seat. "It makes me nervous when you're so quiet."

"Yeah?" She downed the rest of her cola and caught him in her most implacable stare. "Tell you what then. You can fill in the silence."

"I don't have anything else to talk about."

"Sure you do." She put her elbows on the table and leaned in closer. "You can start by telling me where this rave is, and what I have to do to get in."

Chapter 10

Dressed in jeans and a faded T-shirt that read "I have a license to kill," and his most worn leather jacket, Luther escorted Ann into the vacated department store. At the street level, the windows were boarded shut and the doors locked. But around back, through the alley entrance, rough-looking men gave directions to the basement.

In case anyone watched, they said nothing as they crossed the open spaces and located the stairwell that led to the underground area. Halfway down the stairs, they could hear the repetitive music and the buzz of a large crowd.

Girding himself, Luther put a hand to Ann's back and stepped into the rave. The second the door shut behind them, suffocating darkness crowded in. Loud, computer-generated music set his eardrums to vibrating. Artificial fog floated in and out of shadows, highlighted by flashing laser lights.

Luther held Ann's arm until he got his bearings. He could smell weed, alcohol, and sweat. At thirty-two, he'd be one of the older partiers, but as his eyes adjusted, he saw kids in their early teens and adults old enough to know better.

Near Ann's ear, he said, "Remember to stay alert. I've got a bad feeling about this."

Blonde hair loose and makeup overdone, Ann nodded. "Yes, my instincts are kicking up a fuss big-time." She smiled at him, looking like a very sexy knockout. Mort was a lucky guy. "I won't take any unnecessary chances, believe me."

What kind of chance did she consider "necessary"?

Luther made a noncommittal sound. The sweater Ann had chosen showed more cleavage than he'd realized she possessed, and her jeans were so tight they fit her like her skin. She'd be drawing attention, no doubt about it. Already several freaks sent her scurrilous glances filled with lascivious intent.

His hand on her arm tightened. "If anyone tries to give you anything—"

"Oh please." The music blared and the strobe-light effect disoriented. "You don't have to warn me about accepting drinks, Luther. I'm not an idiot."

Damn it, he didn't like this. But Ann was as competent a police detective as he'd ever met. Only her smaller stature and femaleness made her less capable in physical confrontations.

She turned to him. "We should separate."

"No way."

"We'll find out more if we're on our own." She nodded toward a willowy woman with breasts showing through a net bra, and long legs in leather pants. The woman licked her lips at Luther. "We'll each have our flirts and find out what we can. I'll meet you back at the entrance in an hour. If anything goes down, you'll hear gunshots, trust me."

He caught her by the nape of the neck. "*Your* gunshots. Not anyone else's."

"That's the plan."

Knowing she was right, that they would accomplish more apart, Luther finally relented. "Fine. But I mean it, Ann. Take no chances."

"Sure thing, Daddy." She touched his face, then faded into the gyrating crowd, swallowed by bodies and smoke and menacing jeopardy.

Luther saw a woman accept a pill from a man, knocking it back with a shot of liquor. Another man danced with two women, one at his front and one at his back, both of them groping him. A woman climbed atop a table and began stripping.

It was the most outlandish display of decadent immorality he'd ever seen. The majority of young people were already stoned out of their heads.

A mostly naked breast brushed his arm, and Luther geared himself for the role he needed to play. It wouldn't be easy, because for the first time in his life, guilt attacked him during the job.

He had to do this, but he knew how Gaby would feel about it, and damn it, that nicked his conscience.

Doing his best to tune out thoughts of Gaby, he faced the Goth chick with the decorated naked chest. He said nothing, just stared at her.

His scowl must've heightened her interest. She leaned into him, licked his ear, and purred, "Hey stud, you wanna dance with me?"

"Not really." Luther stepped closer, his gaze as direct as he could make it in the alternating psychedelic light and obscure darkness.

When the lights flashed, he saw her smile and her dark eyes, dazed from drugs or alcohol, or both.

She took his hand and led him across the floor and around a distant corner where he could at least hear himself think. Several people gyrated together, their hips grinding in a semblance of dance.

As she tossed her head, glimmering lights shone in her inky hair. Close to his ear, she asked, "You with that other chick?"

"Does that really matter to you?"

She gave an insincere laugh and shook her head. "I guess not."

"Our relationship is an open one." He looked down at her breasts. She had an impressive rack, he'd give her that. As a man, he appreciated the sight. As a responsible person, pity for her dulled the enjoyment. "She's off doing her own thing . . . and I plan to do mine."

"Your thing being . . . ?"

His gaze moved over her, and dismissed her near-nudity as unappealing. "You'll have to find that out on your own."

She looked to be in her early twenties, and was too foolhardy to survive long. Using her didn't suit him. He'd rather arrest her and get her someplace safe—but he couldn't. Not yet.

She pouted. "You're far too steady to have any fun. You want to take some ecstasy or speed with me?"

As if she wasn't already flying? "Depends." Luther put a hand to her bare waist. His skin was clammy, too warm. "Here . . . or someplace more private?"

"Private, silly." Laughing, she started off on a winding path through the crowd of sweaty bodies.

Luther followed, making note along the way of things that should never occur in a public place.

At the back of the room, she went on tiptoe to kiss a hulk in a purple G-string. Ornate tattoos covered his whole body, delineating bulging muscles and even trailing into his very brief underwear.

The man accepted her kiss stony-faced, without inflection of any kind, and then he opened a heavy door for them to pass through. Once inside, low-burning red lights replaced the lasers and strobes, making it easier to make out their surroundings.

Another young lady fell into him, laughing hysterically, unsteady in every way. She twisted both hands in Luther's shirt and held on. "Oh my God. This is off the hook, isn't it?"

Luther pried her loose and relinquished her to a rubbery-legged young man who chortled with her. Red-faced and bleary-eyed, they stumbled off to the side and into a bean-bag chair.

At his sardonic best, Luther commented, "Very private."

"It's for special guests only." She held Luther's hand and walked backward, giggling at him.

"And I'm special?"

"Tonight, for me, you are." She looked down at his crotch. "I'm Desiree, by the way."

In the corner, on a decorated twin bed, two people fucked for a small but appreciative audience. Ahead of him, a woman perched on her knees as a man, holding a leash attached to a collar around her neck, spanked her with a leather paddle.

As crude public displays went, that was distasteful enough. But to top it all, behind a parted curtain, Luther saw a man piercing a woman's nipple with a long, thin needle. A thin trickle of blood dripped down her chest. She moaned and squirmed and appeared to love it as the man leisurely licked away the blood.

Luther never paused as he stepped away from the repulsive act.

He'd expected a grisly scene of drugs and alcohol and possibly rape, but he hadn't expected this orgy of depravity.

The malodor of stale sweat, musky sex, and drugged excitement hung thick in the air, assaulting his nostrils and violating his lungs. The red lights cast a carmine hue over everything, making shadows shift like liquid puddles of blood.

Luther's stomach curdled.

So much wickedness.

Thank God he hadn't broken down and brought Gaby along. He wanted to be honest, to share everything with her and build a partnership where they worked together . . .

But he couldn't imagine her reaction to all of this.

Heads would roll—and then she'd bombard him with endless uncomfortable questions pertaining to sexual perversions.

Luther no sooner had that thought than he felt the forceful stare of someone watching him. The short hairs on his neck stood on end, but he didn't dare look behind him.

He heard no disruption; bodies weren't flying and people weren't screaming. It *couldn't* be Gaby.

Anyone other than her, he could handle.

Desiree said something to him that he missed, and then she stopped before a small, cloth-covered table that displayed an arrangement of colored pills, a few drinks, and a line of cocaine already cut on a mirror.

A tall, thin man with long dark hair and very pale blue eyes awaited them. Given the faint creases in his face and the cynicism in his gaze, Luther put him in his late forties, early fifties.

If his eerie watchfulness wasn't enough, his age made him stand out in the young crowd.

He seemed displeased with, and somewhat wary of, Luther's presence. Desiree moved forward, put her head to the table, a straw to her nose, and inhaled the coke. Giddy, she stepped back, wiped a dainty hand over her nostrils, and laughed.

In a too-polite, too-moderated voice that barely carried over the music filtering into the isolated room, the man asked, "Who is this?"

Now more vague than ever, Desiree stroked a small hand over Luther's crotch. "This is all *mine*," she taunted with a squeeze.

Revolted, Luther again removed her hand. "Not accurate at all."

Undaunted, she clung to his arm. "We just wanted to get a good buzz going before we get . . . friendlier."

The man's gaze slid over Luther with the comfort of sticky oil. "He's not your normal fare, now is he, Desiree?"

"He's bigger," she crooned, now sliding her hands everywhere. "And strong."

Luther stood there, impassive and accepting, when he really wanted to strike out.

Blue eyes took his measure. "You look like a cop to me."

"Maybe the shirt is misleading."

He read the slogan and laughed. "What other license is there for killing, if not under police jurisdiction?"

"I have a hunting license." Luther looked at young Desiree, now pressed to his leg. He levered her away with enough force to show his displeasure at her boldness. "And sometimes I like to hunt pretty women—but only when they know their place."

The man smiled in understanding—but the edge of distrust remained both in his gaze and posture. "Far be it from me to interfere. I'm not a drug user myself, and I have no idea where these came from, but I'm not the moral police, so carry on as you please."

"I'll pass," Luther said. No way in hell was he ingesting anything from this place.

Desiree eagerly took the instruction to heart and again groped Luther's crotch.

Just as the older man started to walk away, something crashed behind Luther. He froze. The man froze. The woman continued to fondle him—until a slender hand reached around Luther, caught her long hair in a fist, and yanked her off her high-heeled sandals.

Desiree screamed as she hit the ground. The man stiffened in affront.

And Luther, throbbing with dread, slowly pivoted to confront the interference.

Eyes bright with fury, Gaby smiled, and it was a chilling sight. "There you are."

Her gaze went past Luther to the man. With that maniacal smile still in place, she drifted closer, put her nose out, and sniffed. "Ah. I knew I'd find you eventually."

Awareness rocked Luther's very foundation, making it difficult for him to tamp down his heightened sense of alarm.

Gaby had *smelled* the man, the same way she'd sniffed those mutilated, corpse-filled garbage bags.

And now she claimed to know him?

Was Gaby telling him that they'd just found their cannibal? If so, that left him in one hell of a predicament. Though he trusted her, he needed more than Gaby's word on something so monumental.

He needed actual proof.

※

Fury burned through Gaby's veins, so hot that it even blurred her vision—but thankfully not her aggrandized sense of smell. The commingling of jealousy toward a vapid tramp, and hatred at malignant turpitude, had her muscles clamping and flexing with the compulsion to strike out.

It wasn't easy to stay contained, to keep from rampaging. But she wasn't a fool. She understood that this was Luther's work.

She would never ruin that.

Later she might maim him for leaving her behind, but she had other things to do first.

Leveling her discontent on the downed girl, Gaby curled her lip. "Get up."

Heart hammering with fear, eyes wide and dazed with drugs, Desiree stared at her.

Impatience detonated. Reaching down, Gaby grabbed her upper arm and hauled her to her unsteady feet. "How old are you?"

"T- . . . t- . . . twenty-three."

Stupid fool. "You act like you're fifteen." Gaby kept her grip tight enough to leave bruises on Desiree's pale flesh. "Find a shirt, cover yourself, and then *leave*. Don't let me see you at a rave ever again."

The girl looked to Luther, then to the other man. "She can't—"

Gaby shook her hard.

When the girl started a high-pitched protest, Gaby smacked her.

Big tears sprung to her eyes and a red palm print rose up on her cheek. Around gurgling sobs and sloppy tears, she wailed, "That's . . . that's assault!"

Closing in, Gaby exposed her true intent and fundamental nature. When she slid her knife from the sheath, she felt Luther stir beside her—and didn't give a damn.

A lot depended on her scaring the girl enough to make an impression. Gaby sensed that if she didn't change her ways, quickly, she'd end up dead.

She couldn't just let that happen. Not if she could alter events.

And if Luther actually believed that she'd hurt an innocent girl . . . well then, he didn't know her that well after all.

Holding the edge of the blade just beneath the girl's heaving left breast, Gaby whispered, "You stupid, fucking little slut, I will carve out your heart. Do you understand me? I will dice you up in little pieces and not lose a second of sleep over it."

When Desiree looked around for help, Luther made a point of offering none.

Knowing he wouldn't have done that if he'd believed, even for a single second, that she'd hurt the girl, Gaby felt emotion course through her. Later, when the time was right, she'd tell Luther how much she appreciated his faith.

For now, she had a point to make, so she let the knife slice through Desiree's net cover. It just pierced her skin, sending a bead of blood to well up.

"No one can stop me, little girl, so don't bother trying to find a way out of this. You put yourself in this situation, didn't you? You knew what could happen. You knew you could get raped, killed, or in my case"—Gaby tightened her mouth into the semblance of a grim smile—"worse."

Face going pale, the girl almost fainted.

Gaby jerked her back to attention. "Go home to your mommy and daddy. Find a safe job in a safe neighborhood. Dress with some pride and don't ever again shove shit up your nose. Got me?"

"Y- . . . yes."

Disgusted that a young lady would sink so low, Gaby removed temptation by returning her knife to the sheath at her back. She watched as the fool raced to the corner, found a jacket and small purse, and, sniffling and weeping, tried to dress herself.

To Luther, Gaby asked, "Is she straight enough to get herself home?"

"How the fuck should I know?"

So he was still undercover—and indulging his own bad mood. Tough tittie. She didn't have time to indulge his mood swings. "Call her a cab."

Jaw clenching in feigned affront, Luther withdrew his cell phone and put in the call, yelling to be heard.

Gaby snagged the girl before she could slink away into the crowd. "You're going to park your skinny ass out front on the curb and wait for a cab. If I find out you didn't, you won't like the consequences. Got it?"

Fat tears tracked down her pale, still-red cheek, mixing with inky makeup. She nodded.

Gaby released her with a small shove. "Maybe now you'll live to see your next birthday."

Dismissing her now that she'd seen to her safety, Gaby turned to the tall man. An electric sizzle sparked in her veins.

Recognition. Wariness.

Her stomach churned with a nameless dread. Never had she felt anything like it.

She knew this man.

In some indefinable way, she was already acquainted with him.

Smothering the aberrant sensation, Gaby stuck out a hand. "Bogg told me to talk to you. But that was before someone trampled him. I understand the dumb fuck may never walk again." She shrugged, showing how little she cared about that probability. "His brother told me you could still be trusted."

Appearing entranced, the tall man took her hand and held it.

Gaby saw it in his eerily memorable blue eyes: a sense of intimate knowledge.

So he felt it, too?

He shook his head as if to clear it. "Tell me. Is there a reason you attacked Desiree?"

"I schooled her, actually. There's a difference." Gaby withdrew her hand, made a show of wiping it on her jeans. "If I had attacked her, she'd be dead." Her voice lowered. "Believe it."

The man watched her hand as she cleaned it, then propped it on her hip. Slowly, he brought his puzzling gaze to hers. "I am Fabian Ludlow."

"Gaby." She met his stare with frigid resolve. She wanted him to know upfront that he didn't matter—whoever he was. "The big gorgeous dude behind me is—"

"Link." Luther held out a hand to confirm the alias.

Gaby slanted him a look. "I was going to say off-limits."

Annoyance growing, he gave a brisk nod. "Obviously that, too."

Fabian accepted his hand, but kept it quick to turn his attention back to Gaby. "You said you'd found me." He all but sizzled with curiosity. "I sense that I know you, but I can't place where we might have met."

"We haven't." Or he'd already be dead.

Fabian didn't believe her. "No, I'm sure we have." He looked her over, walked a circle around her. "Could it have been years ago?"

"No."

"I'm sure we're acquainted."

"Not before now." But somehow they were, and Gaby knew it.

His expression cleared. He wasn't giving up on his theory, but for now, he'd let it rest.

Gaby read him as easily as she did everyone else, and yet . . . there was some mystery to him. Something anomalous and sketchy and very unclear.

He smiled. "So why were you looking for me?"

Pulling up her sleeve, Gaby showed him the healing scar left from the bullet wound. "I want a tattoo to conceal this. Most tattoo artists have told me I have to wait a year, maybe even two."

"And?"

"I want the tattoo now."

He shifted, and as Gaby breathed in his unique scent, she knew she had the right person. That faint aroma of ink and the reek of insanity had wafted from the human refuse he'd dumped—just as it clung to Fabian now.

If he denied being a tattoo artist, that would only add measure to his guilt as far as Gaby was concerned. "I'm told you're the most talented artist around."

Fabian contemplated her for a long time before finally reaching for her arm. "Let me see what we have to work with."

Behind her, Gaby felt Luther loosen a tight breath. Had he expected her to start slicing and dicing? She'd told him she'd try to cooperate with him, would try things his way.

If it didn't work out, she could always go back and kill Fabian later.

Tracing a delicate line around her scar, Fabian explored her skin with his fingertips. It gave Gaby the creeps and sent a frisson of unease down her spine, but no way in hell would she flinch or show her revulsion.

"What did you have in mind?"

Gaby shrugged. "I don't really give a fuck. I just want the scar hidden."

He smiled. "With the jagged edges to the wound, I would suggest a barbwire design. It'd give us more opportunity to tie in each small cut in your skin." Holding her wrist, he looked up at her. "Gunshot?"

She stared at him. "More like 'none of your fucking business.'"

His chuckle showed that the set-down didn't faze him. "I'm not cheap."

She nodded her head toward Luther. "Link is paying, so I don't give a shit what it costs."

Luther made a choking sound. Being treated as a lackey was new for him, but he deserved it for keeping her in the dark about the rave. Before the night was over, she'd make him regret that decision in a dozen different ways.

"By the way," Gaby added, "the big dude wearing the plum smugglers out front? The one who tried to guard the door? He might need some medical attention."

Fabian's brows pinched down. "You injured him?" he inquired with as much aplomb as he could muster.

"Guilty. But, hey, he tried to stop me." She pulled the sleeve back down over her arm. "Big mistake, that."

"I see." Fabian's eyes went cold in consideration. "If he failed, then he deserved whatever you dealt."

"Yeah, cuz, like, I never deal undeserved shit." Smirking, she turned to mock Luther with her sarcasm. "Ain't that right, *Link*?"

Luther gave a low snarl, flexed his jaw, and ignored her. "When can you do the tattoo?"

To Gaby, Fabian asked, "How about—?"

"You'll do it tomorrow, late."

Her bossiness started to wear on him. The small muscles in his face twitched and tightened. "We close at seven P.M."

"Close whenever you want. It's no skin off my nose. But you'll let me in at ten. I want this done on the down-low."

They did a visual standoff, each of them unblinking, unrelenting. Gaby yawned, but other than that, she didn't give an inch, and, visibly perturbed, Fabian acquiesced.

"Fine, we'll do this your way."

"Course we will." Had there ever been any doubt? "My way is the only way I do things."

Fabian wasn't nearly as schooled at hiding his emotions. He was pissed, and it showed in his tense shoulders, the slant of his mouth, the tightness of his features.

Ah, too bad.

Trying to act cavalier, he asked, "Do you know where I work—"

"Sin Addictions." Gaby bestowed on him a menacing stare. She lowered her voice to a provoking whisper. "Come on, Fabian. Did you really think I'd approach you without knowing everything?"

Annoyance heightened his breaths. His shoulders went back, his mouth pinched. "*Everything* is a rather massive concept. Perhaps you don't know me as well as you think you do."

Oh yeah, Gaby thought. *Brag to me, you sick bastard.* "And maybe you're not as slick as you look if you believe that."

Her knife appeared in her hand as if by magic. She touched the tip of the blade to his chin. "Be at the shop at ten P.M. tomorrow. Don't make me come looking for you. You'll find I'm not the most patient person when I want something." Gaby leaned into his space. "And I want that tattoo—from you."

He didn't recoil from her knife blade. If anything, his sarcasm sharpened. "To hide your wound from the cops?"

She tapped the blade against his cheek, then returned it to the sheath. "We sick fucks all think alike, don't we?"

Before anyone could say more, Gaby turned to leave.

Luther stalled her by going to the small table holding the drugs. He began folding the tablecloth up and over everything.

Fabian scowled. "What are you doing?"

"Since you said this isn't yours, no reason to have it go to waste." He saluted Fabian, put a hand to Gaby's back, and started out.

A brief struggle ensued as he and Gaby each tried to take a position in the back to protect the other.

Of course Gaby won, but mostly because Luther didn't want to cause a scene and she didn't give a shit either way.

They had to step over the behemoth in the G-string. He was still collapsed across the entrance.

Luther growled back at her, "Did you kill him?"

"Nah." Gaby gave the big guy a curious glance. "At least, I don't think I did. My guess is he's hopped up on something and that, combined with my fist to his temple, is keeping him asleep."

"We have to find Ann." Stopping in the middle of the floor, the cloth bundle of drugs hanging from his hand, he surveyed the crowd.

"I know where she is." Gaby gave him another push to keep him walking. "I took care of her before coming after you."

Luther turned on her. "Took care of her? What the hell does that mean?"

Her temper pricked. "It means," she shouted over the god-awful techno music, "that this isn't a safe place for either of you boneheads." She took a breath, but it didn't help. Now that they were out of Fabian's range, she all but exploded. "What the *fuck* were you thinking to come here without me?"

Aware of their cover, Luther glanced around, and that infuriated Gaby, too. "Give it a fucking rest, will you? No one *normal* can hear or see in this fucking atmosphere." She forged forward. "Let's go. By now, Ann is probably so pissed off she's ready to kill."

They passed a guy holding a hypodermic, ready to inject a willing woman. Luther paused long enough to lean down and growl something dire in the guy's ear. When the young man handed over the hypodermic, Luther expressed the liquid into the air, broke off the needle, and pitched it all against the wall.

With a shove, he sent both the guy and the girl toward the entrance.

Gaby shook her head at the futility of it. "This place is fucking crawling with imbeciles. How the hell do these people survive, being so stupid and so incredibly reckless with their own lives?"

Looking like a thundercloud, Luther replied, "Damned if I know."

Everywhere Gaby looked, perverse activity took place. She couldn't take it. She wanted to start busting heads—and yeah, that was likely why Luther hadn't invited her along.

Knowing that and liking it were two very different things.

With Gaby leading, they turned a corner and went down a quieter corridor. She opened a lock on an isolated and unused office.

Before she could turn the doorknob, Ann burst out, red-faced and vibrating with fury. "*Damn you*, Gaby. How *dare you* lock me away?"

Stunned mute, Luther stared at Ann, and no wonder. Her hair rioted, her face flushed, and the veins in her temples throbbed.

Resisting the urge to point out her state of disarray, Gaby rested back against the wall. "I dared because that skinny vampire-worshiping boy you wooed had a sedative-filled needle hidden in his pocket. He planned to stick you with it the first time you blinked—with or without your permission."

Ann blanched even as she continued to breathe hard.

Gaby waved a hand. "This whole fucking place—"

"God almighty, Gaby." Luther glared at her. "Find another adjective, will you? Even for you, the language is a bit much."

Gaby tucked in her chin. So now he wanted to remonstrate with her on her guttural speech?

She clenched her fists. "This *fucking* place is filled with perverts and predators hoping for an opportunity to take advantage of everyone else—including you two."

Flattening a hand to her forehead, her eyes showing her shock, Ann sucked in three deep breaths.

Reluctantly, she looked at Gaby again. "How do you know that?"

"How do I know anything, Ann? I just fucking do." Doing her best to tamp down her rage, Gaby shoved away from the wall. But, damn it, as much as Ann irked her, she didn't want the woman hurt.

She didn't want anyone hurt—except the few she targeted herself who had it coming.

Pivoting, Gaby went nose to nose with Ann. "After he had you all pliable, you wouldn't have had much say in anything he did. At least this way, you got to keep your wits and your high-class virtue. I figured you'd prefer that to rape in a dirty corner with a lot of yahoos watching, cheering him on, and maybe taking turns."

Ann's mouth opened and shut with nothing coming out.

"Yeah." Gaby smirked. "You don't strike me as the type to enjoy a gang rape much. You're a little too cultured for that sort of play."

"Gaby," Luther chastised, but he sounded tired.

Knowing she wouldn't get a thank-you, not even expecting one, Gaby added, "I stuck the little creep with his own damn needle and left him passed out on the john floor. Whatever happens to him, I don't much care." She turned to lead the way back out.

Before she'd taken three steps, Ann's hand closed on her shoulder.

The contact was so ripe with emotion, Gaby paused without complaint.

Seconds ticked by with no sound other than the repetitious music. And then Ann said, "Thank you."

Gaby didn't face her. She couldn't.

Luther stepped up alongside her. "Now what?"

Gaby used her elbow to viciously smash a glass cover on a wall-mounted fire alarm. "Now we get wet."

She grabbed the handle and yanked it down.

Piercing alarms cut through the bedlam, and sprinklers sprayed out icy water, dousing everyone and everything and sending the doped patrons to scatter.

"This way," Gaby instructed, leading Luther and Ann to a side exit unmanned by the coordinators of the rave.

Once outside, Luther turned his back on Gaby and pulled out his cell phone. He put in an official call and within minutes cruisers were in the area and had the building surrounded. As he, Ann, and Gaby stood off in the shadows unseen, arrests were made by the dozens.

Everyone with illegal drugs in his pocket or in his blood was hauled in.

Luther and Ann watched the controlled confusion without comment.

Gaby watched them.

Seething tempers formed steam that rose from their damp clothes. They didn't look at her.

They were still furious, but they were safe, and in the end, that's what mattered most to Gaby.

It'd be a long ride home, she knew, but what the hell. She had unspent energy, so if they wanted to fight, she'd oblige them.

Chapter 11

Still burning with irritation, Luther looked at Gaby but spoke to Ann. "We met someone, Fabian, who might be key to all this. Tomorrow evening we'll visit him on the pretext of Gaby getting a tattoo."

"No pretext to it." Gaby shivered with the cold and wet, but tried to hide it. Susceptibility to such commonplace weaknesses didn't jibe with her self-imposed purpose on earth.

Luther reached for her arm, saw her slight flinch away from him, and almost lost his control. He clamped a hand on her, met her furious glare, and hauled her closer. "Let's go."

She tried to jerk away, but he kept a tight hold on her.

"Don't manhandle me." She dug in her heels.

Luther dragged her along. "The car is over here." And then, because the thought of her self-sacrifice infuriated him, he added, "And you are *not* getting a tattoo."

"Wanna bet?" She stuck a foot out and tripped him, which effectively freed her from his hold. Nearly dropping his bundle of drugs, he stumbled and almost hit the ground. He had to stop to grit his teeth, his rage clamoring for release.

Ann touched his shoulder. "Not now, Luther. Let's get out of here first." She shivered. "I'm tired, disgusted with it all, and *freezing.*"

"At least two of us are human enough to admit that." He saw Gaby stiffen and almost regretted the verbal jab.

But damn her, she had treated him like a child, like an unskilled buffoon incapable of handling the very fiber of his job. And on top of that, she planned to get a tattoo just to facilitate a closer inspection of Fabian's tattoo parlor.

Out of habit, and because she was close, Luther put a warming arm around Ann.

As if she had eyes in the back of her head, Gaby stalled in front of them. Slowly, so slowly that Luther could almost hear a drumbeat crescendo accompanying her movement, she turned to stare with deadly intent—at Ann.

Saying nothing, not moving, she stood there until Ann rolled her eyes and inched out of his reach.

"Let's don't provoke her," Ann suggested. She strode ahead of Gaby and opened the car door to get in.

Gaby still glared at Luther, and he met her fury with his own measure. He would not back down from her; not in this, and not with anything else.

Her left eye twitched, and she turned away to join Ann in the car . . . in the backseat.

So he was to play chauffeur?

He'd be damned before he asked her to ride up front with him.

Given her posture, Ann wasn't at all pleased with the close confines of the backseat. Showing her irritation, she nestled up to her car door, as far away from Gaby as she could get.

For her part, Gaby slouched down and propped her knees on the back of the passenger seat. She looked bored. Pissed off and bored.

Luther handed the drugs to Ann. "Hold on to that, will you? And be careful."

"What is it?" Ann loosened the tablecloth and peered inside.

"An array of dope I confiscated before Gaby and I left Fabian. I couldn't blow my cover, but there was no reason to leave it there for others to use. Thanks to Gaby, we just came off as a dysfunctional couple. Grabbing the dope only reinforced our pushiness." He started the car and jacked up the heat. "Be careful with that until I can book it into the evidence room."

"We *are* a dysfunctional couple, and I *am* pushy." Gaby picked at a fingernail. "No stretch of the imagination there."

At least she called them a couple, Luther thought. "I should get to the station to do my paperwork. But there's no reason for us both to go."

"I'm your partner," Ann said. "That's reason enough. And besides"—she gave a meaningful glance toward Gaby—"you have other stuff to see to tonight. I'll take care of it. Drop me at Mort's so I can grab my car first."

He didn't relish the idea of leaving Gaby home alone, knowing she might take off again. But neither did he want to drag her along to the station. He could only imagine the questions that would crop up if everyone witnessed her prickly temper.

"You're soaked."

"So are you. But I have a change of clothes in my locker at work. I'll be fine."

"You're sure?"

"Positive." Ann located her purse, found a tissue, and tried to repair her makeup. "And this way, you'll owe me."

Relieved, Luther nodded agreement. "Gaby, tell us more about Fabian. You think he's our man?"

"He's something." Staring at nothing but the darkness, Gaby kept her gaze out the window. "Definitely a killer, definitely a psycho lunatic. His stench was all over those bags." She looked at Ann, and in infuriating and unnecessary fashion, added, "The bags of inedible human parts."

"Of course." Ann slapped her purse down beside her on the seat. "What others bags would you possibly mean?"

Fearing a real conflict might erupt, Luther said, "Knock it off, Gaby."

Gaby slouched more. "I don't know what you're talking about."

"Gaby . . ." Luther warned.

Insulted, Gaby said, "She's all scrunched up over there like she thinks I'm planning to hurt her. I don't fucking hurt women." She rethought that and added, "Well, unless it's for their own good."

Luther let out an aggrieved sigh, and explained to Ann, "She slapped around the little skirt who was hanging on me, basically just to scare some sense into her."

"I'm sure her tactics worked just fine," Ann said to Luther, and then to Gaby: "But I have plenty of sense already, so I don't need you—or anyone else—trying to bully me."

"When did I?" Gaby asked.

Incredulous, Ann swung around to stare at her in disbelief. "Just before! You know good and well that you threatened me with a look."

Her brow went up. "I was threatening Luther, actually."

"You were looking at *me*."

Gaby smirked. "Yeah, so Luther would know why I was threatening him."

"Of all the ridiculous . . . " Ann reached out to touch

her arm. "That is not how a woman shows a man that she cares."

On alert now, Luther kept his mouth shut and just listened.

Gaby pressed the heels of her hands to her eye sockets. "Look, Ann, I have nothing against you except that Luther likes you so much and you're so fucking perfect. But you can take your advice and—"

"Perfect?" Luther and Ann said at almost the same time.

Ann scowled at Luther, and then said to Gaby, "That's absurd. I'm far from perfect."

Gaby dropped her hands and crossed her arms over her chest. "Bull. You're a fucking saint, and everyone knows it."

Discomfited, Ann tried a different tack. "Gaby, Luther and I are only—"

"Friends, yeah I know." She looked out the window again. "Saint that you are, you wouldn't cheat on Morty, and Luther isn't the type to poach. But for whatever reason, it doesn't seem to matter to me."

Ann and Luther shared a glance before Ann said, "I'm not sure what you mean."

Gaby's sigh was long and exaggerated. "Look, I know you two wouldn't fool around. But I still don't like how close you are." She sawed her teeth together, gave up her scrutiny of the darkness to glare at Ann. "If you want me to spill my guts, then I guess I'm fucking jealous, and isn't that a kick in the backside?"

Always so honest, Luther thought. A modicum of irritation eased, pushed out by warm sentiment.

Knowing Gaby cared enough to be jealous lent him a certain peace of mind, and gave him confidence that eventually things would work out with her.

Pleased with her, Luther drove out of the alley and headed toward Mort's without saying a word.

Ann cleared her throat. "There's no reason to be jealous of me, Gaby."

"Jesus, pay attention will you? I just told you that you're perfect." Gaby reached behind her and pulled out her knife. As she polished it against the denim of her jeans, she extolled Ann's virtues. "You're classy, anyone can see that. And smart. And even though you're really pretty, you're still kind." Voice dropping to a mumble, Gaby added, "Even to a mutation like me."

Ann scooted closer to her. "We've discussed this before, Gaby. You're not a mutation, so don't say that. I think you're brave and honorable—"

"And freakish." She lifted the knife to inspect it. "Admit it. I scare the shit out of you."

"You're unpredictable and I know your ability, so yes, you can make me nervous. But nervousness is a long way from fear."

Letting that go, Gaby made an abrupt change of topic. "Getting a tattoo is a good idea. It'll give me time to dissect the crazy fuck, maybe figure him out. He's our guy, I'm almost sure of it, but there's something about him that's throwing me off."

Since that was something new for Gaby, Luther didn't like it. Usually she saw things in clear-cut, unwavering precision. "Throwing you off how?"

"It's hard to explain. He has the sickest aura I've ever seen. It even lingers around his tattoo parlor, this thick smog filled with pain and misery. But he's got smarts, too. And a higher frequency of light and power. And . . . " She stopped, going introspective.

"What?" Ann asked.

"He knows me." Voice faint with bewilderment, Gaby said, "Somehow, I think the bastard recognized me."

"From the previous crime scene?" Luther shook his head against that possibility. "We were careful. And you stayed in the cruiser . . . "

"No." She shook her head. "I meant that he saw me, who I really am. It was in his eyes, in that messed-up aura of his. When I got near him, it sparked, almost . . . almost like we were connected somehow."

Very glad now that Ann would take care of business so he could get Gaby home, Luther said, "All the more reason for you *not* to let him tattoo you." Hell, he didn't want to let her anywhere near the lunatic, much less have him stick a needle in her.

Gaby shook off her brooding contemplation. "That's a dead issue, Luther. Let it go." She showed Ann her arm. "Besides giving me a chance to dissect his psyche, the tattoo will cover this scar."

Ann studied her arm with concern. "Is that from a gunshot?"

"Bullet just grazed me, no big deal. But you see, *everyone* knows what a gunshot wound looks like, so I need to cover it up. People are too damn nosy as it is. I don't need to go around advertising my life with scars."

"Damn it, Gaby—" Luther started.

Again changing the subject, she said to Ann, "You have a really bright aura."

"I do?"

Luther snarled. "Gaby, we're not done discussing this."

"I'm done, but, hey, if you want to talk to yourself about it, feel free."

Ann's curiosity overrode Luther's irritation. "What does my aura look like?"

Momentarily giving up, Luther glanced from the road to the rearview mirror to see Gaby studying Ann.

"Everyone has an aura, but usually it extends out pretty far until it sort of fades away." Lifting her hands, Gaby moved them slowly around Ann. "Yours is real close to your body, intense and bright, like you're protecting yourself." She sat back again. "You sure you're not afraid of me?"

"I'm *not* afraid," Ann stressed. "I trust in your ethical nature."

"My ethical . . . " Gaby snorted, as if attributing such an asset to her was asinine. "Then it's Mort. I hope you're not leading him on." She pitched her voice low in warning. "I wouldn't like that."

"Neither would I." Ann went silent for several seconds as she searched for the right words. "In all relationships, there's a certain amount of uncertainty. The more important the relationship, the worse it is."

"And your relationship with Mort is important?"

"I've never really been in love before," Ann explained. "At least, not like this. I don't want to rush into anything."

"Especially since you and Mort are so different?"

"I don't think we are. Not when it comes to core values, and that's where it really matters."

Ann relaxed, sounding more like herself, and like the woman Luther knew and respected.

And trusted.

She could be a valuable friend to Gaby if only Gaby didn't feel so threatened by her.

"Understand, Gaby, I've dated pretty boys before, guys who spend the best part of their free time in a gym and salon, ensuring they always look their best. And I've been with wealthy businessmen who live under an umbrella of entitlement. None of them have gotten to me like Mort has." A smile sounded in her tone. "He's very special, and he makes me feel special."

It occurred to Luther that, when not skittish from Gaby's volatile nature, Ann treated Gaby as she did everyone. While Gaby was well used to fear, deference, and distanced caution from those who came into contact with her, Ann spoke to her as she might a close girlfriend.

She even leaned in to bump shoulders with Gaby, startling her and causing Gaby to scowl.

"Mort is the kindest and most sincere man I know."

"Then what's the problem?"

"Love is new to me. And I'm only a woman. I need time to adjust, that's all."

A quick glance in the rearview mirror showed Gaby's reaction to that. She didn't understand Ann, didn't trust the openness and acceptance. And she knew jack-shit about love.

But with any luck, Luther would change that.

Though tension still hummed in her body, Gaby slouched back in a deceptive pose. "Yeah, well. Time won't make any difference. When people are lovers and in love, you can see them both in the same aura. I see Mort's aura when I look at you and yours when I look at him."

Did Gaby have an aura? Luther wondered. And if so, did it show in his aura? She mentioned his many times, but never with any connection to hers.

"It's like Bliss said." Gaby rolled her head toward Ann and gave her a meaningful look. "You're meant to be together, so you might as well stop shying away from it."

"And you, Gaby?" Ann studied her. "Will you stop shying away?"

Luther pulled up in front of Mort's and let the car idle. He was anxious to hear what Gaby had to say, but she disappointed him by saying nothing pertinent.

"Here he comes." She rolled down her window to greet Mort as he rushed out the front door and into the dark night. "Take a breath, Mort. She's in one piece."

"And you?" Mort asked. A streetlamp lent crazy shadows to his features, amplifying his obvious concern. "How'd you fare?"

"Don't ask stupid questions. Who could hurt me?"

It was that attitude that often put Luther into a cold sweat.

Gaby rolled the window back up and glanced behind the car through the rear window.

As Ann hustled out of the car, the bundled drugs in hand, she said to Luther, "We need to make this quick, because we were followed."

"You saw the tail?" Gaby asked, surprised.

"Did you?" Luther repeated.

Gaby rolled her eyes. "Apparently we all did. You lost him a few blocks back, but Ann's right, we shouldn't hang around or we risk compromising Mort." She crawled over the seat to sit up front. "Wait until it's clear before you take off again, Ann. Be cautious. And if anything happens, call."

Wearing an indulgent half-grin, Ann nodded agreement. "Thanks, Gaby. But remember, I am a trained professional." She winked, snuggled close under Mort's arm, and walked away.

Luther squeezed the steering wheel. "News flash, Gaby. You aren't in charge."

"No?" She hooked her seat belt and settled back. "Well, Ann and Mort are already up the steps to the front door, and it really wouldn't be smart to hang around. But, hey, do whatever you want. If some bozo shows up starting shit, I'm sure I can handle it."

Frustration drove heat up his neck. "You're in rare form tonight, aren't you?"

"If by rare form, you mean majorly pissed off at you, then *yes*."

"Why the hell are you mad?" She was the one who'd crashed his cover and taken over, treating him like a nitwit in the bargain. Because of her, he and Ann were breaking protocol by not taking the drugs directly to the station. If anyone got wind of their roundabout trip . . .

"I'm furious because you snuck off without me!" She turned toward him, and added with venom, "And you were *schmoozing* with Ann."

It'd take a while to get used to her jealousy. "We were undercover, that's all."

Her voice rose to match the rage sparking in her eyes. She leaned nearer to give him the full blast of her temper. "And being undercover meant you had to *lie* to me?"

"I did not lie." Luther jerked the car into gear and sped out into the street. The momentum thrust Gaby back in her seat. "I just didn't tell you because I knew you'd take over. And you *did*."

"Spin it however you want, cop. It was a lie of omission, and if that's the way we're playing it still, then fine." She propped her feet on the dash and crossed her arms. "I can play."

Damn it. Every time it felt like he'd made headway, Luther found himself falling back two steps again. Frustrated, he shot through a yellow light, then turned a corner too fast.

After several minutes of steaming silence, Gaby looked at him with pity. "You're going to give yourself an ulcer holding all that rancor inside."

He glanced toward her—and noticed something odd about her features. The fury remained etched in her demeanor, but now something else was there, too.

Something hotter than rage.

As he continued tossing wary glances at her, she made a sound of annoyance. "For cryin' out loud, Luther, I won't crumple, you know. You can blast me if you need to." Her beautiful blue eyes went darker, more intense. "But if you are going to blast me, I suggest you hurry it up."

"Why?" Luther stiffened in dread. Was she about to get a calling? Is that what had so subtly transformed her?

Dark eyelashes shadowed her eyes. "Because once we get to your place, I have other plans."

That did it. "*What* other plans?" If she thought to take off again tonight, he'd damn well tie her down if he had to. He'd lock her in a room. He'd—

"Thanks to you, I'm tense." She flexed her fingers, rolled her neck. "Earlier today I had to pound on two punks who tried to waylay me."

Dear God. "How bad?"

She shrugged off his concern. "Other than a broken nose, busted knee, and maybe a rib fracture, they're okay."

His nostrils flared as he dug deep for flagging control. "You're starting to make a habit of fighting in the street."

"We were on the sidewalk, smart-ass, and my method of dealing with assholes is nothing new. But since I didn't massacre them, I've still got all this pent-up energy. And then Mort let it slip about that stupid party—"

"Rave," he corrected.

"Orgy," she clarified with a black scowl. "I saw more kinky sex tonight than I did when I lived with a gaggle of hookers."

Luther tried and failed to calm the rush of his temper. He knew what she'd seen, because he'd seen it, too. Damn it, he had wanted to protect her, not drive her further away. "And now you're angry, and you want to punish me by taking off again?"

Unhooking her seat belt and, sliding over to him, she growled, "I'm not going anywhere."

"But . . . " Tension vibrated off her. Her hot breath caressed his neck. Her eyes fairly glowed.

Frowning, Luther concentrated on not wrecking his car. "You said you had other plans."

"Fuckin' A." She flattened a shaking hand to his abdomen. "I need you to have sex with me."

Luther almost hit the curb. After righting the car, he dared another quick look, and saw her lick her lips. "You're kidding."

She put her nose to his temple, nuzzled against him, and breathed in with a rough moan. "I need it." Her hand fisted his shirt just above the waistband of his jeans. "I need you."

Luther's brain scrambled. Of all the scenarios he'd envisioned, this wasn't among them.

Steering wasn't easy, not with Gaby moving against him, her own heated scent of arousal filling the interior of the car.

Damn. She wanted him. She could have him. No problem. "I can be home in a few minutes." He pressed down on the accelerator. "Put your seat belt back on."

She bit his earlobe. "I'm not sure I can wait that long. I need to burn off steam. *Now*."

"Now?" Suddenly too hot, Luther fumbled for the switch on the heater. The passing landscape showed enough late-night bustle to keep him from pulling over to accommodate her. "I don't think—"

She put an open-mouthed kiss to his neck, grazed his skin with her sharp little teeth. "It's creeping up on me, Luther, taking over, suffocating me." Her voice caught. "I need it. Now, Luther. *Please*."

No way would he deny her. She was in a bad way; that was obvious. And . . .

And who the hell was he kidding?

It had nothing to do with his decision to pull off onto a dark, deserted side street. Gaby had him so turned on, it wasn't safe for him to be behind the wheel anyway.

He slammed the car into park, turned the lights off, locked the doors, and reached down for the lever to adjust his seat back.

It'd been a hell of a long time since he'd made out in a car, but he wasn't so old that he didn't remember how.

Before he'd even settled back, Gaby was over him, straddling his lap, her hands holding his head and her mouth on his.

In a fevered state of lust, she kissed and bit at him, and made him nuts. He loved her wild like this.

He loved her in those rare moments when she was gentle, too.

Fighting it had done him no good, because, damn it, he just plain loved her.

Always.

Gabrielle Cody was the one and only for him. And giving in felt good.

"Stupid bucket seats," Luther complained when she let him up for air.

Urgent with demand, she put her head back and moved against him, moaning, hurting with lust. Luther shoved up her shirt and found her heaving breasts, her nipples already taut and swollen.

"God Almighty, Gaby." He lowered his mouth to her, drew one stiff peak in against his teeth, teased with his tongue.

Her hands clenched hard in his hair and she cried out. She was already so far gone that foreplay was the last thing she wanted. If he put her through it, it'd only be torment, and she had enough of that in her life.

"You have to get out of your jeans." When she didn't appear to register his instruction, Luther hooked a forearm under her backside and drew her up to her knees. Keeping her there, he fumbled with the snap and zipper on her jeans and managed to work them down enough that he could wedge his hand inside, touch her.

Sink two fingers into her.

They both stilled, and Gaby sank back down to his lap on a shuddering moan.

When he moved his fingers in her, she raped his mouth, all the while rocking against him, on his fingers, clenching and groaning in escalating heat.

It was awkward, but Luther managed. For Gaby, he'd do anything.

A porch light across the street came on, and out of the corner of his eye Luther watched, on alert. Gaby stayed oblivious, and that, too, was nice. Her keen awareness of everything and everyone normally precluded any personal relaxation against her plight with evil.

The door opened and a cat went inside. The light turned off again.

For once, with him, Gaby let her enjoyment override her vigilance. To Luther, that felt like complete trust. Combined with her sexual enjoyment, it was enough to build on.

"I need more," she groaned in frustration. *"More."*

Luther levered away from her. "Get your jeans off." He removed his hand and held her back. "Gaby, listen to me. Shh. *Listen.*"

Eyes heavy and dark, she stared at his mouth.

"Jeans," Luther said. "Off."

"Okay." She fell over the console into her own seat,

and without her usual grace, wrangled the denim down her long legs. It was a sight to see, Gaby perpendicular to him, scrunched on her back in the narrow passenger seat, her legs up in the air . . .

She shoved everything onto the floor and came over him again. "Now you. Hurry up."

While he worked himself free, Gaby kissed him, his mouth, the bridge of his nose, his chin, and his jaw. She licked along his throat and purred. "You always taste so good, Luther."

Before too much longer, he'd get her to taste him everywhere. His heart hammered at the thought.

But not here. Not in his damned car. And not in a suburb.

Her impatience made it difficult to get the condom rolled on, and as soon as Luther had it in place, she came over him again. Locking eyes with him, her hands clasped on his neck, she sank down onto him—and gave a vibrating groan of pleasure. "Oh God."

Rigid from his hairline to his toes, Luther knew he wouldn't last long. But then, he wouldn't need to. Gaby had learned enough to set her own pace, and she wasted no time in riding him hard, rocking the car, fogging up the windows, panting and moaning and clenching so tight around him.

He measured the nearness of her release by the bite of her nails on his shoulders. He loved the sting she inflicted. He loved the out-of-control sounds she made.

He loved her fervor. He loved her.

Acknowledging it felt better and better. So damn right.

"Gaby." Locking his teeth, Luther put his head back and strained for control, for just a minute more until she . . .

Moaning loudly, hugging the air out of him, she came long and hard before going all soft, falling against him until he held her in his arms.

Luther opened his mouth on her throat, immersing himself in her scent, her taste, the incredible feel of her, and it was enough. Clasping her hips, he drove her down on him even as he thrust up, burying himself in her as deep as he could, wanting to be a part of her, to share her burdens—to steal her heart.

Release surged through him, grinding his muscles, shaking his core. As he let himself go, Gaby stroked his hair, making soft sounds of pleasure.

The lethargy in his bones accompanied his still-heavy breaths and knocking heartbeat. He opened his eyes and groaned with the repletion of it. Through the fogged windshield, Luther saw ominous clouds scuttle across the sky, filling the area with creeping moon shadows. Somewhere a dog barked, the sound hollow with distance.

Loving Gaby insulated him from all of it. He felt at peace, whole, and triumphant and renewed.

It was a moment he'd remember forever as a demonstrable change in his future. Gaby had admitted to needing him, wanting him. The concession would forever be etched into his brain.

A deluge of emotion engulfed Luther, and he hugged Gaby to his heart. She stirred herself, but only to get more comfortable. Neither of them felt pressed to move, to leave the dubious privacy of an idling car parked at the curb of a quiet middle-class neighborhood.

He remained inside her, but not so much now. He needed to remove the condom, to restore order to their clothes. But . . . he didn't. Not yet.

After a time, as their body heat faded, Luther reached out and adjusted the thermostat again.

Lazily, Gaby sat back on his thighs and studied him. Luther relinquished a slight smile at her scrutiny. "Better?"

"Mmm." With her fingertips, she touched his bottom lip.

In veneration to the mood, she spoke in the quietest whisper. "You did good, cop. That at least took the edge off."

Her insistence on calling him "cop" usually struck him as an insult. This time, he took it as an endearment. Smiling wider, he brought her down for a soft kiss. "I'm glad."

Her nose touching his, she frowned and said, "I'm still angry with you, though."

"We'll work through it." Luther had faith in that.

A soft sigh brushed his mouth. "It'll require more sex."

"What a hardship." He smoothed a hand over her bottom, along her thigh. She had the softest skin, and a very toned physique without being overly muscular. "But I think I can handle it."

"I wasn't really giving you a choice."

He landed one more grinning kiss onto her mouth, and then lifted her over into her own seat. "Put your pants on."

"Why?" She rearranged her shirt to cover her breasts, and then chafed her arms to ward off the growing chill. "They're just going to come off again as soon as I get you alone."

Luther handed her jeans and panties to her. "Let's just say I'll drive better without the distraction of your nudity."

Gaby grumbled, but obliged. Her comfort with nudity turned him on. Her possessiveness toward him did, too.

After rearranging himself, Luther put the car into gear and turned on the headlights. He turned around in a driveway and headed back to the main road, anxious to get home.

If it weren't for a blood drinker turned cannibal, and Gaby's devout compulsion to eradicate the lunatic, he'd feel like the luckiest man alive.

God only knew when catastrophe would strike again, so he wanted to take advantage of his private time with Gaby while he could.

Chapter 12

Fabian went down the steps to the basement of the old house. Already he'd pocketed his porcelain caps, leaving his jagged fangs revealed. Anticipating the treat that awaited him, saliva filled his mouth.

The woman would be physically weak now, crazed with fear, desperate for any salvation.

He'd promise her none. He wanted only to drink from her, to relish her warm blood for as long as she lasted. If he took too much, if he drained her, well then, she'd make a rewarding meal for the others. He had a new recipe he wanted to try out anyway.

After that hideous excuse for a rave where he'd suffered not only the disturbing encounter with the girl and her man, but also a quick trip to the police station thanks to an absurd bust, he had a desperate need for savage release.

Breathing hard, his body throbbing, he rounded a corner, turned on a light, and found . . .

Empty shackles on the wall.

Disbelieving, he stared at the empty wall where his captive should have been, but wasn't.

With consternation, he took in the scene. Blood trailed along the floor, and at a small puddle he saw the IV tubing that had been inserted into her, and was now uselessly thrown aside.

Precious blood dripped from the tubing, stained the concrete floor. Hollow shock became an inferno of rage.

She'd fucking escaped. *But how?*

"Fabian?" Panting from exertion, a young man trotted down the steps, talking a mile a minute. "They got away from me! Like you said, I followed them but at a distance. But they took a lot of turns and it was so damn dark . . . I'm sorry."

In his rage, Fabian didn't quite comprehend. He turned with burning eyes to stare at the man.

"I . . . I didn't come straight here. I drove around for more than an hour first, just in case anyone was on to me. But no one was. This time of night, the streets are almost empty."

Thundering past the man, Fabian charged up the steps. At the moment, he didn't care about whether or not his lackey had been able to follow Link and Gaby. Whether he wanted to or not, he knew he'd see those two again soon enough. At *her* convenience, not his.

But damn her, his curiosity had forced him to agree to her timetable.

Somehow he knew that peculiar bitch beyond recognizing her physically. In some bizarre way, he felt an affinity to her. He'd have to be in her presence to absorb her energy, and then he could figure it out. There'd be an added benefit involved: in stealing her light, he would also vitiate her ability.

And so he'd agreed to her demands.

He wasn't worried about either of them connecting him to the current overblown headlines. No, given how Gaby had demolished innocent people, she had no connection to the law at all.

Gaby was a freak—and one way or another, Fabian would uncover his bond to her, even if he had to consume her to divine the connection.

But right now, he had something more important that required his attention.

For one of the few times in his adult life, Fabian suffered a loss of aplomb. In a mostly empty main room, he found the others assembled, awaiting his direction.

Only two of them had been at the rave, but as per his rules, they'd both been sober and free of drugs.

A man had to keep a clear head in order to recruit others for a meal.

Behind Fabian, the man who'd followed him back upstairs said again, "I . . . I'm sorry, Fabian."

So furious that he couldn't see straight, Fabian raised a hand for silence. As they all waited, breaths held with anxiety, he took his time replacing the caps over his teeth.

His hands shook, and that infuriated him. He needed to be precise to expedite the problem.

And to mete out punishment.

Marginally composed, he faced the small crowd of four. "Our meal has escaped."

At his announcement, panicked inhalations sounded.

The man behind him sidled away to join the others, feeling a false sense of safety in numbers. Fools. Idiots.

Eyes burning and fury thrumming, Fabian studied the five of them, trying to divine the guiltiest. "One of you is to blame."

Nervous murmurs whispered in the air. The group tightened.

"Who saw her last?" Fabian asked.

Three men and one woman looked to the young nurse. She blanched and shook her head in frantic denial.

Fabian saw it in her eyes. Ah, yes. She was the one who'd fucked up his plans and put them all at risk.

She'd been appointed with obtaining the anticoagulants for their captive. Obviously, she couldn't go free. Not now.

He swelled with resolve. "Shari, isn't it?"

She tried to back up, but ran into the others. "Yes." Her gaze shot this way and that, seeking an avenue of escape. Conspicuous culpability trembled through her limbs.

Fabian smelled her intoxicating fear. He breathed it in and let it infuse his objective, transforming him and how he reacted to the loss.

Holding out a hand toward her, he commanded softly, "Come here, Shari."

The others shuffled back, anxious to separate from the realm of punishment. Shari went pale enough for alarm; if she fainted, what fun would that be?

Annoyed by her lack of immediate obedience, Fabian snapped, "Bring her to me."

The others showed the extant deference he expected. Against her frail protests, they dragged Shari to stand right before him.

While she remained contained by human fetters, Fabian touched her face. "Lying will only exacerbate my temper, child. I suggest we get through this peaceably. Yes?"

Eyes flared so that the whites showed all the way around, Shari gave a faint nod.

"Excellent." Fascinated, Fabian touched the wildly throbbing pulse in her throat. Her blood pumped hard, inciting him, pressing him to haste. "You gave her the anticoagulants?"

A fat, glistening tear slid down Shari's cheek. Lips quivering, she nodded. "Yes."

The most appealing facet to Shari's personality was her extraordinary urge to give pleasure to men. Offered the opportunity, she would willingly scar herself just to make a man smile.

Knowing this, Fabian stroked her hair. "You've been a valuable asset to me, Shari. I hope you know that."

"I try," she said, and gratitude seeped color back into her pallid face.

"Tell me now, how did she get free?" Fabian did his utmost to sound sympathetic. "It was an accident, wasn't it?"

"Yes. I would never have let her go without your permission."

"Of course not." He smiled. "What happened?"

No longer straining against the hard hands gripping her, Shari relaxed. "I gave her the anticoagulant, as you said to do, and she revived enough to tell me how uncomfortable she was. Because her arms were chained up too high, her toes barely reached the floor."

A vivid image flooded his brain. "She was straining? Her muscles stretched taut?" A curl of lust slithered into his guts. Such a delicious picture she would have made.

"Yes." Shari lowered her eyes in apology. "I only unfastened the main chain so I could loosen it to give her more slack."

As if cattle needed comfort? An edge entered his tone. "And?"

Frowning as if she still didn't quite understand how it had happened, Shari swallowed. "She took me by surprise, Fabian. She was stronger than I expected, given the state of her body."

"Fear is a potent thing."

"That must be it, because she struck me and ran, yanking the chain right out of my hand. I was dazed. I swear, Fabian. I tried to go after her, but my head was spinning . . . "

"My poor girl." Sifting his fingers through her hair, over her skull, Fabian located a large lump. "Oh my. She did strike you hard, didn't she?" He pressed a thumb to the spongy lump and felt Shari flinch with pain.

"I . . . I think the wrist manacle got me. It felt like she'd hit me with a pipe."

Working his thumb over the painful swelling, he saw her eyes water, her lips tighten.

But she didn't protest. Not Shari. No, if he wanted to hurt her, if he took enjoyment in that—and he did—then she would suffer him gladly.

Stupid bitch. She took all the fun out of his torment.

Annoyed with her silent submission, Fabian brought his hands down to her throat, encircled the slim white column with an unnerving lack of haste. "How long ago was this, my dear?"

His kind tone led her to misunderstand the precariousness of her position. "Maybe an hour or more. I'm not certain."

Alarm jolted him. Much could happen in an hour. If the cow hadn't died in the street, if she'd made it to the police to bleat about her abuse, they could all be collared. Even now, teams of cops could be circling the house.

Pulling his lips back from his teeth, Fabian rasped, "And you didn't think to alert me right away?"

She tried to draw away, and couldn't. "I . . . I don't know. I'm sorry—"

"Apology not accepted." He smiled—and tightened his hands until her eyes bulged, until her lips parted and she gagged for air. But he wouldn't offer her such an easy death, so he loosened his grip. "You do realize that you have put us all at risk, don't you?"

"She was bleeding out," Shari gasped. Her nails dug at the backs of his hands, but to no avail. "Fabian, please. She was weak, too weak to get far."

"Strong enough to escape you, though?" He wanted to snap her neck. He wanted to drain her of every ounce of her blood and then quarter her flesh for a later feast.

Common sense prevailed.

Jerking his hands away before he changed his mind, he allowed her to sink to the floor, sobbing in pity. He wanted to kill her, and he wanted to sate his ever-growing hunger. But if he killed her here, he'd not only waste precious time better spent escaping, he'd also have the added burden of moving her so that she couldn't be used as evidence against him.

Allowing her to live—for now—meant she would carry her own weight in their rush to vacate the premises.

"All of you, listen to me. Shari made a near-unforgivable mistake, but forgive her we shall." He smiled down at her, and the brainless twit wilted with pleasure at his benevolence.

Sickening. At the earliest opportunity, he would dissect her heart and use it to season gravy.

Drawing a deep breath for clarity, Fabian redirected his talents. "Our efforts must now be concentrated on destroying this site."

Always, as a precaution, he kept tools nearby to use in just such emergencies. Now they would come in handy.

"Get the fuel canisters stored out back. Pour gasoline in the basement. Be certain to douse anything that might hold fingerprints. When that is done, torch it, and get out. I'll contact you later with further instructions. Make it quick."

When Shari started to move away, Fabian grabbed her

arm. "Not you." Leading her toward the back door where he would make a safe escape, Fabian explained, "You will remain by my side."

She licked her lips with nervousness. "You require something of me?"

Dark red bruises encircled her throat, and a definite rasp sounded in her voice, but she wanted only to gain his favor. Pathetic bitch.

With every second, his loathing of her escalated. "Yes, I want you near me where I can ensure you won't err again."

"Oh." Crestfallen at the mild rebuke, she dropped her head and wrapped her arms around herself, following him in silence.

Someone had treated her poorly, someone male, and now she lived only to serve men. Would she willingly give him her blood?

Probably. He'd test that theory once he had them both safely away from the house.

After reaching the reasonably secure position of his vehicle, Fabian and Shari got inside. Watching for any sign of detection, he drove down the empty gravel road to the main street where he blended in with other drivers.

Putting the car in park, he turned to look back through the rear window.

Through the darkness of the night, he detected the flicker of flames in the windows of the old house. Before long, raging fire consumed the building, licking through the roof and sending smoke to billow into the sky.

Somewhere in the distance, sirens went off. Soon the fire department would be on hand.

But they'd be far, far too late to find anything valuable. Only ashes would remain.

"Where will we go now?" Shari wanted to know.

Fabian put the car in drive and eased into traffic. "I'll take you someplace to freshen up." Not his home; never that. He kept his private abode sacred of the foul idiots who so recklessly followed his lead. "And then, my dear, you can begin your efforts at making amends."

Sexual interest darkened her eyes and spiked her breaths. "I would relish the opportunity to show my remorse."

"Of course you would." Fabian favored her with an utterly false smile. With her big innocent eyes and vulnerable demeanor, Shari would help him to gain the trust of the young girl. And once he had her trust, he would enslave her and present her as a gift to the others.

As one, they would commit the gravest sin, an orgy of taboo wickedness, and in that act, he would cement his dominance over them, and secure them all as his slaves.

Filtered sunlight penetrated the bedroom drapes, announcing the dawn of a new day. Gaby stared toward the ceiling, watching dust motes dance in a stray sunbeam. All along her side, her skin tingled in awareness of Luther's proximity. After hours of sexual indulgence, he'd fallen asleep with a protective arm draped around her midriff, one heavy thigh over both of hers.

Through a remarkable infusion of carnal stimulation, he had obliterated her unease.

But the night was long, hours had passed, and the conviction that an anomalous personal defect tied her to a grotesque monster gnawed on Gaby's peace of mind.

Luther stirred, stretched, drew her closer. Voice rough and deep, he murmured, "Good morning."

He sounded so pleased with himself, and with her. She knew men enjoyed sex, so he'd probably appreciated her method of cure.

Gaby turned her head to look at him. "Thank you for last night."

Sexy bristles covered his jaw, his chin, and upper lip. He leaned in and kissed her, soft and light, then rolled to his back and stretched again.

Going up on one arm, Gaby looked at him. He had the most impressive chest, at least to her. In fact, his entire body seemed designed to push her buttons. Before Luther, no man had physically impressed her.

"Today is going to be rough."

He scrubbed his hands over his eyes. "I need coffee before you tell me anything horrendous."

Gaby scowled, but the pinch in her brows faded as he sat up on the side of the bed, giving her a seductive view of his broad back and firm backside.

She sat up, too, and though it stunned her, her attitude softened. "We have time for coffee."

"Glad to hear it." He pushed off the bed and strode into the bathroom.

Grumbling to herself over his cavalier attitude, she left the bed and headed for the kitchen. She was far from domestic, but she could put together a pot of coffee.

However, the longer Luther took, the more her agitation rippled and surged. She listened as he showered, heard him dressing, and a minute later he strode into the kitchen, but pulled up short to find her naked.

Paused in the doorframe, he devoured her with a look, shook his head, and smiled. "We need to get you a housecoat." He walked up to her and touched her face. "How did you sleep?"

"Good."

"Not cold this morning?"

She shook her head. "Luther—"

He put a finger to her mouth. "Whenever possible, coffee first." He got down two cups.

His mood today confounded her. "Nothing has changed, you know. The evil is still out there."

"An evil that we'll catch. I have faith in that." He took two worshiping sips of his coffee, made a sound of pleasure, and sat down in a kitchen chair. "Okay, I think I'm ready. Let's start with what had you so upset last night."

Not an unreasonable suggestion, but she felt pressed to clarify. "I wasn't upset."

"Course not." He sipped more coffee.

Her agitation growing, Gaby got her own coffee and leaned back on the counter.

"I *wasn't* upset. But I did need to burn off steam."

"Because?" he prompted.

Infuriated with his attitude, Gaby jerked out her own chair and sat opposite him. "Several reasons. It pisses me off to like Ann in spite of myself."

"She's a likeable person. And since there's nothing of a romantic nature between her and I, you have no real reason to dislike her."

Reason had nothing to do with her jealousy, so she let that jibe slide. "It *really* had me irked that you deceived me and left me in the dark."

"I do apologize for that." He took her hand, ran his thumb along her knuckles. "I promise, whenever possible, I won't do it again."

Whenever possible? She pulled away from him and curled her fingers into a fist. "And then to see all that crazy shit at the rave . . . God, Luther, I wanted to kill some people, I really did. And I could have." She put her arms around herself and slouched in her chair. "You know that."

"I do know it." He looked down at his coffee cup, but

brought his gaze right back to hers again. "I want you to know how much I appreciate it that you handled things so well."

"But you think you could have done better without me there?"

He studied her for several seconds before speaking. "You're being honest, so I'll try to do the same." After finishing off his cup of coffee, he stood to get more. At the coffeepot, his back to her, he said, "You did great, Gaby. You gave Fabian just the right attitude to keep him interested, and to convince him that you were on a par with him."

She turned in her seat to face him. "I *am* on a par with him." Her chest tightened. "And that's the biggest part of what had me so itchy in my own skin."

"No." Forgetting the damn coffee, Luther reached for her hands and drew her out of the seat. "Not for a single second do I want you to think you have any semblance to a lowlife cretin like Fabian." He cupped her face. "You infuriate me, and you take things to extremes, usually well outside legal limits. But your purpose is always to protect innocents, not take sick pleasure in torturing them for your amusement."

As her agitation grew, Gaby had to accept that it wasn't only her association to Fabian. Something was wrong. Very wrong.

Standing still proved impossible, so she paced away from Luther, but quickly returned to the comfort of his nearness. "It's difficult to explain, but I recognized him on some other level. You saw how he looked at me, that he thought we were acquainted." Her muscles began to tighten. "I think he's right."

Luther rubbed her shoulder, showing his concern. "Maybe you met him during one of your foster home stays. He could have been—"

"No." Before he'd even finished voicing the possibility, Gaby shook her head. "I never connected with any of them. My stays were short-lived and, for the most part, the people who tried to take me in just ignored me. We sure as hell never bonded."

"Maybe he was a member of Father Mullond's congregation?"

Mentions of Father, the priest who had first shared her burden, always perturbed her on a deep level. "Evil is not influenced by morality, so I doubt Fabian is a churchgoer. But it wouldn't matter, because I barely attended myself. Father tried, but . . . " She sent a narrow-eyed look at Luther. "God and I have a more personal relationship. It's not meant to share with the masses."

Luther nodded. "Then where have you met him?"

"I don't know that I have. What I felt wasn't a simple recognition. It was more than that." When she'd looked at Fabian, neared him, awareness had beset her in a panoply of impressions, both emotional and physical. "It's a connection, a bond of some kind. I understand him, Luther. I feel him, know him." Her head pounded, and she closed her eyes tight to admit, "I'm . . . drawn to him."

He showed his dislike of that in the stiffening of his shoulders and the edge in his tone. "What the hell does that mean?"

"I don't know." Gaby pressed a fist under her breast as if she could remove the ache in her heart. "But I feel it, I know it's real. And I have no idea what to do about it."

Chapter 13

Luther pulled Gaby into his arms. When she would have pushed free, he hugged her tighter. "I need it," he said near her ear, "whether you do or not."

At that, she subsided and returned the embrace with enough force to make his ribs ache.

God, what now? How the hell did he handle this?

If he tried to keep Gaby from investigating further, she'd buck big-time. Gaby was not a woman to be ordered around or contained. But if she got close to Fabian, would he have an unnatural hold over her?

The crazy fuck drank the blood and ate the flesh of humans. How the hell could Luther let him get anywhere near Gaby?

Hoping to reason with her, Luther cupped her face. "Listen, honey, I know you're tough as nails. I swear I do. But—"

Luther's cell phone rang, halting him in mid-sentence and bringing on a low curse of vexation.

"Better check that," Gaby suggested as she wormed out of his embrace to grab more coffee.

One glance at the number showed Ann calling. Without mentioning that to Gaby, Luther clicked the TALK button and said, "Yeah?"

"Surly, huh?" With her usual good humor absent, Ann said, "Well shake it off, partner. Something big has come up and I need you."

Luther watched Gaby rest back on the counter and sip her coffee—with her gaze glued to his. No way in hell would she let him escape the room for a more private conversation.

Seeing no other option, Luther gave in to the inevitable. "What is it?"

"I got a call from Sergeant Sutton. He said a couple of his guys patrolling the streets found a half-dead woman late last night, or actually, real early this morning. She was mostly incoherent, in a bad way, covered in blood and naked."

"Did she have any noticeable wounds to explain the blood?"

Gaby's eyes narrowed. Very slowly, she lowered her mug of coffee back to the counter.

"Lots of wounds actually—most of them bite marks. They took her to the hospital, but she was already really weak, and, get this, Luther: she kept babbling incoherently about being the next meal."

Going on high alert, Luther prayed for a break. "She's a victim of our bloodsucker?"

"From what the hospital said, it sure sounds like it. The bad news is, they don't know how long she'll last. They said she's fading fast, in and out of it. I'm already on my way, so get a move on."

Ann told him which hospital to meet her at, then hung up.

Luther's pulse pounded with the possibilities. Naked, Gaby waited for him to explain.

Instincts taking over, Luther went into full cop mode. "We might have a live victim of our guy at the hospital." Tilting his cup up, he finished off his coffee in one long gulp. "Ann's already on her way there. I'm going to meet her."

Gaby didn't argue, but she looked . . . odd. Distraught, distracted, sharply drawn.

Luther rubbed his mouth. There was no time to waste; he had to take her along. "Hustle up if you're coming with me."

She pushed away from the counter. "I'll sit this one out."

Fuck, he didn't have time for this. He knew better than to let anyone or anything distract him from the job. "Gaby, I can't be effective if you're dividing my attention."

"There's no reason for you to be divided. I'm not going to see Fabian, I swear."

"Then what?" He couldn't imagine many scenarios where Gaby wouldn't want to take center stage on this.

"I met a little girl the other day." She drew in a shallow breath. "I need to go see her."

Oh shit. Finally Luther recognized the glitter in her eyes, the clarity of her features, the definition in her muscles. "You're having a . . . " What the hell should he call it? An *episode*? That didn't sound right.

"No, I'm not. At least, I don't think so." She clasped her hands behind her head and briefly closed her eyes. "I know I need to go to her, but not because she's being hurt."

"Then what?"

"I don't know. Whatever this is, it's different. I think . . . " She dropped her arms and frowned at herself. "I think it might just be worry. But I can handle it. Go, talk to the woman, see if you can get her to confirm Fabian's involvement."

"Right." Luther headed for the door with Gaby right on his heels.

"Have the hospital check her for blood thinners. Given their appetites, they probably gave her something to keep her blood flowing. And make them test for muscle relaxers, too. Or a sedative. He wouldn't want a screaming, clawing captive."

"Right. I'll call ahead to get the hospital started on that."

"And look for signs of restraint on her wrists and ankles."

Humoring her, because he'd already thought of each of those instructions, Luther opened the door. "Got it."

Naked, Gaby followed him into the doorway, and when Luther saw a neighbor in the next yard, he turned and backed her into the house and out of view.

"Honey, I've got it." He blocked her from view of prying eyes.

"I know, but . . . when I think of how she's probably suffered, I really want us to get this creep."

Us. Finally Gaby saw them as a team.

Loving her more with every minute, Luther cupped her hip. "I can't have you flashing the neighbors, honey. It isn't done."

She looked beyond him, and scowled. "Sorry."

Damn, she pleased him. "Get dressed. And don't forget your phone. I'll call to update you as soon as I know something."

"Okay."

"And don't forget to call me if you need anything."

That irked her. "I wouldn't need—"

Luther interrupted before her outrageous independence

could ruin the moment. "And, for my sake, try not to pulverize anyone today, okay?" He kissed her hard and quick. "I care for you, Gaby. A lot. Please keep yourself safe."

Seeing he'd surprised her, Luther hurried out the door and to his car. Ann would be waiting, and he had a job to do. He'd just have to trust that Gaby could get by without him monitoring her every move.

At least she'd promised to steer clear of Fabian. That was something. A lot.

For Gaby, any promise was a monumental concession.

No one tailed Fabian.

Giving up his careful watch out the rear window, he continued studying every shadow, alleyway, and doorframe as he drove down the street toward his work, as usual. Although wary of police scrutiny, he knew that altering his routine in any way could draw notice. At the first sign of a trap, he'd flee.

But none awaited him.

His escaped captive had either crawled behind a rock to die, as befitted her, or she'd been too far gone to give away details that might implicate him.

Fabian didn't care which it might be, as long as the bitch didn't complicate his life.

In the future, he decided, he'd cut out the tongue of anyone he deemed suitable to serve as his nourishment. Rendering the captive incapable of speech would be smart. And everyone knew he had a higher level of intelligence than most.

Sated on a morning meal of Shari's blood, Fabian parked behind the tattoo parlor, got out, and stretched. It was a beautiful day. Bright sunshine warmed his face. The air smelled crisp and cool and full of promise.

Shari had been full of promises, too.

He smiled with the memory. Willingly, she'd given him her blood; she'd even put the IV into her own arm, then allowed him to drink his fill until she'd grown faint and confused from loss of blood. After coercing her to call in sick for the day, he'd tethered her to the bed, gagged her for safe measure, and left her insensate at the fleabag motel.

The run-down roadhouse catered to the criminal activity of gangs, drug users, and lowlife prostitutes. The slum location was ideal, so overlooked by everyone that he might keep it for his future assignations—both for quick collation and quiet captivity.

In rapid order, many of his most immediate problems had been resolved.

He felt safe again, omnipotent even.

Shari couldn't talk. The girl couldn't even sit up by herself. And the escaped cow obviously hadn't spilled her guts, or else the police would already be at his door.

Given their own involvement, and knowing he'd make any snitch pay with his life, none of the others would dare point a finger at him in any way.

Fabian smiled in triumph. He'd turned conventional society on its ear, broken every restrictive taboo, and he'd gotten away with it, time and time again.

No one and nothing could ever stop him.

He unlocked the back door to the tattoo parlor and went inside. They didn't officially open for another couple of hours, but he wanted to do some research on his business computer. Before he met with Gaby tonight, he would figure out how he knew her, and the best way to kill her.

He could hire others to dispatch of her, but only he possessed the passion, the skill, the control, to do it properly.

With Gaby, he would do his finest work.

The change in weather did little to lighten Gaby's mood.
Slouched on the curb, earbuds in so she could vibrate her
brain with hard music, she alternately watched the play
area and Sin Addictions.

She'd unzipped her sweatshirt, revealing a T-shirt beneath. Elbows on her knees, she waited for the little girl to
show up. And she noticed when a light went on inside the
tattoo parlor.

Her skin prickled.

Today, something would happen.

What, she didn't know, but she felt it deep inside. Unlike her usual calling that tormented her with twisting pain,
this feeling of expectation sizzled along her nerve endings,
a foreboding of imminent distortion in her life.

To ensure she wouldn't miss a call from Luther, she'd set
her phone to vibrate. At the small of her back, the hard bite
of her knife against her spine lent a degree of comfort.

A cool breeze stirred her hair. A bird dipped in
flight, then circled and landed in a barren tree. Children
laughed.

Off in the distance, a siren squealed, blending with the
lonesome whine of a train whistle. Dogs barked.

Seeing the girl she wanted walking hand in hand with another, smaller child, Gaby pushed to her feet. The younger
girl shot free and ran to join the other children.

Wondering what to say first, how to protect the girl
without alarming her, Gaby started across the street.

The girl glanced up, and smiled a greeting. "Hey."

Relieved that she wasn't afraid, Gaby said back, "Hey."
She nodded toward the other girl. "Who's your friend?"

"My little sister." She moved toward where the girl
played. When Gaby didn't immediately follow, she looked

back. "Come on. She always wants to play, but . . . I fear it might not be safe."

Perplexed by the friendly welcome, Gaby joined her. "You're not afraid?"

The girl crossed her arms over a broken chain link fence. "Now, with you here, it is better. You will keep everyone safe."

"No . . . " Stumped, Gaby turned and leaned her back on the fence. She felt awkward with the girl's innocent acceptance and trust. "I meant, aren't you afraid of me? After what I did, I thought . . . I don't know. It didn't freak you out a little?"

Braided, the girl's long dark hair reached the middle of her back. She wore too-small, tattered jeans, a stained shirt that couldn't keep her warm, and sneakers without socks.

But she smiled when she looked at Gaby again. "I am Dacia. And you are?"

"Gaby."

Dacia stared at her sister. "She is Malinal. I care for her, but it is not easy."

"How old are you?"

"I am twelve." Sunlight glinted on her small nose and long, dark lashes. "Mali is five."

Gaby's heart twisted. She moved a little closer to Dacia, tried to look relaxed when she felt anything but. "Dacia, where do you and your sister live?"

The silence grew louder than the kids' laughter, more deafening than the cawing crows and beeping horns of traffic a few streets away.

Gaby waited, while inside her soul, the turmoil clamored and expanded to immeasurable proportions.

Mali ran after another kid, and Dacia adjusted her position to keep the little girl in her sights. When that required moving a few feet away, she held out her hand to Gaby.

Unnerved by the gesture, Gaby took the small hand in her own, and knew she would die to protect the girl.

"I can trust you," Dacia said as they rounded a big, half-dead tree. "Can I not?"

"You can," Gaby vowed.

"I do not want Mali taken from me."

"I won't let that happen."

"Sometimes . . . " Dacia swallowed, took a moment to compose herself. "Mali cries in the night. And when she sleeps, she holds me so tight. I am all she has."

"You love her a lot, Dacia, and that makes her a very lucky little girl."

Dacia's voice broke. "Sometimes she is hungry."

"And you?"

"Sometimes I am hungry, too." They continued to walk, always keeping Mali in view. "We live wherever we can. Where I think we will be safe. We hide."

Because Gaby had done the same off and on throughout her life, she wasn't overly shocked. Just very, very heartbroken. "It's getting colder, you know. Soon it will snow. You need real shelter."

Dacia bent to retrieve the wing of a dead butterfly. She studied it, and then dropped it back to the ground. "I would rather be cold than be alone."

"You won't be alone. Not ever again." Gaby went down on one knee, and damn it, she felt tears sting her eyes. Dacia needed a strong defender, not a whiny female.

Unfortunately, in the current modification of her life, Gaby could no longer distinguish quite where the paladin ended and the woman began.

"From now on," Gaby said, ignoring her weaknesses, "you have me."

Dacia started to smile, when suddenly she looked past Gaby and fear widened her eyes.

Gaby felt it, the charge in the air, the smothering of young laughter, the halting apprehension. The kids fell silent, and Dacia went pale with dread.

This was what had brought her here.

Without looking behind her, Gaby said to Dacia, "I will handle it. Do you believe me?"

Dacia blinked away much of her fear, and proved her incredible trust.

"Yes." She licked her lips, nodded, and said, "Thank you."

Before succumbing to her injuries and loss of blood, the victim had given Luther the name of a street, and a grisly account of her harsh captivity.

Speeding, with lights flashing atop his car, he drove hell-bent for the scene. He'd called ahead, giving strict instructions for cops in the area to gather quietly, to contain the scene—but not to intrude.

Yet.

If he could apprehend someone still at the house, get a match on the teeth marks left on the victim, maybe some DNA . . . it'd be perfect, a real break in the case. And God knew they needed a break. The bodies were piling up.

Beside him, Ann held herself in brooding silence, no doubt wracked from seeing the shape that poor woman was in. But hell, he didn't blame her; it shook him, too.

To think of someone going through what she had, and then to be chained to a wall to be available for future abuse . . . His muscles constricted with the need for physical violence.

Nasty bite marks, most of which had viciously pierced skin and torn flesh, marred her body. She'd been so bloodless that, other than swollen bruises, her skin looked translucent, ghostly blue. Wild-eyed but frail, she'd whispered of atrocities too horrific to imagine—and then she'd given them the name of a street, and died.

Voice trembling, Ann whispered, "I want to kill him, Luther."

"Me, too." He felt no shame in admitting that.

He heard Ann breathing, and then: "I almost . . . almost want to turn Gaby loose on him."

"No!" Hands squeezing the steering wheel, Luther said again, more calmly this time, "No. Not that."

Ann put her head back on the seat and closed her eyes. After a time, she agreed. "Of course not. It's unthinkable." She rolled her head to look at Luther. "For Gaby, as much as the matter of the law."

"More for Gaby." At times like this, Luther teetered toward the attitude of "fuck the law." Some people, some monstrosities in the guise of human beings, didn't deserve the benefit of societal rules. The savage who had cut up those people, who'd gnawed on that poor woman, fell into that category.

But he wanted Gaby removed from it, both physically and emotionally. The toll it took on her was not worth the end result, not to him.

If it came to it . . . He flexed his hands on the steering wheel, and admitted the truth. If it came down to it, he'd protect Gaby by killing the bastard himself.

Maybe that's why he felt such an affinity to her. He understood Gaby and the demons that drove her to slaughter the most abject evil.

Ann's silence wore on him, forcing Luther to explanations. "Understand, Ann. Gaby suffers for what she does."

"I think I've seen that suffering." She let out a staggered breath. "So why does she do it?"

"Because she suffers even more if she doesn't." Ann had seen small glimpses of Gaby's torment, but she didn't know the depths of that agony. And Luther couldn't tell her without betraying Gaby.

They turned down the street and Luther saw the blackened ruins of a house. "No."

Ann sat up, and groaned. "Maybe it's not the house we're looking for."

No other home appeared in the area. "And maybe the bastard will turn himself in if we go back to the office and wait." Luther brought the car to a jarring halt and sat there, staring at the carnage. Little remained of the house. Even the surrounding grounds were scorched and brittle. "Fuck!"

"I'll say." Furious, Ann yanked open her car door, got out, and started over to the uniformed cops who milled around their cruisers in confusion.

It didn't make any sense, but Luther needed to talk to Gaby. He pulled out the cell phone and punched in her number.

She answered on the fourth ring, surprise in her voice. "Hello?"

"It's Luther."

"Oh, right. Bad timing, Luther, sorry." And she hung up on him.

Stunned, Luther stared at the phone as fury boiled up. He dialed her right back.

This time she answered on the first ring. *"What?"*

He ground his teeth together. "Do not. Hang up. On me."

She huffed. "Fine. Then talk quick."

In his current state of mind, her insults pricked more than usual. "What are you doing that's so damned important you can't talk to me?" Through the windshield, he saw

Ann give him an incredulous look, throw up her hands, and go to the house on her own.

"Actually," Gaby said, "I'm pondering whether or not to beat the shit out of some asshole, if you want the truth."

What else had he expected? Luther straightened in the car seat. "I vote no."

"You're not here and you don't know the situation, so you don't get a vote. Hang on."

Feeling absurdly impotent, Luther listened through the phone as a scuffle ensued, followed by a grunt, a low curse, and then Gaby came back.

"Where was I?" She sounded calm, almost bored. "Oh yeah. I'll try to walk away, Luther, but I can't make any promises. He's not making it easy."

Luther's blood pressure went sky-high. "He who?"

"Bogg's brother, I think." She said to someone else, "You are Bogg's asshole brother, right?"

Luther heard more cursing, another crack or two, and Gaby said, "I really do need to go, Luther."

He closed his eyes, but nothing brilliant came to him. "Is anyone shooting at you?"

"No."

"How many are there?"

"Just two."

The odds weren't bad at all—unless he thought of the odds of the two guys surviving. It was a long shot, but he offered, "I'll send a beat unit your way. They could be there in two minutes."

"No, don't do that." Her voice lowered. "Seriously, Luther, that'd be a bad move."

Frustration crawled over him, sent his temper through the roof, then settled in as resignation. He knew Gaby would be tough to deal with.

"All right." What choice did he have? Luther knew that

even if he had the time to race to her side, she'd have the conflict resolved one way or another long before then. "But promise me that you won't dismember, incapacitate, or otherwise paralyze anyone if you can help it. Promise me, Gaby."

"Party pooper."

Jesus. "And if you get into any real trouble, call me so I can help. Promise me."

"All right. I promise."

"Thank you." Marginally relieved, Luther started to disconnect the call, then thought to add, just to devil her in return, "Gaby? I really do care for you, honey. Remember that."

She went silent, then let out an exaggerated sigh. "You fight dirty, cop."

When the line went dead, Luther realized he was smiling. She'd turned him into a half-wit; nothing else explained the ability for humor during such an awful time.

He stuck the phone back in his pocket and got out of the car.

The rancid stench of burned wood, plastic, and fabric, along with something more noxious, still hung in the air. Staked police tape warned off curious spectators. Ann ensured that no one from their station compromised the crime scene—what was left of it.

She'd backed everyone away from the area, and given strict orders that nothing was to be touched, not even a singed gum wrapper on the ground.

She didn't mention Luther's delay in joining her, but instead launched into business. "The boys said it's the only place on the street that qualifies, so it's ours. The houses here are spaced out, only five on the private road, and the others are occupied with normal, family-type folk." Ann looked up at him. "This one was vacant."

"Or not," Luther said. "I'm guessing our psycho moved in unnoticed."

Ann didn't argue that probability. "He's got enough privacy here that no one would hear a woman screaming for help."

Or in agony. "Probably kept her in the basement." Luther paced along the perimeter. The concrete walls of the house's subfloor remained. In the cement blocks of one wall, he could see what might have been the bolts to hold shackles in place. "You call forensics yet?"

"On their way. But it's going to be a conflict."

"Local fire department?"

"They said they put the blaze out last night, but not before most of the house was already gone. From what they could tell, the fire started in the basement, got into the walls, and up she went."

Just as someone had planned. Luther kept a tenuous hold on his temper. "It's an old place, so not as protected with modern materials as a newer home might've been."

Ann put a hand on her hip. "And get this. The bomb guy and the arson investigators are already on it, because naturally the fire was deliberate. Gasoline, they think. And yeah, they saw the bolts in the wall, along with some other suspicious stuff."

"Like?"

"Broken vials. The type that might've held drugs." She shielded her eyes from the sun. "I'm supposed to get a call from the guy in charge. I'll know more then."

"It's possible they found evidence buried under the ash, and didn't even know it."

"I like a man who thinks positive thoughts."

Yeah, they both knew it was a crapshoot. "Let's talk to the neighbors, see if they saw any activity. Maybe someone can identify a car or give us a description of someone they noticed hanging around."

"Arson guys already did that, but, hey, my dance card is free." She held out an arm for him to lead the way. "I'm in if you are."

Chapter 14

Gaby slid her phone back into her pocket. Why did Luther have to call right then, and why did she feel obligated to honor his request? The cretin in front of her needed a good beating. Or worse. He was a clear threat to the kids, most especially to Dacia and Malinal.

Next to her target, another guy vibrated with leashed anger. "C'mon, Whit, let me teach her some respect."

"Shut up, Mud."

Gaby raised a brow. "Whit? Mud? You're kidding me, right? What kind of lame-ass gangster names are those?"

Whit raised a hand, halting Mud's automatic reaction. Whit seemed to have a modicum more control than his buddy. But not much. He was plenty pissed, and it showed.

Of course, thanks to her, blood dripped from his nose down his chin. He didn't wipe it away. "Is there a reason you struck me?"

"Yeah."

He waited, and when she said no more, his face tightened. "Care to share it?"

She shrugged. "You interrupted my phone call. That's rude."

His eyes damn near glowed. Hazel eyes that, when iced with fury, took on a hue of gold. Freaky. She could understand why the kids feared him. Not that she gave a shit what his eyes looked like. In her lifetime, she'd seen a whole lot worse than him.

She'd slaughtered worse, too.

All around Whit, his aura churned with menace and mental disease. He looked tough, but weakness showed through the haze of abuse. This guy was one who liked to put up a hard-ass front, but he needed someone else to lead him.

Through his teeth, Whit said, "You stepped in front of me."

"Yeah, I know. I didn't like where you were headed." Behind Gaby, the kids stirred. Odd that after her last display in front of them and the bloodbath she'd left behind, none of them seemed to fear her. In fact, she felt surrounded by their support and their confidence.

Goofy kids. They were young, so they'd learn.

Spittle flew from Whit's mouth when he roared, "Where the fuck did you think I was going?"

"Too close to where the kids play." Narrowing her eyes, Gaby wiped off her arm. "I'd suggest you *not* spit on me again. I don't like it."

"It's a public street, woman. More to the point, this is prime real estate."

"For selling drugs?"

His chest puffed out. "I'll go wherever I fucking well please."

"Not if I say different." Damn, she wanted to flatten

him. Hoping he'd make a move, that he'd dare to test her, Gaby stepped away from the kids—and closer to Whit. "I won't have you and the other thugs fighting over this block. Your pissing contests almost always end up in gunfire, so from now on I don't want to see your ugly mug anywhere around here."

Mud twitched with angry energy. "Let me dust her, Whit." He made to reach inside his jacket.

Gaby gave him her steely-eyed attention. "Pull a gun around all these kids," she told him, "and I swear to God, I'll cram it down your throat."

Whit held up a hand, stilling Mud's automatic reaction. "And if I have business here?"

"Don't." Gaby moved in so close she could feel the heat of his tall, trim body. Ensuring that the kids wouldn't hear, she whispered, "Do your business elsewhere, Whit. I'm giving you fair warning. Because if I see you here again, I'll break your bones."

He studied her head to toes, and came to a silent conclusion. "You're the bitch who pulled a blade on my brother."

"Bogg tell you that?" She would love to hear the story. It always sounded more graphic when someone else related it.

"Bogg isn't saying shit."

That surprised her. "No?"

"He got an infection and went into a coma. He might fucking well die."

Huh. She hadn't really counted on that, but . . . "Oh well."

Whit's neck went rigid. His eerie eyes gleamed. "You'll pay for what you did."

"Yeah. Someday, no doubt I will." Gaby looked at his compressed mouth, then back to his eyes. "But we both know it won't be today, and never by your hand. So be

smart, Whit. Stay the hell away from here. Let the kids play
in peace."

Expectation pulsed in the air between them. One second,
two, three. As prepared as she'd ever be, Gaby waited.

Whit stepped back. "Come on, Mud."

Mud balked. "You fucking kidding me?"

Already on his way back to where he'd come from, Whit
snapped, "Move your ass!"

Mud couldn't resist shooting Gaby one last look of caution. He pointed at her as he walked backward, warning her
of his intent.

Gaby held out her arms, inviting anything he wanted to
bring. But, damn it, it wasn't enough. Rage cramped her
muscles, left her guts hollow and empty with the need to
physically attack.

She turned back to Dacia. "Get your sister. It's time for
us to go."

"Go where?"

"Someplace safe. Someplace you'll love." Gaby gave
the girl a nudge and then retrieved her phone. "I promise."

"All right." Dacia ran over to where Malinal played on
the old discarded sofa, and dragged the younger girl back
by the hand.

Gaby noticed how alike the two sisters looked, just as she
noticed how Dacia had set herself up as protector, nurturer,
and provider. "Do you need to gather any belongings?"

Dacia hung her head. "We have little of value, a change
of clothes, and Mali's doll . . . "

Damn. "We'll get everything. Don't worry." Keeping
the phone to her ear, Gaby put a hand on Dacia's shoulder,
offered Malinal a smile, and finally Bliss answered.

"Hello?"

Gaby wasted no time. "I've got a great surprise for you,
Bliss. Are you at the apartment?"

"Gaby? Yes, I'm here, but what—"

"I'll be over in twenty minutes. If you can, have a nice hot meal ready." She looked at the girls, and added, "Enough for three more."

And she hung up before her friend could ask any questions.

❦

Through the sparkling glass in the front window of his shop, Fabian took in the dramatic tableau with great merriment. This altered everything in a monumental way. Already he'd adjusted his objective for the special girl, Gaby.

Heady excitement kept him glued to the spot as he continued to watch her. For such a kick-ass, butch bitch, she feigned great maternal instincts, hustling the little girls away from the area and from any intended harm.

Whit had to be furious, and with good reason. Gaby had backed him down with nothing more than her reputation, loads of attitude, and one punch.

An amazing girl. A girl unlike any other.

Knowing Whit's seething temper, he'd be happy to assist Fabian in what needed to be done.

But not yet.

For now, Fabian just wanted to keep the heady discoveries all to himself.

He savored the telling realizations.

Gaby had a weakness, a wonderful, delectable, easily corrupted weakness. The dirty little urchins she sought to guard were already on his radar. He would have that youngest girl. Oh yes, he would. But he'd also have Gaby and that would prove even more luscious.

Pulling himself away from the window, Fabian left the main room and sequestered himself in his office to wallow more privately in his glee.

He recognized the little savage now. Yes he did. It hadn't struck him until Gaby looked at the child with her steely barriers down. Her softness exposed new dimensions to her personality, and Fabian saw what he hadn't seen before. The resemblance, the similarity in facial traits.

Gaby looked just like her mother.

Unable to contain himself, Fabian put his hands over his mouth and squealed like a schoolboy. It was too perfect, too delicious for words.

Putting his head back, he hugged himself to contain his mirth.

The only true nemesis he'd ever encountered, the only person who even came close to matching his intelligence, cunning, and courage, was an exact replica of the whore he'd used and left twenty some years ago. The timing coincided with Gaby's age.

And given those eyes of hers, light blue and piercing, well, it was plain to him.

He was her father.

It made sense. Gaby was like him in so many ways; among inferior society, they had preeminent significance. They each stood out, in every way.

There would be some conflicts. Two great minds were bound to clash on occasion. But he could work that out with her. He was Gaby's senior near about thirty years. He had more experience.

She was wise enough to bow to him, to heed his excellence.

Fabian couldn't wait to tell her. Thinking of that auspicious moment, he laughed again, and even he knew it sounded maniacal.

And why not? He'd just found a way to outdo his own wicked taboo of eating a child: he would share the meal with his daughter.

And if Gaby proved squeamish, if she disappointed him by being too weak, too narrow-minded to join him, well then, he would do what was necessary.

He would shatter every social doctrine of morality—by dining on his own flesh and blood.

❧

Bliss finished mashing potatoes just as Gaby got to the top of the steps. So industrious in preparing her meal, she hadn't yet heard them. She wore an apron over her jeans and had tied up her brown hair.

Pork chops sizzled on the stove, and green beans boiled in a pot. Warm steam and the aroma of food filled the kitchen. Gaby sniffed the air, and heard Dacia's stomach rumble.

No reason to keep the girls waiting. They had to be hungry. And tired. And still very unnerved by the changes about to take place.

After Gaby dropped their paltry belongings in the foyer of the apartment building, Mali hung back. All timid and uncertain, she stayed behind Gaby's legs. At times Gaby felt the little girl's head on her butt. No matter how she tried to move, Malinal managed to stay tucked back behind her.

Dacia, on the other hand, came to stand at her side, proud but defensive. She awaited rejection, Gaby knew, and the young girl's stoicism shredded her heart.

Putting an arm around Dacia and letting Mali nestle in as much as she wanted, Gaby announced them by saying, "Hey, Martha Stewart. Something sure smells good."

Bliss whirled around with a wide smile, saw the two girls, and went blank-faced. But not for long.

Bliss was no dummy. Whatever misuse had plagued her at home, she kept it to herself and didn't let it taint her open, giving nature.

Until meeting Gaby, Bliss had long lived on the streets, and because of that, she had innate recognition of one of her own. Add to that her intuitive nature, and she was the perfect person to relate to the girls.

God knew that regardless of Bliss's past—or maybe because of it—she far exceeded Gaby in mothering qualifications.

Drying her hands on the apron, Bliss came forward with a slight smile. "Good grief, Gaby. When you said three, I thought you meant three big eaters, not small fries."

"Oh, I don't know," Gaby told her. "I don't think these two have had a real meal for a while. They might take even our share."

Both girls stood there frozen in place. Gaby couldn't even detect their breathing. But then, Bliss did look something of an angel, with her soft, golden aura floating around her.

Bliss reached out a hand to Dacia. "Hi. I'm Bliss. And you are?"

"Dacia." She took her hand and quickly released it. "My sister, Malinal, is hiding behind Gaby."

"Am not," Malinal said, and stuck her head out just long enough to get a gander of Bliss. She tucked away again.

Bliss grinned in very real delight. "I'm a new cook, so I hope I didn't muck up anything. Grab a seat and I'll pour us all some milk. We can get acquainted over the meal."

"I'm keeping them," Gaby said.

"Well, of course you are," Bliss replied, as if it was expected. "You couldn't do anything else."

Gaby blinked at her, then scowled. She was not a predictable person. Even Ann had said so.

And she didn't drag in strays. Except for Bliss, but that was different. Bliss was mostly grown and mostly able to care for herself.

Kids . . . well, kids would need a lot of care. As Bliss said, she couldn't leave them behind, but it stymied her, trying to think of all that would have to be done on a day-to-day basis.

And Luther . . . What would he say? Would he—

"I'll help however I can." Bliss set the food on the table. "And I know Mort will, too. We'll have to figure out legal stuff. I mean, I know I had to dodge social workers to keep from getting sent back home."

"Or stuck in foster care." Gaby nearly shuddered. She looked at Dacia and felt Mali squeezing in behind her, and she knew she wouldn't let that happen. Good foster homes existed, she was sure of that, but she wouldn't take the chance. The little girls deserved more.

They deserved . . . love.

Fuck. What did she know about love?

Dacia looked from Bliss to Gaby. "We have no family searching for us. And I will not be separated from Malinal."

"No, you won't," Gaby assured her. "Come on, let's grab a seat."

It was difficult for her to walk with Mali on her butt, but she managed to pry the little girl off and into a chair. Dacia scooted her chair closer to her sister's. Beneath the table, they held hands.

A lump of emotion, big as a melon, lodged in Gaby's throat.

She sought words to put them at ease. "So, ladies, Bliss is a good friend and a really terrific human being. And best of all, she's been where you're at, so she gets it, you know?"

Bliss nodded while loading up the plates. "I really do."

Dacia frowned. "Gets . . . what?"

Bliss answered. "What it's like to wonder where

you'll sleep that night, if you'll be safe from the drug dealers and the gangs and anyone else who preys on others. I know what it's like to share my bedding with the rats and fleas and other creepy-crawlies. I've stolen food, and when I got lucky, clothes, too." She finally took her own seat. "I wasn't as young as you, but I've been where you're at. I know how it is."

The girls sat there, only half listening as they eyed the feast before them.

Gaby rolled her eyes. "Dig in already." But it wasn't until she and Bliss started to eat that the girls followed suit.

Amazed, Gaby watched their food disappear and accepted that they were bottomless pits. Feeding those two would be no small endeavor. She looked at Bliss, and saw that her friend was also amazed. She smiled as she refilled the plates.

Might as well get it all out in the open, Gaby thought. "I want them to sleep here, with you, for a little while. That's not a problem, is it?"

With a mouthful, Bliss shook her head. After she swallowed, she said, "I'll take the couch and they can have my room, that way they can sleep together in the bed."

Slowly, Dacia set aside her fork. For a long time she just stared at her plate. Finally, her big dark eyes came up to meet Bliss's. "We do not want to take your bed."

Bliss shrugged a rounded shoulder. "I don't mind. You wouldn't both fit on the couch."

Dacia's breathing deepened—and Gaby understood her fear. "Dacia, listen to me. You said you trusted me, right?"

She closed her eyes, but nodded. As if in pain, she whispered, "Yes."

So sad, Gaby thought. *So damned wounded and alone.* No child should ever be put in such a situation. "Well, I trust Bliss. I don't have many friends. Only three actually."

"And Luther," Bliss said.

True, but Luther counted as something very different, she just wasn't sure what. "My point is that I only get close to really special people."

"And I'm special?" Bliss asked, looking very pleased.

"Yeah, you are." What did Bliss think? That Gaby got chummy with just anyone? "She wants you to have her bed. She's not going to hold it against you. She won't expect anything in return. And if during the middle of the night, you need her for something, even if it's just to talk . . ." Gaby had to stop because that damn melon in her throat felt like it was swelling. "Bliss would want you to wake her."

"Yeah," Bliss said. "We could do a girl talk or something until you felt better. Like, we could eat ice cream, or watch TV. Wouldn't that be fun?"

The girls looked flummoxed by such a proposition.

Bliss sighed. "Back when I was on the streets, I used to want someone to talk to so bad. But there wasn't anyone."

"You cannot trust others," Dacia said.

"True enough—when you're on the street. But you're here with me now, and Gaby is watching out for you, so you can always talk to us. Okay?"

Dacia took her sister's hand again. "I will . . . try."

Bliss reached across the table and took the girl's hand. "We'll get everything worked out. But until then, how about pie and ice cream for dessert?"

Dacia looked ready to faint at the offer, and Mali actually gasped.

Gaby didn't know what she'd do with the girls, but she did know that she'd protect them with her life.

And Luther would just have to get over it.

Chapter 15

Luther stood behind Ann at her desk, reading over her shoulder as they perused the findings from the arson squad. Because of the circumstances, the team had been great, giving them the go-ahead on their own investigation with agreement that they each keep the other apprised of findings.

So far they hadn't found much.

A scuffle sounded in the hall, and someone crashed into a wall; nothing unusual in that. Muffled voices reached them. Someone shouted a protest, and then protested louder again.

The squad room door opened with a crash.

Luther tuned out the extraneous noise. This time of day the station always buzzed with activity.

A hooker loudly complained as she waited processing. Two young men kept trying to get to each other to finish a fight they'd started in the streets. The officer who'd brought them in bellowed for them to shut up.

Gary Webb, the mail clerk, came and went as he not

only delivered mail, but coffee and the occasional sandwich or donut, too.

"Hey, Detective. Got a minute?"

While Luther continued to read, Ann looked up.

She went unnaturally still, and then brought her elbow
back into Luther's ribs. "Uh, Luther."

"Yeah?" He lifted another paper, engrossed in the de-
tailing of what sounded like heavy shackles found in the
rubble.

"Luther," Ann said again.

He lifted a finger, asking for her patience. Frowning, he
read about an old freezer found at the house. An appliance
to keep dissected body parts? Probably—but it had been
empty when the fire took the place.

"Luther."

He lowered the paper. "What?"

Ann nodded toward the door with a distinct, "Ahem."

Luther followed the direction of her gaze, and there
stood Gaby with a very flustered sergeant beside her.

Oh shit.

A hundred emotions shot through him: worry, fear, and
that confounding elation Gaby always elicited, no matter
what tragedies happened in their small part of the world.

She had the hood of her dark sweatshirt pulled up over
her head, and she'd shoved her hands into the pockets.
Slouched against the doorframe, she ignored the poor
cop who tried to give her rules about barging in without a
proper escort. She looked antagonistic and ready to strike
out.

Beneath that concealing hood, her pale blue eyes glowed
with a strange intensity.

She looked only at Luther, and explained her presence
with a simple, "I need you."

Dumbfounded, Luther looked around, but so far, there

was enough noise and confusion going on that only a few seemed to notice her.

Those who saw her were definitely intrigued. Their gazes bounced from Gaby to Luther and back again.

Trying to decide the best way to handle things, Luther met her gaze—and felt her urgency.

He pushed away from the desk.

Ann caught his arm before he got far. "She looks upset."

Not to Luther. If anything, Gaby looked ready to take the world apart. She wasn't upset; she was furious.

But Ann didn't understand Gaby the way he did, so she didn't recognize the nuances of Gaby's various moods.

"It'll be fine." He hoped.

Ann puzzled at that, and then said, "The conference room on the third floor is empty. I'll make sure no one interrupts you if you want to go there to talk privately with her."

Third-floor conference room. God help him. He nodded at Ann. "Thanks."

Avoiding the cop's grousing, Luther strode up to Gaby, and when she started to say something, he took her arm to shush her.

"Thank you, Sergeant." His smile felt cold and brittle. "I've got this."

"This?" Gaby bristled.

Luther kept smiling.

"God help you," the sergeant said, and he stalked away.

Feeling all eyes on his back, Luther hustled Gaby across the hall, through a heavy door, and into the stairwell.

Starting up the steps, he said, "You'll get the tongues wagging coming here."

With no idea where he led her, Gaby nonetheless took the steps with him, two at a time. "What do you mean?"

"You have a way of making an entrance, Gaby." Luther hoped that Ann would squelch most speculation, but it'd be tricky, even for her. "Everyone's going to be curious now."

"Too bad." She pushed him to go faster. "I wouldn't have come into a police station otherwise."

He'd already realized that. "You could have called, you know."

"Not likely. Not for this."

Luther's apprehension grew. "You look like you've wrangled a tornado. Did you know your eyes are bloodshot? And your face is flushed?"

"So fucking what?" She jerked her arm free on the third-floor landing. "Where are we going?"

"Someplace private."

"Good." Silent now, she fumed beside him until he stopped before a door.

Luther got her into the room, shut the door, and asked without preamble, "Did you kill anyone?"

"No!"

Hands on his hips, he studied her. "Cripple? Maim?"

"No and no, damn it. That's not why I'm here."

She started to pace away from him, and he brought her right back. "I'm not following."

Grabbing the front of his shirt, Gaby shoved him back into the door and went on tiptoes. "I wanted to do all of that—maim, cripple, even slay—but you asked me not to. You asked me to keep it together. And besides, it might have complicated Dacia's life if I had started ripping people apart. So I didn't."

"Whoa." She was so enraged that she wasn't making sense. "Start over. Who's Dacia?"

Gaby pressed into him. "Later. The point is, I brutally stomped down my natural inclination, and . . . I can't stand it, Luther."

Luther smoothed back her silky, tangled hair. "You're holding it all in?"

"Yes, and I'm ready to *implode*. You have to do something."

"Do . . ." Starting to catch on, Luther looked at her bright blue eyes, her parted lips, with shock. "Something . . . as in . . . what?" But he had a feeling he already knew what she was going to say.

"I need you to make it go away. Right now."

"Gaby . . ." Damn, she could give him a boner so easily. "I'm at *work*, honey."

"Tough." She jerked him down to her. "If you don't fix this, *right now*, then I swear to you, I'll fucking well go back and I'll find that son of a bitch and I'll—"

As an expedient way to quiet her raised voice, Luther kissed her.

She took that as concession and attacked. Before he realized where her busy hands had gone, she had his belt unbuckled.

"Gaby . . ." He tried to think, but God Almighty, she took his dick in her hands and put her tongue in his mouth.

He was such a weak ass.

He gave in with hardly any struggle at all.

Looking around the room, Luther saw a somewhat-sturdy, mostly empty table and figured it would have to do. While Gaby stroked him to madness, he reached behind himself and locked the door.

If he got busted, God only knew what the repercussions would be. But they couldn't be any worse than if Gaby murdered whoever had brought on her wrath, especially now that she'd shown herself to the station full of cops.

He didn't work with dummies. The hood of her sweatshirt would not be an adequate disguise against their scrutiny. She'd come in still fuming from an encounter, making herself more than noticeable.

Thinking that gave Luther a moment of sanity. "You're not hurt?"

"Shut the fuck up." She attacked his mouth again.

Okay, not hurt.

"This will have to be a quickie."

"Fine."

"Do you understand me, Gaby? I can't . . . do everything I'd like to do, maybe not everything you need."

Holding his face, she looked at him. Her eyes smoldered and her lips trembled. "I only need you inside me, Luther. Nothing more."

Luther's heart tried to escape his chest. Her heartfelt claim provided the impetus necessary for him to regain his control, and his gentleness. This would have to be brief, so he'd make every second count.

He made quick note of the time on the wall clock, then lifted Gaby. She wrapped her legs around him and went back to kissing him.

After carrying her across the floor, he propped her bottom against the edge of the table. With his hands freed, he touched her everywhere, testing her readiness, teasing her, before opening her jeans and working them down her hips. "Turn around."

She never questioned the order. Breathing hard, she turned and braced her hands on the table.

What a mouthwatering sight. Gaby might be slim, but her body did it for him in a big way. He loved seeing her like this, submissive to him, needing him. There was something very sexy about a woman with her jeans to her knees, her bare backside offered up to him.

Luther put a foot between hers and nudged her feet farther apart. "Open up for me, Gaby. As wide as you can."

When she did that, he smoothed a hand down her spine to her hip. "Arch your back." As he watched her do that, he fished a condom from his wallet and prepared himself.

Holding her hips, he said, "Brace yourself," and as soon as he saw her shoulders flex, her hands curl into fists, he thrust into her.

Her moan was long and deep, her movements sinuous as she accepted him, squeezed him.

Luther bent over her, cupped her breasts in his palms, and thanked God that Gaby never wore a bra to hinder him. The table scooted with each hard thrust, and though he worried about bruising her hip bones, Gaby made it clear that she loved it.

Would she ever love *him*?

He quickly abolished that black thought in favor of seeing to her pleasure.

"Luther."

"Come for me, Gaby." He abandoned one breast to press a hand between her legs, seeking, enflaming her lust. He'd barely stroked her when he felt the tightening of her inner muscles in signal of her release. She bit her own forearm to muffle her cries, and Luther opened a mouth on her shoulder for the same reason.

Every time with her seemed more intense, more mindblowing. Another year or two of this and they'd be combusting from the heat and friction.

As Gaby's pleasure faded, Luther slipped his arm under her to support her, lifted her back against him, and sank to the floor with her in his arms.

She still breathed hard, but now all her rigidity had melted until she felt fluid against him.

Taking advantage, despite his own relaxed state, Luther kissed her forehead and said, "You know what this means?"

"Mmm."

He smiled, and took a big chance. "Rather than me being a hindrance to you, to what you do, I'm an asset."

She opened heavy eyes and studied him. "I'll have to think about that." She touched his mouth. "Sex with you is the antidote to my rage when it starts to boil. Is that a good thing? I don't know yet."

"Making love with me," he corrected. "It's more than sex."

"Since I've never done it with anyone else, I'll have to take your word for it." She looked around him to the clock. "Under ten minutes. Great job, cop."

Luther had to laugh. "Only you would think a ten-minute bang a good thing, Gaby."

"Bang?" She tasted the word, considered it. "It was something of a bang, huh?" With a groan, she added, "I need to get out of here before other, less friendly cops intrude. Now that I'm not stewing, I'm not at all happy being in a police station."

She was right; the longer they lingered, the greater the risk of exposure. But Luther held her in place anyway. He had a point to make, and he wouldn't let her deflect him.

"Your life is changing, Gaby. *You're* changing."

She stretched. "Yeah, in leaps and bounds."

Very little scorn sounded in her tone. Not that long ago, the idea of changing had alternately infuriated her and unnerved her. She'd wanted none of it.

Now, she seemed at least accepting, if not eager.

"With me, it isn't such an odious prospect." Luther tipped up her chin. "Is it?"

"Odious? No." She lifted her hips and pulled her jeans and panties up. "And the side benefits are awesome."

He laughed. "Hussy."

"Getting there." She stood, and held a hand down to him as if he needed the boost up.

Luther shook his head, took her hand, and allowed her to haul him off the floor.

The dress slacks were now dusty and wrinkled, his shirt creased, his tie crooked.

Gaby eyed him head to toe. "You'd better straighten up before you go back, or everyone will know just what you've been doing up here with me."

"No joke." He turned his back to remove the condom and drop it into a trash can. He moved some crumpled papers over it. "Will that bother you?"

She snorted. "No. I don't care what cops think of me. If I did, I'd never have survived this long."

Luther looked around, but he had nothing to tidy up with. Cringing, he tucked himself away and restored order the best he could.

When he faced Gaby again, she wore a droll look with her brows raised.

He tightened his tie and asked, "What?"

"Modesty, Luther?" She patted his chest. "I just didn't expect it, I guess. But it's okay. Don't worry about it." She started for the door.

Flustered, because she was right—he had suffered a streak of modesty—Luther followed after her. "Where are you off to now?"

He almost plowed into her when she stopped dead in her tracks, her shoulders frozen . . . in dread?

Afternoon sunlight cut through the grime on the windows, sending dust motes to dance around her bowed head. "Gaby?"

She pulled her hood up again, hiding her silken, tousled hair. "I've got some stuff I have to do, that's all."

Here we go again. Sighing, Luther put his arms around

her from behind and nuzzled past the hood to kiss her temple. "Can we move beyond that brick wall of yours? At least until we get that bloodsucking, cannibal creep off the streets?"

She deflated without a fight, surprising him. "Yeah, okay." Looking at him over her shoulder, she added, "But you might not like it."

Everything inside him clenched in preparation. From anyone else, a statement like that might not have meant much. With Gaby, God only knew what he had in store for him. "I'm properly braced. Let's hear it."

"No matter what you say, I'm not changing my mind," she forewarned him. Before Luther could address that, she turned in his arms. "And I'm not going to let you interfere."

Butting heads with Gaby gave him a constant headache. "*Why* would I want to interfere?" If he started with that, maybe he'd eventually know what she planned.

Fisting her hands in his shirt, she held onto him, her expression serious, maybe even grave. "Because you're a cop down to the marrow of your bones, that's why."

Luther's understanding of Gaby went beyond the comprehensive acceptance of her singular perspective on things. Nothing else explained why he got the gist of her complaint, if not the implied content. "I'm also a man who knows right from wrong, whether it's within legal bounds or not. I've proven that to you, haven't I?"

"Maybe. Sometimes."

"Trust me, Gaby." He waited, holding eye contact with her, and saw the moment she acquiesced.

"I took two girls off the street."

Luther waited, but she said nothing more, leaving his imagination to take over. Gaby had spent quite a bit of time hanging out with hookers. Had she found new friends in that arena? Not that he'd be quick to judge. Bliss had once been a hooker, and she was a real sweet girl driven by circumstance, not a lack of morals.

"They were homeless, Luther."

Were, meaning they no longer suffered that unfortunate state? "So . . . now you're tussling with another pimp?" The last pimp who had tried to come between Gaby and the women she'd befriended had not fared well.

"For crying out loud, Luther!"

Her affront over the suggestion threw him off. "So, no pimp?"

"Of course not. In fact, there's no one. The girls are all alone. That was the problem. They had no one."

Suspicion sparked. "How old are these girls?"

"Kids." She waved a hand. "Dacia is twelve, but she's mature way beyond that. Her sister, Malinal, is only five. It's hard to tell though, because she's so small and . . . well, what do I know about kids?"

Luther's head started to pound. Now he had to deal with Gaby taking in children? The repercussions of that boggled his mind.

But most of all, he hated that she shortchanged herself. Gaby knew that kids needed to be protected and cherished. He figured that was more than enough. "What did you do with them?"

"I left them with Bliss."

"Oh." He considered that, and nodded. "Yeah, I can see Bliss looking after them." Hopefully for the short-term.

"Yeah, she's got that mothering instinct thing down pat. When I left she was feeding them dessert and promising all sorts of things."

"So why do you look so put out?"

"Bliss gave me a list of stuff they'll need, including clothes with sizes, toys, and books." Gaby pulled the list out and looked at it with dismay. "Problem is, I don't know shit about any of this. What toys? How many books?" The list crumpled in her fist. "I barely shop for me, and I've never shopped for a kid, so how does Bliss expect me to get any of this right?"

Luther took the list from her, smoothed it out so he could read it, and recoiled. That wasn't a small compilation meant to tide things over for a night or two. It looked more like Gaby planned to settle the children in for a lifetime.

"Gaby . . . "

"You're not interfering with this, remember?"

A knocked sounded on the door, and Ann called in, "Wrap it up, Luther. The eyebrows are starting to waggle."

Damn it, he'd already been upstairs too long, but he couldn't leave something this monumental open-ended.

"Hold that thought, Gaby." He strode to the door and opened it for Ann.

She started to speak, paused, and gave him the once-over. She shook her head. "Shame on you, Luther. A little decorum is in order. This *is* your workplace."

Luther dropped back against the door frame with a sigh. "It's that obvious?"

"You do have a glow about you." She smirked, looked beyond him to Gaby, and smiled. "Nookie in the conference room. Scandalous. It's amazing how you've gotten him to loosen up, Gaby. I'd say that's not an altogether bad thing."

Luther waited for Gaby to turn defensive the way she often did around Ann, and instead she looked at Ann like all her problems had just been solved.

"You should make a run for it now," Luther told her.

Ann hesitated. "What are you talking about?"

"Ann." Coming closer, note in hand, Gaby said, "You're into fashion, right?"

"Uh . . ." Ann looked between them, fearful of a trap but unsure how to avoid it. She smoothed a hand over the front of her expensive, tailored suit. The almond color made her skin glow and showed off the highlights in her blonde hair. "Yes, I like to think so."

Amazed, Luther watched as Gaby reeled her in.

"You probably even enjoy shopping, don't you?"

"Sometimes . . ." Unwilling to commit, Ann dragged out the word and then flung her distrust at Luther. "What's going on?"

Luther opened his arms toward Gaby. "You'll have to ask her, because I haven't a clue."

Gaby handed Ann the list. "How about you pick up that stuff for me?"

Ann glanced at the list, and her eyes widened. "All of it?"

"Yeah. We're starting at ground zero here. The girls have what's on their backs, and a pathetic bundle of rags. But don't worry, I'll pay you back. Oh, and the sooner you can get on that, the better."

She started past Ann as if that decided it.

Luther caught her arm and swung her back around. "Hold up, Gaby."

"Don't you have some detecting to do?"

It was unfortunate that Ann stood there, still too stumped to remember etiquette and extend them a measure of privacy. She just stared at the note, tallying, perhaps, all that her shopping trip would entail.

"Tell me about the girls."

Gaby folded her arms and met his gaze. "Sure. I'm keeping them."

"Keeping them?"

"Yeah. They can stay with Bliss for now. She's good with kids. But I'll provide for them."

"Gaby—"

"You are not going to call social services, Luther. I forbid it."

That snapped Ann out of her trance. "Oh, perhaps I should wait outside." She made as if to do that, but didn't quite leave the room.

"When you get the stuff," Gaby told her, "drop it off for Bliss, okay? The girls could really use a bath and all, but they need something clean to change into first."

She turned back to Luther. "I won't have them put into a flawed system, separated, and left with . . . with . . . "

"With the kind of foster homes you had?"

Her chin shot up. "They wouldn't. I was—*am*—a scary oddity. But the girls are sweet-natured and easy to be around. It's just . . . "

"You won't take the chance."

"Stop finishing my sentences for me!"

Instead of obliging her, Luther hauled in close. "I know you, Gaby. I understand how your mind works." He took a deep breath. "And I promise you, we'll work this out together to find the best solution for the girls. Okay?"

If she'd expected real resistance, Luther surprised her.

"How?"

"I know people. I have friends who run social services. We can do a lot off the radar, maybe even find the perfect adoptive parents for them." She wanted to protest, but he didn't give her the chance. "The names sounded Hispanic."

"They are, I think. Dacia has an accent. I haven't heard Malinal say much yet." A fond smile showed in her eyes, if not on her mouth. "She's pretty shy."

Always amazed with Gaby's capacity for caring, Luther hugged her close. "So the kids would probably like a surrounding of their own culture, don't you think? It's something to consider."

Skeptical, she nonetheless shrugged. "I guess."

"Either way, I can ensure that they stay close, so you can still watch over them. What do you say?"

The idea had merit with her, given her lack of complaint. "You promise you won't let them go unless we know for sure—"

"That they'll be safe, cared for, and loved? What do you think?"

She glanced at Ann, let out a huff. "Yeah, you wouldn't. You're too nice for that."

"Thank you."

Ann stepped into the discussion. "You know, Gaby, the girls will need school. It's important for them to be around other kids their own age. But if you're doing things outside the law, you can't enroll them."

Gaby put a hand to her head. "Shit." She paced away, turned back. "I've got a lot to think about."

"At least for now, they're someplace warm and safe, right?" Ann squeezed her shoulder. "You did a very good thing, Gaby."

Her eyes softened, a direct contrast to the words that left her mouth. "Yeah, well, I wasn't going to let those drug dealers get to them."

Luther did a double take. "More drug dealers?"

"A brother, and an even bigger asshole than the one I cut up."

Luther groaned; Ann cleared her throat.

Gaby paid no attention.

"His name is Whit, and I'm sure I'll have to deal with him again, but don't worry. I didn't tear out his spine yet—even though I wanted to." She kissed Luther quick and hard. "And thanks to you, I no longer have the urge to go back and find him and do it even though you asked me not to. So thanks."

Left floundering in his own mixed emotions, Luther watched her go.

Folding the list, Ann whistled. "She's something else."

"I know."

"I think I'll take off early while you finish studying those arson reports."

"Shopping?"

She shrugged. "I have my own soft spot for kids." She paused. "Does Gaby really have money to pay me back?"

"Yeah, she does." Luther thought of her graphic novels and wondered if she'd be writing again soon. Feeling his own amazement, he said, "She's a lot more resourceful than you'd ever imagine."

"I doubt that, Luther. With that one, my imagination is always on overdrive." Ann grinned while tapping the list on her thigh. "I'll take care of the shopping, and then be ready by tonight."

Luther wished for some way to have backup handy when he and Gaby went to see Fabian. His gut told him the night would not end well, might in fact be even worse than Gaby foretold.

But he didn't have legal grounds to call out the SWAT team, and with Gaby around it was always dangerous to involve other law enforcement anyway. Few would back her on her slash-and-dash-them philosophy of fighting crime.

The plan was for Ann to stay nearby outside the tattoo parlor, her radio in hand, and at the first indication of mayhem, she'd call it in.

Luther hoped it'd be enough. Gaby, naturally, would consider Ann's presence overkill. "I have a real bad feeling about this, Ann. You have to be extra careful. If Gaby is right, Fabian is beyond unbalanced. And we still don't know if he's working alone, or with someone."

"Don't worry about me. If it does go down, you better

have an explanation ready because the lieutenant won't be happy that you kept him in the dark."

Having no reason to delay leaving the conference room, Luther held the door for Ann. "Yeah, well, it's not like he'll get a chuckle if another body shows up, either. This is the only way I know to stop him, to nail him, so let's just hope it works."

Chapter 16

Gaby had to admit, the cell phone was handy as she touched base with the girls time and again. She felt like a fool, pretending to have mothering qualities when she didn't, but the girls played on her mind, and talking to them alleviated the clamoring in her brain.

She also talked to Bliss. She wanted to ensure that, if something should happen to her, Bliss would see to the kids' safety. Bliss thought her nuts, but then, her friend didn't know about her planned meeting in less than an hour.

Dread was yet another new sensation for Gaby, and she didn't like it worth a damn. Especially since the dread was diluted with anticipation. She *wanted* to meet with Fabian, to expose his noxious lunacy and then dispatch him with appropriate, grinding finality.

But not knowing how or why Fabian felt familiar hung like a harbinger of sinister proportions over her head, clouding her perspective and her judgment.

"You okay?" Luther asked as he parked far enough

away from the tattoo shop that Fabian wouldn't be able to read his plates.

"Just ducky." Keenly aware of their surroundings, Gaby stared out the window and studied every shadow, every shift in the wind. "Why?"

"I feel your tension." He cupped a warm hand to the back of her neck, underneath the fall of her hair. "Remember, Gaby, I care, and in caring I can't control my concern for you."

"Yeah, I got it." She studied two women sitting on steps, smoking cigarettes and bemoaning circumstances. "I care for you, too, so if I could do this without you, I would."

He went very still, as if unsure what to say.

Gaby glanced his way. "I'm trying to work with you here, Luther."

"I know."

"Then what has you all shell-shocked?"

A slow smile tilted his sexy mouth. "You admitted that you care."

"Haven't I before?"

"I don't think so, but if you did, it wasn't this sincere."

She rolled her eyes. "Come on. Get the lead out. I've got a tattoo waiting."

He opened the car door. "I still think it's a stupid idea to mark your body just to hide a scar that's damn near gone already."

"Noted."

"The way you heal is . . . "

"Incredible, I know. Just another of my many talents." Gaby stepped out to the sidewalk. She breathed in the air, held out her arms, and let her senses pick up each small clue.

Hands on his hips beneath a light jacket, Luther cocked a brow. "We're a block away."

"And that means what?" Sensing nothing amiss, just the usual misery and despair, Gaby started down the sidewalk. "You think he's too stupid to be as cautious as us? Not likely. Don't underestimate him, Luther. It could cost you."

"I would never risk you that way. Believe me, I'm on guard for anything that might happen."

He fell into step beside her, and it felt . . . right.

Comfortable.

To be doing this with Luther, to have him with her, changed everything. His impressive size and strength, his unwavering integrity edged by badass determination to see good prevail, lent Gaby a fresh perception on everything she saw, all that she touched and felt, wanted and needed.

She could do what had to be done. Always, without fail.

But she could also retrench, she could stay in herself instead of drowning in the zone. Because of Luther's nearness.

The ways he effected constructive change in her used to alarm her. But not anymore. Not now.

While she'd always felt akin to a lethal tool used to bludgeon evil, now she sensed her own humanity. She remained an aberration, but hand in hand with that, she was a woman with a mind of her own, making her own decisions.

Looking to the sky, hoping He heard her, she whispered, "This feels as right as anything could. This is the path I choose for myself now."

The sky didn't fall on her, so Gaby accepted that God allowed her the growth. With Luther.

It had probably been His plan all along, and if she hadn't remained so stubborn, she might have realized it sooner.

Gratitude, for what He had bestowed, and what Luther shared, burst inside her, leaving her chest tight again. Emotion could be a son of a bitch when it came at the wrong times.

Headlights hit them and Luther turned, walking backward, as he verified Ann's arrival. "Right on time," he whispered.

Gaby glanced back, too. Ann didn't look at either of them, didn't in any way give up her association or her purpose in being there.

"I like her," Gaby confided.

"Since when?"

"Since she showed up at Bliss's with several bags of necessary and not-so-necessary stuff for the girls. Dacia was speechless, disbelieving in that way of hers because not much good fortune has come her way. But Mali . . . she turned into a chatterbox. I could hear her laughing over the phone, so loud that Bliss got drowned out."

"When this is done," Luther told her, "we can take them to the park. And the movies, and the zoo. I'd love to see you at an arcade. You'd probably break the machines with your reflexes."

Gaby didn't know anything about an arcade, and just then, she didn't care. She nodded ahead of them.

Luther turned back around and the tattoo parlor came into sight.

"Everything okay?"

Gaby nodded. "Yeah, I'm just adjusting to the idea of doing this your way."

"As opposed to your way, which would be . . . what?"

He didn't need to ask, and they both knew it. "I'd kill him, no questions asked. I look at him, and I see his black soul, the ugliness of his purpose, the sickness of his pleasures." She put her hands in the pocket of her hooded sweatshirt. "If shit doesn't roll out right, I'll kill him still. Gladly."

Luther waited.

"But I'm willing to give it a shot your way first."

"That means a lot, Gaby."

"Yeah, I know."

Luther grinned, but the show of humor faded under the weight of the task before them.

Through drawn blinds, a faint light shone in the front window of the tattoo parlor. It gave the illusion of warmth inside.

But outside, shrouding the tidy brick-and-mortar building, a brume of depravity slunk and swirled, shifted and regrouped.

"He's inside, plotting, anxious." Gaby shook her head. "The sick fuck is giddy about something."

Because Luther looked ready to drag her away, Gaby changed the subject. Luther didn't understand about auras, or about her special sight that showed things even he, an intuitive cop, couldn't see.

"I asked around about tattoos so I'd know the process. I don't want him to slip something into my skin that could poison me."

Far from bolstered, Luther drew up short. "I hadn't even considered that."

"Don't worry about it. I'll know if he tries that." Gaby kept walking, giving Luther no choice but to keep up. The sepulchral thudding of his boots on the pavement echoed over tall brick façades and crumbling stucco, faded into alleyways.

Gaby made no noise at all. "Stay here."

Luther started to protest, and she said, "I'm trying it your way, but you've got to compromise a little."

He nodded. "If you're not back around front in one minute, I'm coming after you."

Gaby left without further discussion. She followed the

perimeter of the building to the side, where she checked an old window and found it secure. In the back, she twisted the doorknob. Locked. The other side of the building didn't have a window. Back around front, she told Luther, "Everything looks fine."

The front door opened. Palest light radiated from inside, backlighting Fabian's body, casting a sinister glow around his cadaverous form. "Of course." White teeth shone in the darkness. "Were you expecting a trap?"

"Still am," Gaby told him as she took the lead up the stoop and to the door. "So don't fuck up—or I'll kill you."

Luther acquainted himself with the shop under the pretext of awe. Dark green paint and wood trim accented yellow walls. Padded stools, a special chair, and wood cabinets had been organized efficiently.

Image suggestions lined each wall, and glass cases displayed a variety of body jewelry. Some of it was beautiful, but some of the heavier pieces looked deliberately painful.

"I had no idea tattoo parlors were so heavily equipped." On shelves, he saw tattooing guns, inks, sterilization machines, a copying machine, and a supply of alcohol, swabs, and bandages.

A more private room, possibly an office, jutted out toward the rear, leaving a narrow hallway that led to the back door. On the other side of the hall, a closed door indicated a storage room.

Luther listened, but heard nothing more than his own breathing. The room smelled mostly sterile, with only a faint hint of ink.

Fabian had set out a tattooing apparatus and sealed needle, along with a selection of paints.

Ignoring Luther, he gestured to the chair. "Sit, Gaby."

She bestowed on him the most noncompliant look imaginable.

Fabian amended the order with, "Please."

Gaby sat. She eyed the many ink bottles and said, "Just black. Nothing fancy."

"I understand. But I thought we could edge it in blue or purple—"

"No."

Shooting for pragmatism, Fabian crossed his arms behind his back and took a breath. "I am not without experience in this. I know what will look best, how to give the tattoo depth and light and movement."

"Just. Black."

Luther stood behind Gaby, staring down at her head. She was so cold, so distant, he didn't know what to think. Was it part of the act, or a real reaction to Fabian?

"Yeah," Luther said, "I like the idea of simplicity, myself."

Jaw clenched, Fabian nodded. "As you wish."

To lighten the mood, Luther asked, "Is that your license on the wall?"

"I display it for the comfort of patrons. Getting a tattoo can be a big decision. I want them to know they're in good hands."

"Yeah, I bet." Luther grinned, but the bite remained in the words.

Fabian took his seat. "Remove the sweatshirt, please."

Gaby pulled it off over her head and handed it to Luther. Left in a thin T-shirt, she retook her seat and said, "Can we get on with this?"

"In a hurry?"

"Let's just say I'm not one for idle chitchat."

Fabian studied her. "You're worried about the pain? I hadn't expected that."

"She's not," Luther told him with great certainty. Gaby couldn't care less about a little pain. But he couldn't very well tell Fabian that it was his black soul disturbing her.

Unconvinced, Fabian broke into what sounded like a rehearsed speech for his customers.

"Pain tolerance is a unique thing. Everyone reacts differently. In case you didn't know, the ink is injected into the dermis, the deeper second layer of skin, not just the top layer. I can liken the sensation to being stung hundreds of times by a hornet. Some find the pain nearly unbearable."

Luther snorted for Gaby. "She'll be fine."

But it worried him. Gaby was tough as they came, and she never experienced discomfort as much as others did. But this would be different.

She'd be doing this as a woman, not a paladin.

"I promise not to cry," Gaby told Fabian with sharp-edged sarcasm.

"Very well." He lifted her arm by the wrist and bent to examine her scar.

Most of the shop remained mired in shadows, with only one harsh, powerful light directed on Gaby's arm. The glow of that lamp lent added distinction to Gaby's features. It sharpened her jawline, defined the bow of her upper lip, the length of her inky lashes.

Disturbed comprehension palpated off her in waves.

Luther saw the wary preparation in her, even if Fabian remained obtuse.

"My God," Fabian said when he saw how much she'd healed. He couldn't conceal an odd satisfaction. "The wound is nearly invisible now. It's amazing, isn't it?"

"Some of the scar will remain." Gaby never took her burning gaze off Fabian. "That's why I want you to cover it."

"As good as it looks now, that won't be a problem at all."

He sat back in his seat. "There are several things I need to do first to prepare for the ink." He patted her arm with paternal pride. "Sit tight."

Moving to a sink set in the wall beside the sterilization equipment, Fabian scrubbed his hands. When he finished, he returned to Gaby with swabs and alcohol and cleaned the entire area of her arm that would be tattooed, then let her rest her arm on a sterilized towel.

The alcohol had to burn the areas of her arm not completely healed yet, but Gaby never even blinked.

And Luther felt so much pride, he wanted to burst.

Gaby was the toughest person he knew, and still she had the biggest heart and the most giving nature.

He watched as Fabian opened up a single-use needle, put it in an odd machine, and settled comfortably before Gaby.

"Ready?"

"If you take much longer, I'll be asleep."

Fabian's mouth quirked in a smile. "I'm going to make an outline of the design now." He started working, his head bent to his task.

Luther winced every so often, but Gaby remained as immobile and unflinching as a brick wall.

"So, Gaby." Fabian glanced up, then back to his work. "I saw you across the street today."

A muscle tightened on Gaby's face. "Do tell."

"You were butting heads with one of our more colorful denizens. A drug dealer, I believe."

Belying her tension, Gaby sounded bored when she asked, "You know him?"

"I've done most of the tattoos for the dealers in the city. They want the best and, foregoing modesty, I can say with confidence that I'm by far the best. My designs come alive."

"Bully for you."

"And they can afford to pay my prices, so . . . " Fabian shrugged. "I'm acquainted with many of the more reprehensible sorts."

"Of course you are."

Fabian shot Gaby a look, judged her comment to be only more cynicism, and dismissed it. "This morning, before you left the area, you rounded up some of the area children to take with you."

She said nothing, just stared at him.

He cleared his throat and nodded at the design. "What do you think?"

She didn't release him from her gaze. "That it?"

Fabian flashed an indulgent smile. "I need to fill it in yet, but that's the outline of the barbed wire design."

Hoping to break the tension and help Gaby settle down again, Luther leaned over to look.

But Gaby was already saying, "It's fine. Finish it."

Raising a brow, Fabian used yet another sterile towel to wipe away a few spots of blood. "You're a curious woman, Gaby." He began swabbing the area again with soap and fresh water. "Cody, is it?"

Luther took a protective step forward, too shocked to censor his reaction. How the hell could Fabian know Gaby's last name when she'd *never* given it? Something was going on, something more than he knew, and he didn't like it.

Gaby shifted—a subtle indication for Luther to cool his jets.

Her faint amusement reassured Luther; Gaby would know if imminent danger existed.

"That's right, Fabian." Her slow nod gave Fabian points for ingenuity. "Gabrielle Cody, if you want the whole shebang."

"It's a lovely name." He replaced the needle with a new, sturdier one and went back to work. Occasionally he glanced up at Gaby to gauge her discomfort at the puncturing needle, but she showed none.

If Gaby felt anything at all, she hid it well.

When Fabian had finished, he smiled with pride. "Well, what do you think?"

Gaby approved the overall effect with a dismissive shrug. "Looks fine. It does what I wanted it to do."

Stung, Fabian said, "It entirely conceals any scar and even though you limited me in color, there's a certain dimension to it that's quite unique and appealing."

Gaby said only, "Yeah, you'll get paid."

Frustrated with her lack of appreciation, Fabian scowled. "Let me just bandage it up and we're done." As he saw to that, he detailed more precautions. "For the next twenty-four hours, keep it bandaged. After that, you can wash it with antibacterial soap, but don't soak it. Stay out of hot tubs or long showers. Don't pick at it, either."

"Got it." Gaby started to rise.

Fabian caught her wrist. Even Gaby's glare didn't make him release her.

"I know why you really came here, Gaby."

Luther kept his stance loose, but ready. "Think so, huh?"

Fabian spared him an annoyed frown. "I see the news. I know all about the body parts found." Lip curling, he said, "The headlines have been ludicrous, painting the person responsible as some kind of perverted predator."

"You don't think that fits?"

This time Fabian didn't even look at Luther. He beseeched Gaby instead. "You're wondering if I had something to do with it."

Gaby curled her hand into a fist, tightened it so that her

muscles flexed and rippled under Fabian's hold. Finally he released her.

She lounged back, at her leisure. "Actually, Fabian, I'm not wondering about that at all."

"I . . . " He closed his mouth, at a loss, but not for long. "Then you've already drawn your conclusions."

Hearing a small sound, Luther eased away from Gaby on a pretext of looking at more designs. Concentrating, he listened for any unfamiliar noise—a breath, the scuffle of a shoe.

He heard nothing. But . . . Fuck. He didn't like this. He didn't like it at all.

His visceral reaction was to shut it down, right now. He drew a breath and held off.

"I know what I know," Gaby told Fabian. "No doubts at all."

"I see." Fabian regrouped, and changed tactics. "You know, Gaby, it might interest you to find out that I have some of the same . . . special talents that you have."

That announcement hit Luther like a shock wave. He ended his perusal of the shop and returned to Gaby's side.

While he tingled with a foreboding of doom, Gaby didn't look in the least perturbed. A half-smile cast her features in sinister shadows. "What kind of special talents do you think you have, Fabian?"

He grinned in absurd camaraderie, leaning forward to create a more intimate nature to their discussion. "I knew you were familiar to me. You felt it, too. Admit it?"

She shrugged. "I sensed a deeper knowledge of you."

"I knew it! In the very same way, I recognized you and your symptoms. The extraordinary things you do are not so far-fetched as you might think."

Luther couldn't stand it. "What the fuck are you talking about?"

"Yeah." Gaby slouched lower in her seat. "This is getting interesting. Enlighten me, Fabian."

He couldn't hide the hatred he felt for Luther. "Perhaps you'd be more comfortable discussing this without his intrusion."

"Not on your life," Luther told him.

"He stays," Gaby added.

"Fine." Fabian stood. He moved to a cabinet, touched a flower pot holding an overflowing, glossy philodendron. "The talents you have are symptomatic of a special breed of person. A higher power, if you will."

"Let me get this straight." Gaby smirked. "You think you're a god?"

Fabian snapped a leaf off the plant. Sizzling with fury, he turned to face her. "You have a knack for running with amazing speed while not tiring. You see extremely well in the dark. You have remarkable reflexes, better hearing, smell, and taste than the pathetic majority that chokes our streets. You, Gaby Cody, are superior. And so am I."

Gaby sat up, but said nothing.

Fabian took his chair again. With hesitant daring, he traced his fingertips along the fresh bandage wrapped around Gaby's arm. "It was confirmed for me when I saw your increased recuperative ability." His voice went soft with awe. "It's almost as if you've bathed in blood and taken the healing properties of it."

Luther wanted to rip the nutcase out of his chair and well away from Gaby. But this could be the confession they needed. "Have you bathed in blood, Fabian?"

With Gaby's attention now focused solely on him, Fabian ignored Luther. "You are not meant for the peons of this world, Gaby. Please believe me."

"What do you suggest?"

Luther knew Gaby baited Fabian, but he was so wrapped

up in his recruit of her, he didn't appear to see through her tactic.

"I know that you hurt, Gaby," Fabian said. "I share that pain with you. But you see, I can explain it, teach you how to marshal it, control it." He held out a hand to her. "The truth is, my dear, you and I are more alike than you know."

"That doesn't flatter me, Fabian."

Luther shifted his gaze from Gaby to Fabian and back again. Gaby sounded fine, but he sensed her gathering pain and rage. Before much longer, she would break—one way or the other.

"Well, it should." He drew a breath, let it out, and stated, "You're a psychic vampire. Do you understand what that means?"

Luther spoke up. "You've been watching too much late-night television."

If looks could kill, Luther would have been thoroughly slain by Fabian's stare.

Gaby tipped her head as if curious. "Why don't you tell me what you think it means."

Keen to do just that, Fabian grew bizarrely animated. "A psychic vampire feeds off the life energy of others—those who are unimportant. It's harmless, really. I can partake of your energy without you ever realizing it. That is to say, you, Gaby, would know, because you're one of us. But he"—Fabian tossed his head toward Luther in clear disdain—"would be clueless. Those such as him are emotionally susceptible and can be easily left drained and lifeless, to sleep for days."

Luther laughed. "Yeah, right." He gestured with a hand, praying Fabian would redirect his focus from Gaby. "C'mon, Fabian. Drain me." And then with a taunting smile, "Dare ya."

Fabian snarled. "There is a propensity in the *lesser* specimens of humanity to oppose anything that tests preconceived notions. Those narrow-minded attitudes are why we superior beings are often forced to live in secret, instead of celebrating our unique qualities."

"Your insanity, you mean."

Gaby raised a hand to quiet Luther. "Fact is, Fabian, I'm not whatever it is you think I am. Trust me on that."

He composed himself with effort. "You hurt, Gaby, I see that even if he doesn't."

Luther bristled, but kept silent. Gaby wanted to handle this, and he trusted her to do so. No matter how hard this might be, she would always be strong.

She would always do the right thing.

"The pain is caused by your need to take, to absorb energy from those weaker than you. The agony can be alleviated that way." Fabian braced himself. "But it can be obliterated altogether . . . by drinking and feeding."

Red flags went up for Luther, but again, Gaby didn't react at all.

"Most times, Fabian," she told him, "I don't think of food. What I do, what calls to me, isn't sated that way."

Fabian relished the close confidence, the way she shared with him.

He closed the space between them. "Only because you haven't sated it properly. By taking from others, you fulfill yourself and enhance your abilities." More vivacious now, he snatched both her hands. "I alone understand this."

"Just you, huh?"

"Yes." He went taut with expectation. "I understand everything about you, because you inherited your talent . . . from me."

Time seemed to stand still.

Luther heard the wind stirring outside, the ticking of the

clock on the wall, his own heartbeat. He felt the whirlwind of emotions gathering inside Gaby and put his hands on her shoulders to help ground her. He prayed that his touch would be enough to calm her.

"Just what the fuck are you saying?"

Luther started, unnerved to his bones by that whisper of sound from Gaby.

"I am your father."

Luther's heart dropped into his stomach. Gaby blinked, swallowed audibly. The unexpected bomb had thrown her; he felt it, but didn't know what to do about it. In a show of subtle support, he squeezed her shoulders.

She didn't notice.

Fabian removed an aged photo from his pocket. He laid it on the table and turned it toward Gaby, then slid it over to her. "The woman beside me is your mother."

Hands folded over the counter, Fabian smiled at Gaby, magnanimous in his claim, heedless to the inferno he'd just ignited.

"As your own flesh and blood," he announced, "as one equal to you in our elevated capacity, I'm inviting you to join me in my quest for divinity. Partner with me, Gaby, partake of life with me, share my conquests. Be my family."

Eyes glued to that old, creased, and crumpled black-and-white photo, Gaby shook her head. Hand trembling, she traced the faded outline of a woman's face.

Her hand dropped away.

"Join you?" Very slowly Gaby looked up, and danger crackled in the air. "Father mine, I will destroy you."

Before Luther could surmise her intent, Gaby upended the heavy steel table and all the tattooing implements, sending inks, needles, alcohol, and more, crashing to the floor.

Fabian stumbled out of his chair and backed up in haste, but it was fury on his thin face, not fear. "You dare!"

Gaby held her ground, heaving. "If you think . . . " She had to stop to draw air, to collect herself enough to make the words sound as more than a raw-edged growl. "If you think telling me that you're the son of a bitch who left me behind will in any way ingratiate me to you, you're even sicker than I thought."

"I did not know your mother was pregnant when I left her," Fabian rushed to tell her.

"Would you have cared?" Gaby whispered right back.

Luther saw it on Fabian's face, the consideration to lie or tell the truth.

Truth won out.

"No, likely I would not." He sniffed, brushing at a splash of alcohol on his sleeve caused by Gaby's eruption. "Your mother, child, was a filthy whore, and a pathetic one at that."

Gaby's knife went through the air without warning, embedded to the hilt in the cabinet beside Fabian.

Fabian's eyes widened as he finally experienced an appropriate dose of alarm for his current predicament.

In two big strides, Luther moved between Gaby and Fabian. Had she missed on purpose? If so, why?

Gaby snagged Luther's arm and started around him with a heavy, deliberate stride. Luther tried to stop her, but this was Gaby at her most dangerous.

Fabian scrambled back, but he had nowhere to go. "Stop right there."

"Not until you're dead at my feet."

He stopped retreating, and a glint of rage entered his eyes. "I think not."

Just as Gaby reached Fabian, he called out, *"Now,"* and the interior door to his office slammed open.

Luther had his gun out just as quick, but when he saw the sight before him, impotent fury froze him.

Gaby remained near Fabian, but unmoving.

Gleeful, Fabian said, "Did you really think I'd meet you without backup? Gaby, Gaby, Gaby. My dear, you disappoint me."

Mouths gagged, hands tied, Dacia and Mali stood clamped close to the side of a man with venom in his eyes. His friend held a gun on the girls.

Smiling, the fellow said to Luther, "Drop it, and kick it toward me, real slow-like, or I splatter brains all over this fucking place."

It galled him to do so, but Luther complied.

The man picked up the gun, then said to someone behind him, "Get in here," and two more hostages came forward.

Bloodied and wet with tears, Bliss fell to her knees before the men. She looked at Gaby in abject apology and shame. Luther's heart broke for her.

Next to her, Mort stood rigid, his eye bruised, his nose bloody, the gag cutting into his face. But he didn't fall, and he didn't cower.

Gaby's influence on him showed in his inner strength, his brave composure. Mort stepped nearer to Bliss, trying to shield her from the men, lending her what protection he could.

Fabian had attacked everyone dear to Gaby, and in the process, attacked her where she was most vulnerable.

Fuck procedure, Luther decided. One way or another, he would kill Fabian for this.

Before the night was through, the man would be dead—at Gaby's feet—as she had wished it.

Chapter 17

In a single heartbeat Gaby took in the situation, assimilating the various scenarios about to unfold. She prayed Morty wouldn't try some foolhardy stunt. He looked ready, almost anxious to do that.

God love him. He was the dearest of friends.

And Bliss . . . she was like a sister to Gaby in every way that counted. And these men had harmed her, frightened her.

Gaby couldn't look too closely at the girls. Doing so might impinge on her tightly strung control, might send her into the mindless zone of a paladin. Right now, she needed to stay clearheaded and in control of her own faculties.

"Mort, do nothing. Do you understand me?"

Whit laughed. "He's not that stupid."

"No, but he's that brave."

Scowling, Fabian said, "You know his thoughts?"

She peered at each of her targets, and felt that small smile slip into place again. "I know what each of you is planning." That wasn't entirely true. She could read Mud and Whit, but Fabian's thoughts, perhaps because of the familial connection, mostly eluded her.

But she could still gauge what a lunatic in his position *might* do, so she felt confident in her assumptions.

Unable to speak, Mort nodded to her. In his eyes, Gaby saw trust and confidence. He believed in her, even now, after what had been done to him—because of her.

And it *was* because of her; she had no misunderstanding about that. In his own cunning fashion, Fabian had threatened Gaby with her inner circle, those closest to her.

And in the bargain, he'd signed his own death warrant.

Because of his visibly unstable rage, she considered Mud to be the most immediate threat. Keeping her gaze on him, she reached out and wrapped her fingers around the hilt of her knife. Slowly, making sure they all noticed, she jerked the blade free of the cabinet.

Mud raised the gun, but Fabian waved him down.

Daddy dearest saw no real threat in her being armed.

And he called himself her father?

No, blood meant nothing to her. Not anymore.

There was a time that it would have been everything, her whole world. Back when she'd been a scared, ostracized child, and later, an aberration of society, an outsider from everyone and everything ordinary in life . . .

Yes, back then she might have welcomed a monster into her life.

But since meeting Luther, she'd come to understand that family was more than blood ties. A lot more. God had blessed her with a quirky, meddling, hodgepodge group of people who remarkably enough cared for her. They were all the family she needed.

And Fabian threatened them.

Gaby held the knife to her side and waited for the right

opportunity. Thoughts fluttered through her mind with the rapidity of a film projector.

Had Ann spoken with Mort before he was taken? Had he somehow alerted her? Would she realize the threat and enter?

No, if Ann knew Mort was in danger, she'd have already come in with a force of uniformed cops to protect him. She loved Mort that much.

Unless there was some kind of ruckus, Ann would remain outside, waiting. But if Gaby threw Mud through the front window, would the girls get hurt before she could get to them?

Disarmed, Luther seethed beside her. Please, God, don't let him do something heroic that might get him hurt or killed.

She looked at Luther, waited for him to meet her gaze, and then said, with no inflection, no fear at all, "I've got this."

Luther, bless him, didn't look skeptical. He simply nodded.

When Gaby heard Bliss sob, she turned next to her. "It's okay, Bliss. I promise. Are you hurt?"

She shook her head.

"Good. Now I don't want you to worry. Any of you."

Whit and Mud were speechless at her confidence.

Fabian was amused. "Enough. These meager beings are nothing to you, Gaby. Less than nothing. You will see." Fabian straightened his shirt. "But you, my dear daughter, you are divine."

"You're right about that." Even now, without going into the unseeing, killing zone of a paladin, Gaby felt the acumination of her own skillfulness. She could hear the fast and shallow breaths of more people crowded into that small back room, and with the same instincts, she knew they weren't a real threat.

She sensed Fabian's omnipotent bias, and apperceived it as his greatest weakness.

She felt Luther's caring, Dacia's trust, Mort's poise.

Under her cool skin, her muscles rippled and ripened in preparation.

Never before had she summoned the talents without losing sense of self; this time, she administered control of those skills with a clear head.

"You've gone to a lot of trouble here, Fabian. What is it you want?"

He laced his hands behind his back and moved to face her, to study her. "It is lonely at the top, daughter. I have had no true adversary, no true companion, none to equal me in intelligence or daring. But you have impressed me."

"Just wait." Gaby met his gaze without fear. Oh, she'd impress him, all right.

Fabian shook that off. "You are not quite of my level, not yet, but you will now join me. You will grow, expand your knowledge and experiences." He looked at her under lowered brows. "I insist."

Slipping an arm around her, Fabian foolishly put himself too close to her.

But with everyone she cared for in peril, Gaby restrained the urge to break Fabian in two.

That would come. *Soon.* For now, she had to let her natural sagacity guide her instincts.

She had to react as Luther would prefer.

Fabian's heated breath brushed her ear. "Once you've tasted the sweetness, once you've bathed in the blood, you'll understand the supreme joy of it, how it rejuvenates the soul and enhances every function."

Gaby stared straight ahead, repulsed but determined to time her first move to the best advantage. She'd have to take out someone, stun someone else, immobilize through fear.

Whit laughed at her. "Stupid bitch. You're still calculating. I can see you doing it. You think you have it all figured out, don't you?"

Ah, the perfect segue. Gaby smiled at him. "If I do, Whit, then you'll be the second one dead." She shifted her shrewd gaze to Mud. "Right after him."

Again Mud aimed at her, but Gaby preferred that to having it aimed at the children. She knew he wouldn't dare pull that trigger, not without Fabian's order.

And Fabian had other plans for her.

She asked him, "How did you find the girls?"

"Oh please, daughter. They've been on my radar for a long time." He strode over to Mali and stroked her small, red cheek above her gag, sending her cowering and whimpering to her sister's side.

Dacia went frantic, but she couldn't move for Whit's bruising hold on her.

Fabian grabbed Mali's hair and pulled her tight to his side, deliberately crushing her, enjoying her abject fear. "This one is most sweet." He bent down and licked her cheek. "All baby plumpness and rosy flesh. She will be delicious."

Gaby shook her head at Dacia, quickly trying to calm her. "Dacia, no. Dacia . . . *Look at me*."

When the girl did, Gaby said, "I told you it's going to be okay, remember? He's not going to hurt her. He's not going to hurt anyone."

Fabian found her faith hilarious. Whit and Mud laughed with him.

"I had located the girls a few days back, and had planned this one as a meal."

Even Whit and Mud seemed repulsed by that—but were still unwilling to alter the outcome.

"Then I saw you with them, saw you sheltering them and looking so . . . well, so much more human than usual. That's when I detected the similarities. You look a lot like your worthless mother, you know. But you lack her pathetic, spineless conduct. You took your character from me."

Gaby snorted. "I claim nothing of you. Ever."

His hand tightened in Mali's hair. "When I saw you leaving the area with the girls, I had one of the other street youths follow you. Not close, you understand. You would have detected that. He stayed back, and then found out the rest by asking around." Fabian laughed. "It's amazing what a few dollars will buy you from those who are hungry and alone. You see, Gaby, you were betrayed by the same foul parasites that you seek to protect."

"I don't blame those in need." She regulated her breathing, loosened her muscles. "I know who is evil, and who isn't."

Fabian waved a hand. "Enough of that nonsense. Come. There is much to do yet this night." Shoving Mali back to Mud, Fabian went into that small back room. Gaby and Luther followed, with Mud and Whit forcing the others in behind them.

Inside that small room, Gaby discovered a shocking, bloody tableau of Fabian's intent.

Two young men and one woman stood around, anxiously waiting for instruction. So these were Fabian's underlings? The mindless cattle he directed in his twisted pursuit of perverse pleasure? She looked into their eyes, saw they were already high and mostly ineffectual.

What had Fabian given them? And then she knew: they'd needed coercing to attack a child. Huh. Even they had some scruples. Not that it'd matter in the long run.

Gaby nodded to the naked body hanging over a stainless steel tub splashed with blood. "Who is she?"

Limp hands shackled together and attached to a chain bolted in the ceiling, the cadaver hung there, ghostly white and quite dead. Bite marks marred the body, and deep slashes had been cut into her inner forearms from her wrists almost to her elbows. There was no doubt she had been bled to death.

"Shari was once a devoted follower, but she erred by letting our last sacrifice escape."

"I saw your sacrifice in the hospital, you sick fuck." Luther stepped to the side of Gaby, deliberately widening the space between them—giving her room to perform when she needed to. "You tortured her."

"She nourished us. There's a difference. It was her great privilege, a noble sacrifice, not that I expect you to understand. I had planned to keep her alive awhile, but it's just as well that she died."

"Not before she told us about the house."

Fabian smiled. "We burned it to the ground. You found no evidence there."

"Wrong."

As Luther spoke, Gaby noticed the newest members to the party looking very ill at ease. Between the drugs and the thick ambiance of danger, they were already edgy. Now Luther worried them with feigned details; a perfect ploy.

"Vials were recovered—with fingerprints," Gaby lied. She really had no idea if there were clear fingerprints or not.

Unease shifted in the air.

"Nonsense." Fabian dismissed their concerns with a laugh. "Now, Shari here loved to please men. She lived for it." He stroked a hand along her side. "She offered her blood to me, and now she pleases me greatly by providing the blood you'll drink and bathe in."

Gaby eyed the small, squat tub, the awkward way Shari's

dead weight dragged on that ceiling bolt. It was a chilling setting, and she hated that the girls were witness to it.

"No thanks."

"Difficult to the bitter end, huh?" Like a little boy on Christmas morning, Fabian shook with his excitement. "Let me see if I can change your mind."

Gaby watched as he tugged on a tooth, removed a cap, and then another and another, until his smile showed a frighteningly sharpened, jagged bite.

He sighed, shook back his hair, and closed his eyes. As if in ecstasy, he ran his tongue along the edge of those serrated teeth.

When he recovered, he said to Mud, "Bring the little one to me."

"I'll kill you," Gaby whispered.

Mud hesitated. Whit shot his beady gaze from Gaby to Fabian and back again.

"Do it," Fabian roared.

Mobilized, Mud handed the gun to Whit and grabbed Mali's squirming, sobbing body. He started forward with her, closer and closer to Gaby.

When he was within reach, Gaby moved with phenomenal speed, swinging her arm up, burying her knife blade deep in Mud's face through his left eye. Without a single second of hesitation, she twisted, then pulled her knife free.

Blood, gore, and brain matter dripped from her lethal blade to the floor.

Mud collapsed without a struggle. Mali raced back to Bliss and Dacia, all three of them shrieking through their gags, hysterical as only females could be. Mort cowered over them, trying to shield them with his body.

Gaby tuned them out and looked at Whit with a smile.

Near to hyperventilating, he panted, raised the gun . . . and Fabian screamed, "No," even as Whit fired.

The gun jammed.

Thank you, Gaby silently whispered.

She was on Whit before he could think to pull that trigger again. In three rapid punches, she stabbed him in the chest, yanked the knife free, and kicked him to the ground.

He collapsed in a useless heap.

Chaos ensued. Fabian shouted; Mort tried to corral the girls out of harm's way; Luther kept the other two men from escaping out the back door. He held his own against them and even managed a quick punch to the woman's jaw, knocking her out.

Fabian, having snatched up Whit's gun, fired into the ceiling.

Ah, Gaby thought, just the summons Ann needed. She told the girls, "Stay still," and slowly turned to face Fabian.

Gaze locked with his, she swiped her blade over her denim-covered thigh to clean it.

"Don't." He didn't aim the gun at her; he aimed at Luther's head. "I just proved the gun will not fail again, and as in most things, I'm a superior shot."

"You're a superior ass, I'll give you that."

"One more word," Fabian growled low, "and I will shoot him in the leg. And then in the gut. And then—"

"Yeah, I got it. You'll keep shooting him." Gaby started toward Fabian.

"Ah, ah, ah. Not another step, daughter dear, or your boyfriend will be wearing some new holes."

Gaby stopped.

"Get rid of the knife."

Shrugging, Gaby slid it into the sheath at her back—not even close to gone, but out of sight at least.

Fabian let it go.

"Into the tub." He gestured with the gun. "I want to

see you drink. I want to witness your understanding when you feel all that beautiful, slippery blood on your skin, soaking in, redefining you, elevating your strengths." He breathed hard, and then as if he'd just snapped, he yelled, *"Do it!"*

"All right, all right. Don't get your panties in a bunch." Gaby went over and looked into the tub. Blood still dripped from the woman's body, sending ripples across the surface of the bath. She could smell the fresh blood, tangy, thick, and dark. And she smelled the woman's death, her fear. The scents commingled in a nauseating emanation, a tumultuous assault on her senses.

"Don't do it."

Luther's voice was raw, hurting.

Gaby looked over her shoulder at him. "You know, Luther, before you, I didn't know anything but destruction and duty and pain. I didn't know how to smile. I didn't know how to . . . love."

Luther's back stiffened. His jaw locked, his eyes glistened. "You don't have to do this for me. Not for anyone."

She smiled, proving her words. "Don't you know there's nothing I wouldn't do for you?" At peace, Gaby stepped into the tub. While she crafted her next move, blood soaked into her shoes, the bottom of her jeans.

It still held warmth from the woman's body.

But the scabrous circumstances didn't faze her—they inspired her. Luther thought she was without options? He had to know her better than that.

"I'm glad you're so willing to accommodate me." Keeping that gun on Luther, Fabian edged over to the side and grabbed Mali.

Her struggles only seemed to further excite him, but Gaby knew she couldn't calm the girl right now.

"Drink it, daughter." Fabian licked his lips while stroking up and down Mali's side. "Drink your fill, and then we'll feast on this one together."

When Dacia would have raced across the room, Luther caught her and tucked her behind his back. "Shh," he said to her, to all of them. "Trust Gaby. Always."

Yeah, trust me—please. She made a sound of disgust. "Do you expect me to drink from that dirty tub?"

"It's not dirty." Fabian spoke around his accelerated breaths, so excited that he could barely talk. "It's brand-new, I promise you." A maniacal light shone from his eyes. His laugh sounded demented. "Drink."

"Not from the tub. No, sir." Knowing what she would do, Gaby lied, "I'll take her down and find a fresh vein." She reached up and gripped the chain above the cold, hard handcuffs.

"No." Fabian lowered the gun, distraught at her actions.

"Hang on," Gaby told him, pretending to misunderstand. She put a foot to the wall for leverage—and pulled.

Fabian went crazy. *"What are you doing?"*

Gaby pulled again, and felt the bolt loosening from the ceiling. "Actually, Fabian, at this moment"—she tugged again, straining, any second now—"I'm thinking of the many ways I'm going to kill you."

"God damn you!" Screaming, hauling Mali up off her feet, he rushed toward Gaby.

The bolt in the ceiling popped free.

Going with the momentum and using her hold on the chain, she wielded it like a medieval mace. With Mali in range, the aim was close. She utilized extra care, swinging hard and fast, and the heaviest part of the restraint missed Mali, but struck Fabian's temple.

The sick thud of impact rebounded in the small room.

As blood gushed from Fabian's head he went stumbling

backward, releasing his hold on the girl. Mali raced back to her sister.

Fabian's lips pulled back from his terrifying, sharp-edged teeth and he fell, dropping the gun.

Gaby eased the corpse down into the bath of her own blood. Evil or not, this pathetic girl hadn't deserved such a death.

Luther fetched Fabian's gun and held the other three at bay, not that they'd posed much threat. Without Fabian directing their every move, they caved to their own cowardly natures, behaving like the cattle Fabian thought them to be.

Looking around, Gaby tried to decide what to do next.

Bliss looked to be in shock, white-faced and too still.

The girls were huddled together, bawling their eyes out, sobbing so pitifully that Gaby couldn't swallow.

Mort knelt down and made soothing sounds, trying to reassure them.

They were all so scared, so wounded by what they'd just seen.

Gaby couldn't go to them. Not like this, not covered in blood. *What to do?*

"Evil bitch."

Gaby jerked around—and found Fabian propped up against a file cabinet, one drawer open, a smaller handgun held loosely in his fist. Fresh flowing blood filled his left eye, ran over his mouth and lips, along his jaw, and into the creases of his neck. He licked at it—and smiled, a smile so diseased that Gaby felt the short hairs on her neck stand on end.

"You won't send me to jail," he told her. His words slurred, and he wobbled. "I won't waste away there among the servile scum of humanity's mistakes."

Blood and spittle punctuated each uttered word.

"You, you wicked bitch, are no daughter of mine. I disown you." He spat toward her. "I curse you to everlasting hell."

"But we were just getting to know each other." Trying not to spook him, Gaby reached behind herself for her knife. Did he remember her blade?

A demonic light shifted in Fabian's eyes, glittered with purpose. "You have to pay." He tried and failed to lift the gun.

"Everyone pays, eventually," Gaby agreed. As unsteady as he was, she didn't think he had it in him to shoot her. She could just as easily—

"Goddamn you," he swore. "I will *kill* you." He used the cabinet for leverage, almost fell, and tried again. The gun lifted . . .

A blast sounded.

Gaby jerked, stunned that he'd gotten a shot off. But she hadn't felt a thing.

And then she saw the blossom of blood on Fabian's forehead. In an anticlimactic finish, he slumped back to the floor. His head drooped to his shoulder, and his life ended.

Gaby spun around. Luther stood there with the gun in his hand, his expression set, defiant, and satisfied.

"You didn't have to kill him." But it was one hell of a good shot.

"I love you, Gabrielle Cody."

Her mouth opened, but nothing came out. He'd shot Fabian. *For her?*

Luther Cross, by-the-book super-cop, had put a bullet in her father's brain. "You could have . . . could have overpowered him."

"I love you," he said again. "Now. Always."

Well, crap. She had friends waiting for her to finish this,

to ease them, reassure them. She couldn't go all mushy emotional. Not right now.

"Gaby?" This time Luther's voice was softer. "Baby, I love you."

Gaby nodded. She looked at Fabian, gone forever from her life, and the greatest relief washed over her. "He needed killing."

"I know. But not by your hand."

Luther had spared her. Because he . . . *loved* her. *Wow*.

Gaby looked at Luther again, but he had turned away to remove Mort's gag and untie his hands, while still keeping the gun trained on the three stooges who were lost without Fabian's leadership.

Causing additional commotion, Ann charged in, gun drawn, shouting for Luther and Mort. She saw the blood everywhere and drew up short. "Dear God." Looking around in horror, she spotted Mort, and quickly got it together. "I called it in," she assured Luther. "Units are on their way."

Still speechless, Gaby stood there, ineffectual, uncertain. She looked again at her father, and thanked God that the man had never sought her out. Her life had been twisted enough without him being involved.

Then something hit her around her legs and she realized that Ann had untied Dacia and Mali. They clung to her like little spider monkeys. They didn't care about the blood.

From the tightness of their holds, she could tell they wanted only to be comforted.

Sinking to her knees, Gaby gathered them close. She breathed out the scents of death and despair, and instead filled her lungs with the sweet scent of their acceptance.

Smoothing back Dacia's hair, she asked, "You're okay?"

"Yes."

But tears tracked the girl's face and marks from the gag

still marred her jaw. Without thinking about it, Gaby kissed the injury, then turned and did the same for Mali.

Sirens sounded.

Over Dacia's shoulder, Gaby said, "Bliss? Talk to me, please. I need to hear your voice."

Luther helped Bliss to her feet. She swallowed, nodded. "I'm okay."

But she wasn't, and Gaby knew it.

Luther put an arm around her, but he had eyes only for Gaby.

Such beautiful eyes, so dark and sincere. Such a powerful, altruistic, amazing man.

As his aura of strength and protectiveness grew, spreading out to warm the room and chase away the gloom of depravity, Gaby saw herself.

Her aura twined with his, and in doing so, looked brighter, clearer, than she'd ever thought possible.

Her breath caught. "Bliss? You were right."

Some of the shock waned and color seeped back into Bliss's face. "I was?"

"Oh yeah, my friend. You were very, very right."

Cops swarmed in and quickly cuffed the now-cowering woman and her two male cohorts. Ann stood with Mort, touching his face, fussing over him. He had an arm around Bliss, hugging her to share his warmth.

Luther spoke briefly to the one in charge, then he came to Gaby.

He held a hand out to her, and when she took it, he hauled her to her feet. "Let's get these kids out of here, okay?"

"All right."

He lifted Mali into his arms, took Dacia's hand, and together they stepped outside to a full moon, a brisk, cool breeze, and fabulous possibilities for the future.

Epilogue

Luther woke to an empty bed. He sat up, immediately concerned until he saw the faint light beneath the closed bedroom door.

Slipping from the room, he went down the hall to the spare bedroom Gaby liked to use.

He found her on the floor, dressed only in one of his T-shirts, a box pulled out from beneath the bed. A gun had been tossed atop the guest bed, unneeded, out of the way. Papers were everywhere.

So Gaby had been hard at work on her *Servant* series. He should have known.

Beneath the overhead light, her dark hair shone and her lashes left shadows on her soft cheeks. She had papers spread out around her, ink in hand as she drew with a fevered intensity.

Contentment settled over Luther and he leaned into the doorframe. For a long time he watched her.

Finally Gaby paused, studied her finished drawing, and without looking up, said, "I didn't mean to wake you."

"I don't mind." Of course she'd known he was there. She had tempered the prodigious paladin inside her, but her acute perceptions remained—and he was glad.

She wouldn't be Gaby without them. "We need to get you a proper desk."

She looked up with a small smile—a genuine smile that stole his heart and made him feel like life could never be more perfect.

"I don't mind the floor. When I need to work, I can do it anywhere."

After a trip to the hospital to ensure everyone was okay, Luther had used special connections to guarantee that the girls were released back into his and Gaby's care. Bliss was better, but still too frazzled to deal with two children. The exhausted kids slept in a room together, peaceful, secure in the knowledge that Gaby would protect them.

As she protected everyone.

Gesturing him in, Gaby said, "Look at this."

In his boxers, Luther joined her on the cold floor. Gaby didn't complain about the chill, so he did the manly thing and sucked up his own discomfort.

The still-wet ink sketch she held depicted two girls— and a family.

Unsure what it meant, Luther took it from her to better study it. Her artistic skill forever amazed him. But then, anything Gaby did, she did better than most.

"Dacia and Mali?"

"Yes." She lifted the previous pages and showed them to him. "I finished up my story with Fabian."

Luther laid the paper down and tucked her hair behind her ear. "You didn't want to catch a little sleep first?"

"It's . . . cathartic for me. You know, to get it out. Sort of my way of putting it to rest."

"I understand." He couldn't stop touching her. She was his now, and he'd keep her. Forever.

"I had wondered if my duty would be done. But . . . She searched through the papers and found a specific one. "I think we're just going to keep working together, you know, like we did tonight."

At the thought of going through another night like the last one, a knot twisted in Luther's guts. But what the hell. He could live with that.

He couldn't live without Gaby. "If that's what you want, it works for me."

"After I write some more, I've got that picture of the girls. We're going to find the perfect family for them. It won't be us, but they'll stay close to us all the same. We'll have a role in their lives."

If she said it was so, Luther believed her. "I only want you happy, Gaby. If you want the girls to stay with us, then—"

She shook her head. "We're going to be busy. The girls need someone who will give them a routine dinner and bedtime, and attention with their homework." She glanced at him and grinned. "That's not us."

Probably not. But he'd try his damnedest to adjust for her.

"I don't know what will come up next, but this picture sort of drew itself."

He took the paper she handed him. It was a depiction of the main protagonist of the series, a female paladin who stood outside, hair blowing back. In the distance, a sun rose.

She was alone. Luther didn't like that. "I know that woman is you, Gaby."

"It is." With the tip of a finger, she traced the sun. "This is like your aura, Luther. Always touching me, changing me."

"And that's okay?"

She nodded. "It means a new beginning, you know?"

"With me." It wasn't a question.

Laying the paper aside, Gaby turned to him, crawled into his lap, and hugged him. "Yes, with you. I never knew love until I met you. I couldn't even dream it, because I had no idea what it should be." She leaned back and touched his face. "But it's you. With me. What you feel for me . . . and what I feel for you."

Luther's heart pounded hard. "You love me?"

Very slowly, Gaby nodded. "I wasn't sure at first, only because it's so new and different, and kind of weird."

Luther grinned. "Weird, huh?"

"I woke up ready to write, and for the first time that I can remember, I felt no dread. I felt only contentment. With you, everything is easier. Being me is easier."

"That's because you're a really wonderful person."

She let out a breath. "Only because you say it, can I start to believe it's true."

He hugged her tight. "I'm glad."

"I used to curse my life, but now, with you, I look forward to the future and what we might accomplish. Together, it all seems more possible."

"Your duty to save others is not an easy one, Gaby. It's understandable that you disliked it."

She shrugged. "Well, I might have the duty of saving others, but you saved me. I bet that was a whole lot harder." She grinned. "I know I'm not always easy to be around."

Luther laughed. "You do keep things interesting."

"I love you, Luther Cross."

Finally, she'd said it. Or rather, blurted it out in a rush. But the impact was the same.

"Do you need to do any more writing?" He desperately needed her. Right now.

Gaby looked at him, knew his thoughts, and her features sharpened in awareness. Eyes glittering, she said, "You know, cop, I do believe the writing will wait."

Luther scooped her up, more than ready for what the future would bring. With Gabrielle Cody, he could hardly wait.

And now a special preview of

BACK IN BLACK
by Lori Foster.

Coming soon from Berkley Books!

Gillian Noode stood against the back wall of Roger's Rodeo, the popular bar where many fighters hung out. She was close enough to observe him, but not close enough to be noticed. Yet. At least, not by him. Plenty of other men had already given her the once-over, showing appreciation for her trim black skirt, her low-scooped white blouse, and her strappy sandals. A few had even tried to strike up a conversation. Though tempted, she'd politely declined.

She'd come here for a reason, and Drew Black was it.

Dressed in well-worn jeans and a comfortable black T-shirt bearing the logo of the SBC fight club, the president of the extreme sport sat at the polished bar. Currently, he held close conversation with two long-haired lovelies whose bloated busts defied believability. No woman *that* slender had breasts *that* large.

But Drew showed no signs of disbelief. Like a king of his own making, he ogled with commitment to the boob ruse. Appreciating his commitment, the girls played with their long hair, flirted, and *giggled*.

Gillian fought a gag.

From the many interviews and television spots she'd watched, as well as her current scrutiny, Gillian surmised that Drew Black had a fighter-type physique, not quite as shredded as the actual fighters, but sculpted with honest muscle rather than the steroid-induced kind. He looked strong and capable.

Obviously his ego demanded that he stay in shape. After all, he was often surrounded by younger men in their prime, elite fighters with rock-hard bodies and astounding ability.

Drew Black intrigued her beyond the job at hand.

As an entrepreneur he showed great intelligence; no one could have accomplished what he had without a lot of smarts. He'd taken a mostly dead sport, banned in many states, and turned it into an astounding success.

And motivation? The man had it in spades. He couldn't possibly sleep more than six hours a night, given his enthusiastic workload and insane social calendar.

Good looks, great body, intelligence, enthusiasm and money . . . Drew Black would be quite the catch if he wasn't such a sexist, foul-mouthed jerk with the tact of a mountain goat.

With her external analysis now complete, Gillian moved closer, just a short way down the bar. She could hear Drew's deep voice—not that she expected much enlightenment from his conversation.

But Drew surprised her.

"Will you call me?" Bimbo One asked him with a pout.

Lacking malice, he gave a low and mellow laugh. "No, I won't."

Look-alike Bimbo Two said, "How about me?" She

toyed with his ear in a way that made Gillian twitch. "I can promise you a *really* good time."

"I just bet you can." Drew took her wrist and moved her teasing hand away. "But I have to pass."

Gillian raised a brow. She'd expected him to suggest a threesome, and instead he'd rejected both of them.

Interesting.

The bimbos combined their whining complaints and attempts at persuasion until Drew appeared to get annoyed. "Girls, what the fuck? C'mon, I have shit to do and it doesn't include having my ears ring. Go find something— or someone—else to do, okay?"

"But, Drew, we waited a long time to get to talk to you," Bimbo One whined.

Drew leaned around the woman to eye his male companion. "A little help here, Brett?"

Gillian recognized the other man as a fighter. Grinning, he held up big, capable hands. "Sorry, Drew. I have a girl waiting at home."

"We aren't at your home, damn it."

He smirked. "Yeah, well, Spice doesn't like to share me."

Drew pulled back. "Spice? What the fuck kind of name is that?"

"The kind that suits her." Unruffled by the implied insult, Brett finished his drink. To Gillian, it looked like juice. She gave Brett points.

"Look," Drew said to the closest bimbo, "you're too fucking young and, frankly, too damned pushy."

"We have to be pushy to get near you. You're just so popular—"

"How about I give you a couple of tickets to the next SBC fight instead? Good seats. How's that?"

The girls bounced with enthusiasm. Gillian couldn't

take it. She asked the bartender for a martini. By the time she'd been served and had taken a few fortifying sips, Drew was alone at the bar with Brett.

"You're brutal, Drew."

"Did you see those girls? Not only were they phony from head to toe, the damn giggles were wearing on my nerves." He worked his shoulders, as if releasing tension. "Jesus, I do have some standards, you know."

"Yeah? Like what?"

"You want the whole list, huh? Well, it doesn't apply here, but she has to be less than forty. Older broads are too independent."

Brett laughed. "Those two together weren't forty."

"No, but young and *not stupid* don't have to be exclusive."

Brett grinned. "So what else?"

"She has to be childless, because, let's face it, the whole kid thing is a major pain in the ass. No way am I fucking anybody's mother. And before you say it, yeah, I know, those two are still children themselves."

Brett saluted him with his juice.

"On top of being good-looking and sexy, she has to have a modicum of intelligence—at least enough that I can carry on a conversation with her. And no squealing. God Almighty, I detest broads who squeal."

Brett commiserated. "They were squealers."

"Can you imagine how loud they'd be in the sack, riding out a big O?" Drew laughed. "I'd need fucking earplugs."

Brett grinned. "Braggart."

That nasty mouth of his, Gillian thought as she shook her head. *Riding out a big O.* Who talked like that? The things Drew said, the crude language he used, were not befitting the force behind the fastest growing sport in history. That mouth had gotten him into trouble, whether he realized it yet or not.

It was her job to clean up his act, and to make him a more presentable figurehead for the SBC franchise.

A daunting task, but maybe not impossible. She always enjoyed a challenge.

The trick would be to beat him at his own game, to always keep the upper hand, and to grow a skin so thick that her feminist core wouldn't be damaged in the process.

She'd also have to remember that he was a grade-A jackass toward women, albeit a sexy one, so it would behoove her to keep her emotional distance. Trusting him, in any way, would be a mistake. She could not let herself be drawn to him.

Sadly, he was the first man she'd found exciting in a very long time.

He was the *last* man she could ever get involved with.

Picking up her glass, Gillian moved down the bar and slid onto the vacated seat beside Drew. Slowly she crossed her legs. While sizing him up, she removed the olive from her drink and bit into it.

Both men stared at her, not so much because of her looks, which she knew to be average, or because of her figure, which was a little more voluptuous than currently popular. But because she'd invaded their space—and was now staring back.

Drew swiveled around on his stool to fully face her. Without a word, he checked her out, lingering on her legs, her cleavage, and then her mouth.

When his gaze finally crept up to hers, he said low, "Hello, there."

Oh, men were *so* easy. Smiling in triumph, Gillian held out a hand. "Hello."

A very warm, firm hand, twice the size of her own, enveloped her fingers—and held on. "I'm Drew Black."

"Of course you are." Still smiling, she retrieved her hand from his. "Gillian Noode."

"Nude?"

Of course he wouldn't let that one slide. With a chastising look, she spelled, "N.O.O.D.E."

His mouth quirked. "Hell of a name."

"Yes, and I've heard every joke there is from every grade school boy out there." She reached beyond Drew to the fighter. She'd heard Drew use his first name, but she liked proper introductions. "And you are?"

He took her hand gently. "Brett Bullman, ma'am."

Unlike Drew, who shaved his head, Brett had shaggy brown hair that was a little too long, a little too unruly. His gorgeous green eyes showed good humor.

He also had a name familiar to her. "The Pit Bull, right?"

His mouth twisted with chagrin. "I hear that's what they're calling me."

"I've read about you, Brett. You're touted as a self-taught phenomenon taking the fight scene by storm." Gillian tilted her head at him. "You don't like your nickname?"

He shrugged with indifference, and shared a friendly smile that had surely melted many female hearts. "Long as the contenders know who I am, I don't care what they call me."

She lifted her glass at him. "You've certainly earned some respect."

"Maybe. The thing is, I haven't really been challenged yet." He gave a nod at Drew. "But we're working on that."

So it was a business meeting. "And I'm interrupting. Shame on me." She stood to leave. She could wait for their negotiations to conclude. "Congratulations on your recent success."

"Thanks, Ms. Noode. But please, don't leave on my account. We're all talked out now anyway. I was just finishing up my drink."

Drew agreed. "I'm all yours, honey, so why not park your pretty ass back up on that stool so we can get better acquainted?"

Gillian's teeth locked, but her smile didn't falter. To Brett she said, "Call me Gillian, please."

He nodded. "All right, Gillian."

"When is your next fight?"

"It's still being set up. After that last win, I got recruited by a great team, so I'd prefer to train with them for a while first." He shrugged. "But if Drew wants me to fight, I will."

"No more going it alone, huh?" Gillian had read that Brett taught himself by watching taped fights and then practicing the moves.

His grin personified charm. "No, ma'am. I only started out that way because I didn't know how to get in with a good team." He flashed her that white-toothed smile again. "But I'm always open to learning from more experienced guys."

Drew lounged back, elbows on the bar, and copped an attitude over being ignored. "After some promotion, I'll give him a main fight on a pay-per-view. I just want to build him up a little more first."

"I find it fascinating how this all works. Thank you for explaining." Gillian turned back to Drew but did *not* reseat herself. "So, Drew." She let out a big breath. "I suppose we really should talk."

"You heard Brett. I'm all talked out." His brown eyes challenged her. "But, hey, you got something more physical in mind, count me in."

Gillian might not have had an extensive romantic background, but neither was she obtuse. Drew was sexually attracted to her. After having seen how he'd sent off the young bimbos, she felt marginally flattered by that. But not enough to play the fool. "I'm sure nothing more than talk will interest you."

A brow went up. "The hell it doesn't."

This time her smile was snide. "But I don't meet your many requirements, Drew."

His gaze went over her again, slower this time, lingering in a way meant to discomfort her. He paused on her chest. "Honey, I think you fit the requirements just fine."

Rather than be offended by his near-tactile scrutiny, Gillian felt . . . warmed. And that annoyed her. So he was confident. And take-charge. He *did* possess a type of raw sex appeal.

But it was so raw as to be dangerous.

She put an arm on the bar and propped her chin on a fist. "But Drew, I'm forty-one," she lied. "That puts me well beyond your age stipulation."

His mouth twitched into a grin and he took up the game with practiced ease. "You sneaky broad. You were eavesdropping on us."

"Guilty. But you see, on top of being elderly, I have five . . . " She paused for effect. "No, let's make that *six* children."

"You're a terrible fibber." He turned his head to study her waist in the snug skirt. "I'd put you at no more than thirty-three, tops. And any idiot can see those are not the hips of a child-bearing woman."

Brett gave a choking cough, and made a point of looking at the ceiling.

"Hmm." Gillian leaned in closer to Drew. "Perhaps you're right." She gave him a quizzical frown. "But why ever do you think I'd lie about such things?"

"Modesty?"

She pursed her mouth as if in thought. "Or *maybe* I stretched the truth to deliberately disqualify myself based on your list of suitable criteria. You know"—she waved a hand—"to avoid your personal interest."

Drew got closer too, so close she felt his breath on her lips. He stared at her mouth. "Ah. So you assumed I'd be personally interested, did you?"

"Accurately, it seems. After all, you did suggest certain things you'd like to do."

"To you. Yeah." His gaze locked on hers. "If you need more details, they involve you baring yourself, and getting a little sweaty. So what do you say?"

Good Lord. The man showed no decorum at all. "Umm . . . no. Afraid not." For her own peace of mind, Gillian moved away from him again. "You were probably too hasty in sending away the enthusiastic groupies who, I'm sure, would have been much more accommodating."

"But they didn't interest me." His appreciative attention held her captive. "They were too artificial for my tastes."

"The laughs?" she guessed.

"The boobs." He nodded toward her cleavage and smiled. "I like things a little more natural."